Lance C

Not of Sound Mind

This novel is entirely a work of fiction. The names and characters and incidents portrayed in it are the work of the author's imagination. Any resemblance to actual persons, living or dead, events or localities is entirely coincidental.

First published on ebook Kindle 2013-02-01

Copyright © Lance Clarke 2013

Lance Clarke asserts the
moral right to be
identified as the author of
this work

The catalogue record for
this book is available from
the British Library

ISBN: 978-1-291-35267-2

All rights reserved. No part of this publication may be reproduced, stored in a retrieval system, or transmitted in any form or by any means, electronic, manual, photocopying, recording or otherwise, without the prior permission of the author.

This book is sold subject to the condition that it shall not, by way of trade or otherwise, be lent, re-sold, hired out or otherwise circulated, without the author's prior consent in any form of binding or cover other than that in which it is published and without a similar condition including this condition being imposed on the subsequent purchase.

PublishNation | London
www.publishmation.co.uk

Dedication

This book is dedicated to all those who suffer dreadfully from a mental illness, triggered by some long-standing condition or by a single occurrence. It changes their characters and the lives of others around them – leaving them imprisoned in a shell of despair.

Ira furor brevis est
(Anger is brief madness.)

Acknowledgements

To all those who patiently proof-read this novel and advised me on the technical aspects, especially ex-police inspector Peter Martin Surrey Police and Sue Doughty who was at the time Liberal Democrat Member of Parliament for Guildford.

Other books by Lance Clarke

Thirty Days,

Horizons.

Chapter One

Robert Ackroyd awoke slowly, his senses swimming with the smell of ether. Then a sharp searing sensation burst up throughout his body; he screamed in agony. Along with the pain came the sound of heavy blows that caused it. Every time he tried to move his arms the jagged pains in his hands made him scream out loud.

Slowly his eyes focussed then tears flowed and as they did his vision cleared. In front of him, her face flushed, stood a woman holding a large hammer. As he looked up at her she deliberately brought the hammer down on a large nail that pinioned his hand to a wooden barn door. The pain was so terrible he almost lost the use of his voice as his throat closed involuntarily.

"Oh dear, does it hurt?" said the woman sarcastically. She was panting now and had little dribbles of saliva and foam at the corners of her mouth. Pausing for a moment she tilted her head to one side and pursed her lips as she continued. "Tell you what, now this is really interesting, so listen very carefully. If you are an old lady and in your late seventies and some bastard thug does this to you, your bones shatter and guess what? It really hurts, just like this..." then she brought the hammer down on the nail attaching his left hand to the barn door. He screamed again, even louder. Blood trickled from his bruised and broken hands in slim rivulets down the wooden surface. Again and again the blows rained down sometimes bending the nails in half or missing them completely, pulping the flesh and exposing sharp pieces of bone.

By now tears were streaming down the woman's face and she began shouting, "You bastard," over and over again, repeatedly smacking his face with wide powerful strokes of her arms. Ackroyd screamed some more, but then as the shock and trauma of the broken bones, the full force of the slaps and pain got the better of him he slipped mercifully into unconsciousness.

The woman fell to her knees and put her hands to her face.

After ten minutes she got up, dried her eyes and looked at the body of the young man nailed to the barn door without any feeling or pity. It had been easy to entice him away from the public house. He was boisterous and loud, having successfully avoided being charged for the crime of murder and so full of himself from some other criminal act, no doubt perpetrated against another innocent vulnerable elderly person. She tapped into his arrogant confidence and got him to believe he had pulled an attractive and willing, older woman. Administering the ether was difficult, because he had been quite drunk but she had practised this move endlessly with a large first-aid dummy before she was certain that she could render a medium sized man unconscious then drag him to a vehicle to be transported to the barn. The preparation had been worth it and ensured the job was done easily and effectively.

She turned her back on the crumpled heap and walked away without a second glance at the barn. The question was: what now?

But then deep in her heart she really knew – it didn't end here.

A fuggy, sticky early spring mist clung to the ground around the Farm Museum just off the A12, a mile or so outside Chelmsford, in Essex; the sun would need to work hard today to burn it off. It was so dense that it blurred the flashing blue lights on the parked police vehicles, spreading the bright blue light in different directions. Detective Inspector Jack Rollo's large frame stood to one side of the building as a young police photographer moved around eagerly to get the best photographs of the boy who had been nailed to the wooden barn door. Rollo was glad to leave the detailed work to the scene of crime officers, known as SOCO. This kind of thing didn't happen often and his preference was for the endless burglaries and other crimes usually committed by itinerants. He tried to busy his thoughts by looking around him at the collection of wooden buildings, old agricultural machinery and stables that formed the museum. A full English breakfast sat uneasily close to his rib cage and he wished he could be somewhere else. It was the sight of the boy's swollen, blood-stained hands and his face screwed up into an agonised shape, evidence that he had suffered horribly before he had died, that made Rollo want to throw up.

The police doctor arrived and it didn't take him long to pronounce the boy dead and estimate an approximate time of death at about four in the morning. He said that the actions that caused death would have happened over a prolonged period before that. He found evidence of a major heart attack, probably brought on by shock, but this would be more clearly established at the autopsy.

A man in a green wax jacket, wearing a flat hat, leaned against the barn wall his head bent forward between his outstretched arms. A policewoman was calming him. It was the museum manager who had turned up early and found the victim. Rollo thought it reassuring to know that someone else was feeling so ill.

The SOCO donned white suits and over-boots a little way from the outer cordon, which had been marked out with blue and white tape bearing the words, 'Police. Do Not Enter', by the local police who were first on the scene. Their job now was to look for clues and to ensure that the crime scene was not contaminated. They began a close fingertip search of the crime scene behind the inner cordon. Whilst this work went on, a constable some distance away spotted signs that something had been dragged to the barn from a lay-by on the main road nearby. Jack gratefully grabbed the opportunity to move away from the murder scene. He carefully studied the tracks and drag marks that clearly led to the barn; this was a crafty move by the killer. If a vehicle had driven down the main track to the museum comprising a mixture of grit and mud, it would almost certainly have left tyre tracks or perhaps other indicators as well as traces on the vehicle. The lay-by revealed nothing at all because of the nature of the firm composition of the road surface.

He slowly walked back towards the crime scene not really wanting to see the boy's body, hoping that it was now long gone, but conscious of his responsibilities. What on earth had impelled someone to do such a thing? A smoke seemed like a good idea, but had given it up some several months ago. If he stayed here any longer he would most definitely start again.

After a number of hours, the body was put onto a stretcher, in the usual plastic body bag, and taken to a waiting ambulance stationed some distance away. The whole operation had been complicated. It was necessary to cut away a large chunk of wood surrounding the

3

several large nails embedded in each hand, into clear plastic bags and clinically labelled.

Jack had never seen anything like this in his eighteen years with the Essex Force, and he couldn't help thinking that it looked like the kind of punishment dealt out by the Mafia and the Irish Republican Army. Neither group had any scruples about what they did to individuals that crossed them. He was ex-British Army, Royal Army Ordnance Corps, a veteran of Northern Ireland and remembered finding a middle-aged Catholic informer nailed by his loose skin, hands, arms and his feet to a wooden floor in a warehouse. It took the army two hours to get the nails out and in the meantime the man died. He wondered if it could be drug-related or perhaps some kind of retribution?

Whatever it was, this young chap had really annoyed somebody.

Chapter Two

Thick fog drifted barely a mile or so inland from the North Sea and hung low over St Thomas' Church cemetery in Bradwell-on-Sea not far from where the North Sea meets the Essex coast. The sound of the sea birds was strangely missing as Angie MacPherson stood by the graveside while her mother's coffin was lowered slowly into the cold dark earth. Tears streamed down her face and her shoulders shook until she could hardly breathe. Her life had been such a tangle and now she had lost the most wonderful person in the world.

A friend of her mother called on the telephone to tell her that her mother had been attacked in her bungalow and was seriously ill and in the intensive care unit at the local hospital in Chelmsford. Angie raced to the hospital and was greeted with the sight that she most dreaded – her mother was attached to dozens of tubes and monitors and her face and arms were a mass of red and purple bruises. She was hardly recognisable and even Angie had to look twice. The policewoman on duty was faultless as she followed all the proper procedures and Angie's heart sank as she told her that her mother had been attacked that evening by a burglar. It had been a vicious assault and her mother's last words to the ambulance crew who attended to her were: "Why did he do this?" Then she lapsed into unconsciousness.

Angie could tell that the policewoman was a probationer and relieved her of the necessity to say anything else. She told her of her previous position in the Hertfordshire Police Force and she could be left alone. The young girl was visibly grateful and went on her way; no one likes the 'bad news shift.'

She walked to the window of the intensive care ward and pressed her face against the warm glass. Her heart thumped like crazy and she gripped her hands tightly hoping for the best. Angie's thoughts did what everybody's did in such situations. Memories of happy days as a child floated by, days by the beach, her first period and Mum's gentle care and advice and Christmases enjoyed without a wastrel of a father who left when she was a only a toddler. Her mum married again, but that was short-lived. Perhaps he had found it difficult to penetrate their strong and loving relationship? He left and that was all there was to it.

She felt the tears well up in her eyes.

Then, unexpectedly, there was a loud continuous bleep and she caught sight of the monitor that showed a straight green line where she knew it should display a wavy heart pulse. Nurses rushed past her and she stayed rooted to the spot. They did all they could, but despite electric charges, large doses of adrenaline and cardiac massage, nothing more could be done. Her mother was dead.

So here she was on a foggy morning in May, watching her beloved mum being lowered into the cold earth.

The Essex Police Criminal Investigation Department, CID, was confused about the nature of Robert Ackroyd's murder. It was vicious and extraordinarily vengeful, almost as though it was some kind of retribution. They did their best to contact all local snouts to find out just who would or could have killed someone in such a fashion, but without success. Akroyd had a lengthy list of crimes to his name, but he was a small-time crook, with no trace from him to any of the major criminals on the police files. They knew of only one brother, by the name of Tom, and he worked on a North Sea oil platform. Robert Ackroyd was despised in the community, even amongst the criminal fraternity; he was a loner and had no male friends and certainly no girlfriend.

Several victims of his crimes were interviewed, but they were all, without exception, quite elderly and could hardly lift a hammer let alone drag a body to a barn door. One alleged victim was dead: Mrs Alice McNulty and she was without a partner having been divorced twenty-five years ago with no recorded children as next of kin. They drew lines under all these contacts and concentrated on the possibility of it being the result of some kind of punishment meted out in a drug gang feud.

The CID team was forced to leave it to the snouts to come up with something and rely on luck whilst they continued to widen the net – that was always the way in the early days of investigations. But the murder was so bad it was attracting a lot of attention from the media and the authorities, and they felt decidedly edgy at the emerging prospect of not finding a killer.

The court case had been a farce. The evidence against Robert Ackroyd was at best circumstantial and nothing could be proven 'beyond all doubt'. Angie Macpherson's blood seethed as she heard him lie once he was cornered. Then his solicitor offered a plea of not guilty to murder and said that he would however admit to burglary, driven as he was by a crushing need for money to buy drugs. He went on to say that Mrs McNulty had insulted and goaded him and another man, whom he called John, about getting a real job when they called to see if she needed any odd jobs doing. He said that he stole from her because he was angry at her remarks and needed the money. He had only shouted at her and it was the other person, this man called John, who he left behind in the house who must have committed the vile act, not him. It wasn't his fault and he swore that he left the other person alone with her; he was a victim himself.

Ackroyd's solicitor was masterful and the jury was moved to find him not guilty of murder or manslaughter; there simply wasn't any direct evidence to convict him. He was given a two year suspended sentence for burglary with a bundle of drug rehabilitation sessions; great play was made of the fact that he voluntarily turned himself in. The fact was that he knew the police were on his trail.

The other party was never found and everyone knew that this phantom friend never would be.

For months after the trial Angie had withdrawn within herself and she started drinking heavily. She had nightmares and visions, and sometimes felt as though the very room she was in had closed in on her, inch by inch. Days flowed into nights without any divide whatsoever. She tried to pull herself together and bought newspapers and groceries; but the papers went unread and the food mostly went out of date and remained uneaten.

Seven months earlier, Angie had left the Hertfordshire Police Force where she was a successful detective sergeant. Her personality was not quite what the chief constable wanted from his officers and she was often skirting close to a disciplinary interview when she cut corners to achieve positive results or stood up to her politically correct superiors. She was growing to despise the criminal justice system that shackled good police officers and seemed to featherbed criminals. The inevitable list of warnings, cautions and then suspended sentences allowed criminals to keep pushing until almost reluctantly the authorities put them behind bars – only to parole them as quickly as possible afterwards. It was almost inevitable that she would be caught sounding off about criminal justice just as the chief constable entered her office, but sad for her that he was in the company of a group of local members of parliament. She refused to give ground and, full of pride, she resigned a few days later after a blazing row.

The past months provided her with a chance to review her life and reset her objectives – it was a time of rebirth, to do something different. She benefited from the removal of the daily stress of police life and was a different person - until now that is.

Her flat in central Welwyn Garden City was modern and the décor minimalist and stylish – it was all that a career policewoman deserved. But it now looked like a tip, with rubbish strewn all over the place and dust thick enough to write your name in. She opened another bottle of malt whisky and poured a large glass. The radio was playing as it did now twenty-four hours a day – without it she believed she would have cracked up. Some neighbours complained so she turned it down a little, but it stayed on – it had to. After several more glasses of scotch, she ate some stale bread and mouldy cheese without even noticing the rank taste and settled back in the leather settee to drink herself into another night's sleep. Memories of her mother came flooding back, followed by tears and a terrible, deep, tight pain in the chest.

She stood up and looked in the mirror. Angie could hardly believe her eyes. Her face was blotchy and hair waxen and greasy; she had always been particularly fastidious about her appearance, but that would be difficult to see now.

All this agony was because of the action of some little thug; some little bastard who had no respect for life or property, with no conscience and a streak of cruelty who set out to rob and maim. Her fists balled and she wanted to scream. She stood back and wobbled slightly on her feet moving closer to her image. She detested the pathetic creature in the mirror and wanted to hurt it. Angie looked like a victim – but she never had been nor would she ever be. Her eyes caught sight of a paperweight on the coffee table next to her and without a moment's thought she picked it up and threw it directly at the mirror. It shattered into pieces and some shards flew outwards cutting her bare arm, but she felt no pain. Papers and envelopes that had been neatly placed into a small Chinese lacquered box fell to the floor. Then, miserable, she walked to her bedroom and fell face down on the duvet, blood oozing from the cut in her arm defacing the white satin cover and bed sheet.

    She cried herself to sleep.

Chapter Three

Angie MacPherson awoke as soon as she felt the warmth of the sun that streamed in through her bedroom window. She sat up straight and brushed her short brown hair back against her scalp. She felt strangely alert and was filled with boundless energy and a remarkably clear head and her mind raced all over the place almost trying to think of two things at the same time. This really surprised her, because her mouth felt like sandpaper and she had expected a hangover. It was quite surreal, as though she was floating and not part of real life. She had an anxious feeling in her chest as though she was scared and yet she was completely focussed. She raised herself slowly from the bed and then showered and dressed.

After a breakfast of toast and coffee she read a few old local newspapers over and over again. Her head throbbed and she felt that she no longer owned her body or her personality any more. What had she done? Her whole life had been serving the rule of law and now she was no better than a common criminal – worse: a murderer. But as soon as she thought that, her head hurt and grew tight and she heard a voice goading her. It told her that she was soft and if she had any honour at all she would act to avenge the helpless; she had failed as a policewoman; she had failed her mother. Just thinking about this guilt set her nerves on edge. Her mother, Alice McNulty, had worried about her when she left the Police Force; the older generation clung to jobs whatever the situation and she couldn't understand how Angie's principles got in the way of paying for a mortgage. Then her mother moved house barely three weeks before she was murdered from nearby Southminster, to a small terraced, wooden-board fronted house in the village of Bradwell-on-Sea. Angie had been too busy searching for a job to help her with the move or even go to see the new house, always putting things off to a future weekend. Too damned busy, she shouted loudly, too damned busy! And so her mother sought help from elsewhere.

Upset and guilty, she felt inexorably driven to plan what she was going to do next. In her heart she knew it wouldn't be nice, but then she didn't feel disposed to be nice any more. She was going to put the world to rights and Akroyd had been only the beginning.

But Angie faced a dilemma: whatever she planned, she had to divert attention and her work as a police officer in the Hertfordshire Police Force. It was inevitable that some smart police investigator would eventually trace her as a next of kin to Alice McNulty, and she would have to explain her whereabouts at the time of Ackroyd's death. Her tart remarks to the Hertfordshire Chief Constable and robust views on crime and punishment were well known and that could arouse interest. She knew that investigations would not stop until every avenue had been cleared and she was certain to be a prime suspect. Now was the time to sit on the other side of the fence and plan ahead.

The first hurdle would be easy to negotiate. There was a strong possibility that the investigators would not get up to full speed on a single murder; this was because of the logistics and effort needed to set up a major crime incident team – called the MCIT – and allocate a wide range of tasks. But, of course, that would all change speed when a series of murders were committed. As she doodled on a notepad, she realised that there would be more murders - some bad people were going to die.

Then the police would start afresh as the pressure mounted and start again. They would retrace connections back from the murder of the thug Robert Ackroyd and link his name to the death of her mother. But even then she was able to buy time. Her mother's name was McNulty and her first husband died in a factory accident. She was childless and married a widower, Michael MacPherson, who brought with him a baby daughter, called Angie. But he turned out to be no more than a wife-beater and lazy lout. She divorced him, but paid him off to on the agreement that she would keep Angie and he would stay away from the family home forever. Then she reverted to the name McNulty. Thus Angie grew up a MacPherson whose mother's name was different.

With luck, any initial search of data would not reveal this and her mother would be considered to be without relatives. But Angie knew this would not last long and a thorough quality audit of information would eventually identify an adopted daughter. She needed to use the time available to her to develop a suitable low-key role as Alice's daughter, living locally, that would stop further investigation that might trace to her former employment as a detective sergeant in the Hertfordshire CID. She had to create a new personality to fit the local identity and this meant that she first had to pay attention to her physical identity. So she powdered down her face to look pale. Then she padded her body and went back to the hospital and coroner's office several times to place this image firmly in their minds. Angie had received a small legacy from a distant aunt some years ago and had enough money for the work she had to do. She rented a small, two up, two down, semi-detached house in a tiny village called Steeple, in Essex, not far from where the family home used to be in Southminster and got a job in a local bakery for a few weeks. It was one of those family businesses that didn't ask for references for casual staff. Then she moved on to a superstore in Malden, before finally taking a job in the smaller local store in Latchington near where she rented her new home in Steeple. All of her employers would confirm the slow, laborious way she talked and moved around – almost listless and not too bright – and the fact that they didn't really know her that well. She doubted she needed such elaborate cover, but wanted to be certain.

So Angie developed a new personality. Eerily, from the night she broke the large mirror in her flat her lovely mother appeared to her quite often, she approved of her plans, but thought it a shame that Angie had to look so dowdy. Her mother said that she looked so bad that it legitimised her treatment of Ackroyd – he was a wicked boy and deserved his fate. Angie told her that everything would be okay and it was a sacrifice that had to be made. She kept repeating that she was sorry, so sorry, but whenever she did that her mother simply smiled and disappeared, leaving Angie calling after her. But her nightly appearances were a great comfort to Angie – they gave her strength when she doubted herself and her mum helped her with her plans.

She would soon be ready to deal with more bad people.

Flickering sunbeams danced through the Chelmsford library windows their rays occasionally interrupted by passing clouds. It was a mild day and the library was full of elderly people who wanted no more than to talk to someone and students who needed to research the extensive reference collection and sleep off their almost endless round of hangovers.

Angie MacPherson, dressed in a dark hooded tracksuit, with matching T-shirt underneath and cheap grey training shoes, sat at the microfiche reader calling up past local newspaper records and printing selected pages. It was as though she was entranced as she worked steadily through the records staring intently at the screen and turning the wheel to allow her to scan every detail. She reached up with both of her hands and ran her fingers through her hair several times then returned to her search. She knew she was lucky. Not many libraries had these facilities. Occasionally, she looked up and saw someone at staring at her. Faces seemed to change shape and to take on a lumpy, ugly sneer; she looked down, her temples throbbing and concentrated hard on the screen. Oddly, she didn't question this strange situation: why she was doing the research – she simply accepted it, moving through life like a programmed automaton. However, she knew what she was looking for.

After she finished her reviews, she gathered up the copies of the printed press cuttings, she'd found a lot of them, closed down the microfiche terminal and printer, and walked towards the door and the fresh air. As she did so someone called out to her. Angie's nerves jangled as though they were connected to an electric current, she was sure that this person might want to kill her. Turning around with fear in her eyes she saw a middle-aged woman running towards her. The woman seemed to be running with her feet ten inches above the ground, holding an axe in her hand. Angie was transfixed and closed her eyes; then, despite fear that seared into her belly, she opened them again and saw that the scene had changed. Standing in front of her was a perfectly respectable, elderly, grey-haired and bespectacled lady.

"Here you are, dear," said the lady's kindly voice, "it's your temporary library ticket, you mustn't forget that. You also paid too much for your copying."

She proffered the loose change.

Angie wasn't afraid of her now, but wanted to get out of the library.

"Thanks, it's okay, keep the change," she blurted, turned and almost ran for the door.

Eventually, after five minutes of fast walking through the streets, she stood breathless, in a shopping arcade by a large stone column. There may be spies in the town so she had to be careful whom she talked to and what she said. Angie closed her eyes again and breathed deeply, her heart was pumping and she was convinced that she was hyperventilating.

"Must get a grip," she repeated quietly several times, "must get a grip."

She could do it; her mum kept telling her that every night - she knew she could do it. With her back to the cold stone column, she managed to settle down and her thoughts focused on the next part of her plan: to purchase a knife - a good sharp knife. She looked around like a frightened animal. No one noticed the pathetic figure avoiding imaginary followers, ducking from doorway to alleyway and keeping her head down all the time. Angie was living in a wholly different virtual world to those around her. She weaved around supporting stone columns in the arcade and finally found the shop she was looking for: **Ansells Kitchen Shop**. She went in.

It wasn't difficult to find the section that specialised in knives and other implements needed for the preparation of meat and vegetables. Her eyes roamed over the collections of blades – some shiny, some long and thin and some short with serrated edges. She touched them gently with her right hand – they looked beautiful, black or wooden handles, shiny blades all with stainless steel mouldings. Then she settled on a carving knife that was about twelve inches long. She held it in her hand and it seemed to vibrate. Looking towards the open doorway, it seemed to beckon and she wanted to run out of the shop and away into the distance. As she thought about doing so, her mum appeared immediately in front of her.

"Don't be so silly, dear. You were always very silly, my sweet little girl, weren't you? But not now, dear, you have important work to do. Avenge your guilt, Angie. Go and buy the knife, now," said the mother figure and Angie obediently turned, took hold of the carving knife and went to the cash desk where a weary looking young girl stood chewing gum and doing her nails. Without saying anything, she wrapped the knife and then announced the price in a high-pitched irritating nasal voice:

"Twenty-three pounds and fifty pence, madam, it's expensive but these are new in the country, they're made in Italy." She squinted at Angie, whose mind interpreted this as an act of aggression; Angie looked away, her heart beating madly, then put twenty-five pounds on the counter and made for the door, refusing high-pitched calls to return to get her change and the sales ticket.

Once outside she made her way to a nearby Costa Coffee café, where it would be noisy and crowded, which was just what she wanted. This would provide her with the anonymity she needed; she could hide in noise. She entered and was pleased to note that customers were trying to talk over the noise of coffee grinding and steam machines and no one looked up at her - it was perfect.

She ordered her coffee black without sugar, then sat in a corner seat and began to read the content of her plastic file. Her eyes flicked back and forth as she read each newspaper cutting from the library at breakneck speed, turning each page with flicks of the wrist, making a snapping sound. Several people looked at her strange antics, but returned to their coffee and conversation without taking any further notice.

It was all there. It wasn't only her mum who had been so terribly violently assaulted and robbed; lots of other people had been too. Time and time again she found details of muggings, aggravated burglary and murders against vulnerable, ordinary, everyday people, like her mum. She also found much evidence of people being defrauded out of their life savings, or being treated badly by landlords. Not every guilty party got away with a lenient punishment, but she was appalled at the evidence in front of her that a significant number did and more horrifying was that they seemed to have crime sheets as thick as telephone books and were mostly recidivist by nature.

The more she read the angrier she got. Her eyes welled up until she couldn't see to read. Her mum was right; it wasn't just her that suffered. An elderly man saw her distress and leaned towards her, smiling.

"Are you all right my dear?" he said warmly.

Angie jumped like a startled rabbit, grabbed her papers, thrust them into her bag and, head down, and hurried to the door. As she did so, she knocked over her coffee and the man yelped as it spilled down his trouser leg. Half turning she looked at him, one hand on her papers and the other tightly gripping the handle of the carving knife. She wanted to stab him in the eyes to stop him looking at her – then she wouldn't be in any danger. But her body seemed to impel her out of the café.

He shouted after her, "I was only trying to bloody well help!"

But she took no notice.

In any case, no one could help her now.

Constables Colin Robbins and Richard Dawson walked steadily along the side of an industrial estate just outside Colchester. The town was famous for its Roman history and for military people, its military prison. It was a warm day and they chatted amiably about football, the state of the world and so on. They were both local men who had served over ten years on the local police force.

Both of them were big men who were sometime players in the Colchester Rugby Club first team. Their sense of humour was well known inside and outside the local police force and they were respected as being two exceptionally good 'beat' coppers.

Constable Robbins stopped abruptly as he saw a youth loitering near a haulage contractor's fence. He was dressed in ill-fitting jeans and wore a thick black hooded fleece jacket. His hood was up and, hands in pockets, he was peering over the fence. The company had been turned over several times losing costly computer equipment and items from the outside stock. It was difficult to police every inch of the trading estate and local criminals knew it.

"Well I never. It's our little friend from the Traveller's site, Alfie Bishop. Shall we say hello, eh, Ritchie? You go around the road to the right and I'll approach him direct and when we have him cornered we can ask him some meaningful questions."

They both closed in on the boy who spotted Constable Robbins and made a run for it. Constable Ritchie Dawson stopped him by stepping out from behind a van. Bishop crashed into him and fell to the ground, winded.

Constable Robbins stood over him menacingly and hauled him up by the scruff of the neck.

"Alfie, how nice to see your smelly self. Now what would you be doing here? Casing the joint for another evening visit? About to give them some advice on their reception layout, or, don't tell me, you're going to do some landscaping in that shit-hole that you and your family live in at Clandon Hill Traveller's site? Such a busy world isn't it?"

"Fuck off, filth. I ain't done nothin' and this is 'arassment. My dad's got an ace lawyer and he'll see you sued and off the streets. I got my rights, y'know," yelled young Alfie.

Constable Robbins boiled inside and he felt the bile rise in his throat, but he didn't let it show. Years of practice had taught him that much. But he was mad, mad as hell. He knew only too well the chaos and misery that Alfie Bishop and cronies caused local people. He just wanted to grab the boy and beat the steam out of him. He knew of this boy's antics more than anyone else did. No one was safe from the attention of him and his evil clan and they did indeed enjoy the services of a particularly clever lawyer.

"Your rights, Alfie? Well now let's see, as an honest and upright citizen of this country you indeed do have rights my son. Only problem is that you are not honest and upright." He looked around him and saw no members of the public – his colleague simply nodded approval of what he automatically assumed he was about to do.

Robbins attention returned to Bishop and he continued. "In fact you are a dishonest and vile little shite. You are the lowest form of vermin and if I had my way I would flush you down the toilet."

The boy stood his ground, but moved uncomfortably under Robbins' grasp of his collar.

"I'll 'ave you for sayin' that, you filth, copper, filth. There's nothing you can do to me. Nothing anybody can do to me, twat!"

Inside his soul Constable Robbins knew that this was true. Short of getting the boy to sit down, take coffee and cake with him and politely offer to own up to the dozens of crimes the local nick simply knew that he had committed, there was really nothing that could be done. So what the hell? He reached forward and grabbed the boy's sideburns. Alfie yelped in pain.

"Yes, that's right, Alfie, painful is it?" he said.

Alfie was standing on tiptoes as the constable held tight to the small patches of hair at the side of his head, level with his ears and raised his hands slowly higher and higher until the hair threatened to part company with the flesh.

"Ow, God, stop it, you bastard. I'll bloody 'ave you," yelled Alfie, instinctively raising his hands to try and prise Robbins' fingers apart.

"Oh, you will, will you? How about this then?" Robbins loosened his left hand, raised it then slapped the boy's face hard, once, twice then again. The boy howled with pain, but couldn't move because he was still tethered by the right-hand sideburn. Then Robbins jabbed him several times in the rib cage with his knuckle.

"You know what would make my day. I would just love to hear you say sorry for all the pain and aggro you and your kind cause local people. Go on, say it for me?"

At first Alfie refused, but the pain around his left ear made him think again and he repeated the words that the constable wanted him to say.

"That was music to my very ears, you little arse-wipe. Now, you see this," and he took out a small cellophane packet containing white powder, "I'm gonna make a note in my book that we stopped a young man who we suspected of drug dealing to a group of youngsters and searched him. We found this 'ere powder on 'im, but unfortunately he ran off. Now you are of course aware of how many years you can get for possession with intent to supply class 'A' drugs? Especially someone as popular as you?"

Alfie paled. Then the constable put his face close to the boy's.

"So why don't you just piss off back to your hovel where you and your retards live and we'll say no more about this, okay?"

Alfie smelled Robbins' breath on his face and chose the option of least resistance. He walked off, then, far enough away he turned and shouted, "Bloody bastard, I'll get you for this, I swear I will."

"See you in hell, arse-wipe!" shouted Constable Robbins.

Then he called in to base and told them they were taking a lunch break some distance away from where they actually were; just in case. They both walked across the road and sat on a wall to eat their sandwiches and Constable Robbins reached into his pouch pocket and pulled out the small cellophane bag with the white power in it.

"Want some salt with your boiled egg, Ritchie?"

"Thanks, Col', don't mind if I do," he said, "don't mind if I do, indeed. By the way, never saw a thing. But I enjoyed every minute of it. Little bastard!"

They both chuckled, but inside, Constable Robbins knew that he had come very close to causing the boy real damage.

He knew he must never let himself go like that again.

Chapter Four

Carl Stevens was a good-looking young man. He was of medium build, but muscular, the result of frequent trips to the gymnasium. He had wild fair hair and sparkling blue eyes. They were the kind of looks that most mums would swoon over if their daughters brought him home to tea. But this aura of innocence was illusory; his sexual appetite was voracious and aggressive. Local girls soon got to know him and took it for granted that he would hit on them for a date; a few took him up on the offer – but most didn't. The few that did regretted it and never dated him again. Carl's modus operandi was to have a good night out then offer some soft drugs to heighten the experience. If a girl seemed at all reluctant then he administered the date-rape drug Rohypnal, it never failed to work.

Carl didn't particularly care how he got his sex and, although he would have preferred a little more physical movement, date rape gave him ultimate control as well as sexual satisfaction. But as with all kinds of activity involving the 'pleasure principle', he hankered after something more stimulating. He fanaticised on rough sex without having to induce a coma; this meant premeditated violent rape. Eventually, desire and fantasy got the better of him. Lying in wait in Chelmsford Park, it wasn't long before a young female jogger came running towards his lair in the bushes. He looked around carefully; no one was in sight.

The jogger, a girl called Janet Anderson, had been only a few yards from a bush he was hiding behind, when he rushed out and put his hand tightly over her mouth and nose. Her body went limp with fear and she fainted as he hauled her back into the bushes, then his body became aroused with the power he had over her.

He removed her clothes, fitted a condom and as she regained consciousness he held his hand over her mouth and raped her; she was clearly too scared to scream or move. When he finished, he carefully removed the condom, put it into a handkerchief and then into his pocket. He stood up, towering over the girl and she automatically curled up into a foetal position. Sneering at her, he gave her a kick in the buttocks, but in his haste to leave, didn't notice her face. She had been on a date with him once and had refused his invitation to sex and this enabled her to put a name to her attacker. He was arrested soon afterwards, but by then had changed his clothes, putting the discarded ones into the washing machine. They had no evidence to go on and only the girl's statement – it was never going to be easy getting a conviction.

The resulting trial was an ordeal for the girl as inevitably they always are. On the one hand, she had a positive identification, but absolutely no reliable DNA or other evidence. He also had an alibi – he had a wide circle of friends with a similar violent taste in sex, all too happy to stand by his statement. But more devastatingly, his lawyer ran rings around the prosecution. It was firmly put in the jury's mind that she was mistaken in picking Stevens' face out of an identity parade. He had after all only recently dated her and she must have mistaken the rapist for him. The girl was nervous, upset and extremely emotional. To top it all she was unused to speaking in public, let alone having her sex life and the events of that terrible night being exposed in every intimate detail to a bunch of strangers in a court of law. Her nerves got the better of her.

She was forced to admit that she was not a virgin and that she had taken recreational drugs a few days before. And so it went on - the trivia mounted and slowly but surely it overtook the real facts as the case progressed. Her character was impugned and she was so worn down and confused that the jury had to cast doubt on her mental state and reliability, and Stevens was eventually acquitted.

Janet Anderson was destroyed and Carl Stevens held his arms aloft in victory.

But retribution was coming to Mr Carl Stevens.

Angie had been drinking again and the room in her flat whirled around her and the floor felt like a waterbed. She sat half on the brown leather couch and leaned forward over the large coffee table on which were dozens of press cuttings. Each one of them outlined in great detail the suffering of victims of crime, focussing on the unfairness or ineptitude of the legal system. But one cutting seemed to stand out above all others. She felt a sudden well of hatred for a man called Carl Stevens as her eyes skimmed over the report of the rape case. This was a familiar story and she had seen this sort off travesty many times before when she was a detective sergeant. This girl had been innocent. She had been savagely abused and, like Angie's poor mother, the perpetrator had sought to place the blame on her, the victim. It is terrible to be abused and worse still to be blamed afterwards; a double whack.

Big tears rolled down her cheeks. She cried as she imagined how it must be for someone to lose all hope in the criminal justice system that was supposed to be there for protection. Then to have to try and build their life anew knowing that the criminal who dealt out the most appalling terror was still at large, free to come and go as he pleased.

Angie's hand gripped the coffee table as the world around her whirled, rose and fell and the pictures and shapes on the walls of her house seemed to lose all kind of shape and form, resembling melted images, like Salvadore Dali's portrayal of a clock. Then the dizziness passed and she looked up and saw her lovely mother standing in front of her. She could rely on Mum to tell her what to do and felt instantly better. Mum spoke and her voice sounded as though it was an echo and she could swear that she felt her tender touch on her face.

"He's a bad man, Angie - a bad man. What did that lovely girl do to deserve that? Nothing is what I say, absolutely nothing. He deserves all he gets. Cut his bits off, that's it, cut 'em off." Then she turned away looking haughty and raised her chin as Angie remembered she would do when she got above her station and her mum wanted to reassert her authority. "Cut his bits off. Do it for me Angie and that other lovely girl. Do it, Angie – think on, you might be next y'know?"

Angie cried some more and reached for the whisky, "I know, Mum, I know, yes, he bloody deserves it, Mum, just like Ackroyd. I won't let you down."

Then the room went dark and she fell forward onto the coffee table, banging her nose and making it bleed slowly onto the surface.

Carl Stevens couldn't believe his luck. He hadn't even been into the nightclub and some bird started making eyes at him as he stood in the queue for two-for-one lager. She was a stunner too, intelligent looks, black hair and heavy make up with red lips, almost like an older Gothic style of chick. He thought that perhaps she was a kind of thinking man's crumpet? But he cared little about her intellect and was sure that she was up for sex – it was written all over her face.

He thought it a bit strange at first, but she seemed to want to avoid crowded situations, always appearing in the shadows and smiling directly at him. What the hell? After exchanging a few words with her, it was easy enough to let her lead him across to the Central Park in Chelmsford and down to the riverside. They kissed, then after a short while, too short for Carl, she pulled back slightly and he thought she had changed her mind. To his surprise she produced a small bottle of wine and two plastic glasses from her large handbag. How cute, he thought, she wants to soften me up; and he went along with her request that they drink a toast to an exciting evening ahead. Poor slut, he would certainly give her a good seeing to, that was for sure.

He had never liked white wine. Horse's piss was his usual assessment. So he put his head back and gulped it down in one. Unseen, she poured hers away. She excused herself for a pee and to his amusement, went behind a bush. He thought of creeping up and watching her, but didn't and idly went over his sexual repertoire in his mind. In fact it was Angie who was doing the watching, as the large dose of Rhohypnol took effect on Stevens' muscular frame. At first he shook his head as he began to see double and tried to focus on the distant lights and full moon, but without success. The world seemed to take on an alarming tilt. Then he tried to walk, but his legs would not let him and he fell to the ground.

Angie's chest tightened as she walked from behind the bush and then she saw her mother standing by a tree near where Stevens lay, laughing at him and calling him names as he tried to stand up, but he kept staggering around and bumping into trees before falling over again. She shouted at him that he was evil but he didn't seem to hear her. She turned to Angie, her face glowing, almost translucent.

"Hurt him, hurt him like I've been hurt. He's evil. Evil. Evil. Do it for me," she implored.

"Yes, yes. I love you mum, you're right, he's evil and he has to be hurt."

Angie rounded the bush and stood over the body of Carl Stevens that was by now still and completely unconscious. It took a while, but she dragged his heavy frame to the tree and tied his arms behind him and around the trunk. Then she removed his trousers and underpants, and parted his shirt. She folded his underwear and formed it into a gag over his mouth, using his leather belt. Then she removed the carving knife from her bag. In the moonlight its sharp edge glistened. She sat cross-legged in front of Stevens, her mother close beside her and waited. It would take quite some time for the drug to wear off, but she would wait.

This had to be done when he woke up.

Chapter Five

Detective Constable Jenny Ellis vomited violently several times into a plastic supermarket bag. The sight in front of her was awful. The emasculated body of a young man with his arms tied behind him and around a tree in central park Chelmsford was truly sickening. The perpetrator had literally hacked away the man's parts rather than cutting them surgically. The man's face was contorted into an agonised grimace and the features seemed to have frozen in this state. He had died of blood loss and the ground beneath his torso was dark red.

Jenny addressed the doctor and almost choked the words out of her mouth.

"I suppose it's difficult to determine the time of death?"

"Yes it is really," he said, looking at her sympathetically. Then he touched her shoulder, "why not leave it to your colleagues to sort out? They are all kitted up and seem to know what to do. You will want to check his identity and follow up on all sorts of other things. You've done all you can and the other teams are here now. It really is very nasty and there's no sense in you staying any longer."

Jenny accepted his kind guidance. She felt dizzy and sick. The police team who were immediately on the scene were now thoroughly searching the area and Jenny had the man's wallet and some other papers from his jacket in a plastic envelope. She would go back to the station and start to look up his details. Turning the bag over in her hands she read the details on a number of papers inside; Carl Stevens was his name.

Poor sod!

The Essex Chief constable, Alistair Blackley, was briefed on the latest murder. He was a tall imposing man with greying hair and a normally friendly face, but today his features were taut, making his mouth seem like a mere pencil line on his face. He was concerned – very concerned - because the horrific mutilation of a young man called Carl Stevens was barely four days after the last horrific murder. Something told him that this wasn't going to be the end of things – he had that uncanny feeling about the situation and was rarely wrong.

He was an old fashioned copper. Although he was the first to admit that he had been overtaken by modern police methods, he had been smart enough to embrace them. He was a man with a history of service to the police force, many credits to his name and able to keep up with the times. Above all, he felt that he needed to support his Force in the light of continual unfair criticism from the public and veiled remarks from the media and even government sources eager to distance themselves from problems, but keen to dissemble when it suited their political wrangling. He was an outspoken critic of the indiscriminate use of bail and the de-motivating effect this had on the morale of an already hard-pressed police force.

The Chief Constable knew that the Essex police would need a particularly good team to investigate the two recent gruesome killings; it had to be the best of the best. He would need to closely keep in touch with the situation and the only way to ensure success was to appoint the right person to lead the inquiry.

Almost on cue, as he put the briefing notes down onto his writing desk, his personal assistant, a bright and intelligent young female secretary, brought in his morning coffee and biscuits.

"Morning, Chief Constable. You need to know that Her Majesty's Inspector of Constabulary, Sir Peter Robinson, left a message that he is going to call you soon." She winced and half smiled at the Chief Constable, whom she liked as a boss and was a decent person, and said guardedly, "he, er, sounded a bit strained, sir, quite a bit strained in fact."

She left without waiting for a reply.

He sat back in his leather chair and thought that it would be good to pre-empt what the great man wanted and called in his aide, Superintendent Graham Howlett.

Howlett entered with a smile on his face.

"Morning sir. I heard that God called and left a message. I've been counting the seconds until your summons."

The Chief Constable laughed, "I trust I didn't keep you waiting too long? But then that's why I picked you to be my aide, Graham; you've got the biggest nose in the business. Now then, if I had to set up a major crime investigation team to solve two grisly murders who should I select to lead it?"

Howlett scratched his chin playfully and, staring at the ceiling, he theatrically thought out loud. "Okay. Hum, let's see, difficult murders. It's probably going to be a high profile case the way things are going. I suspect that there are more on the way – gut feeling that's all. We therefore need someone who is ruthless, driven and will shift heaven and earth to succeed, taking no prisoners along the way, and oh yes, will enjoy the limelight. Well sir, it's easy really."

Then they both said, with more of a scowl than a grin, "Ramsden it is then!"

The Home Secretary, Ralph Hardacre, listened to the soft evening rain patter against his window as he sat, glumly surveying his latest and seemingly never-ending list of 'fire-fighting' items. He was normally quite an affable man, but the strains of office, particularly this office, had made him belligerent and tetchy. The usual issues raised their ugly heads again, illegal immigrants, identity cards, a major passport fraud and so on. But at the top of the briefing paper, prepared by his aide to describe the contents of the box, was an asterisk, which cross-referenced the paper to another one in the box with a red tab on it. This usually meant 'read this quickly'. He had excellent staff and followed their judgement on key issues; so what was up today he wondered?

He reached into his box and pulled out the relevant paper. The note on the top was clear:

Suggest you read this item which was taken from the daily law and order reports to the PM. A murder in Essex is attracting much attention. His note at the top of the document is very clear that he expects some action to be taken to reassure the public of the government's intention to take tough action on criminals, etc, etc. The Criminal Justice System is under siege from time to time and we need to buy time before applying lubrication.

Ironically, this had been written a few hours before the Prime Minister was booed by a group of protestors carrying placards criticising the government's poor record on crime, who had waited patiently in the late spring rain for his car to leave 10, Downing Street. The Home Secretary read the notes on the Essex killing. Putting the two together, he realised that this needed a classic fire-fighting task to ensure an effective and quick solution to extinguish concern. He thought carefully for a while then pressed his intercom and asked his PA to bring him some coffee. He had an idea; he would get someone to arrange a local press briefing, the usual stuff, orchestrated with planted questions, plenty of party members present and good PR. But he needed someone uncompromising and thick skinned to lead it.

He picked up his telephone handset and dialled the number for Elizabeth Curtis MP.

Chips Johnson slowly turned the pages of the local newspaper having read about the recent murders in Chelmsford and paid attention to the letters page, where indignant local residents lamented about the state of the criminal justice system and vented their anger on local policing. He was one of those hacks to whom popular journalism came easily. He had been a secondary modern schoolboy with few educational qualifications and a big attitude problem, who joined the Ford workforce at Dagenham. He followed his father onto the shop floor. The youngest of six boys he learned how to gain attention or avoid his fathers flaying right hand, the hard way. But it did instil a strong sense of self-preservation and canny eye for opportunities.

He became a trade union representative and through sheer hard work and tough negotiating was renowned throughout the industry for striking fear into the heart of any motor trade management that abused its workers and even some that didn't. His demeanour was stern looking and enhanced by grey hair slicked back off his flat forehead and large spectacles that he peered through. He dressed in an old-fashioned way in cheap clothing in dull colours that had the effect of making him blend into the background. Insignificant and nerdy he might look, but those who took him for granted always regretted it. It was as though he was permanently at odds with the world – angry at everything.

Chips took early retirement from Ford at the age of fifty-three and decided to become a newspaper reporter. At first he went to work on a local newspaper based in Chelmsford and did some good work for them. But he hated the day-to-day stuff such as interviewing charity workers, covering village fetes or listening to the incessant complaints of local people about the borough and county council. It irritated him that many of them were too slack-arsed to ever go and vote in council elections and use the democratic machinery that was available to them. It reminded him of his Ford colleagues who would smile and pat him on the back when he won them a concession or pay rise, but changed their tack when the company raised its game and significantly increased benefits, but at the expense of a few hundred redundancies. It was always every man for himself. That's why he had a passion for sticking up for the underdog.

Inevitably, boredom caused by the lack of a really challenging environment led him into trouble. He blotted his copybook when he deliberately misquoted a local Member of Parliament, thus causing a terrific storm of protest from local people who believed what was printed. With characteristic journalistic licence he misquoted the Chelmsford MP Joyce Abbot as saying, "What's wrong with a special housing estate for asylum seekers in Chelmsford, or for that matter in any town in Britain?" He mischievously knew the effect this would have on the city fathers. He was subsequently sacked, not because the article touched the hearts and minds of local people, but because what he had said was a lie. He knew that was fair and left with good grace. Besides, he wanted a more exciting kind of journalism.

Nevertheless, this incident increased his standing. Being an independent journalist suited him, as well as the newspaper industry; he was their 'wild card'. They could take his stories or leave them. More often than not they took them. They could give him the dirty jobs to do and he accepted – for a price. He was building quite a reputation for himself, especially where investigative journalism was needed and people felt they had nowhere else to turn. There was much to be angry about in society.

His nickname 'Chips' came from his early days in journalism when he was hounding a local dodgy businessman who had allegedly cheated hundreds of elderly local people out of large sums of money. He virtually camped out in a fish and chip shop across from the business in question and bombarded the directors with requests for interviews, reporting on those who arrived at the company and those who left, what they did and what they owed local people.

During a period of eight weeks the owner of the fish shop swore he only ate chips; so the nickname stuck. He was canny and realised that the nickname was memorable and gave him a certain edge in the market – it made him easily well known and in some areas extremely popular. But popularity had to be maintained and he had to work hard to keep his profile high.

Today, he sat at home, eating a healthy breakfast of fruit and yoghurt, quite different to his reputed eating habits, reading the local newspaper. Two things hit him. First of all, was the report about another terrible murder and secondly, the killings had encouraged mounting public disquiet about law and order in the county. He smiled with some satisfaction. That's what it took to wake people up.

It was not difficult to understand. The fact was that all around the country people found themselves at odds with punishments meted out to criminals in magistrates' and crown courts, lacklustre political solutions with their seemingly never ending and pathetic sound bites, and a genuine fear of violent crime. It was all bubbling up, and not before time; just the way he liked it. He had his own axe to grind and reflected ruefully on the action of the police force in Essex after they had wrongfully arrested him some time ago. That incident had stuck in his craw – it would never go away.

He cared little about the deaths of two miserable thugs if it meant that the police would get a good kick in the pants from the general public. He knew that he was being presented with a unique opportunity to foment bitter debate in the press, aimed at the Chief Constable, concerning the policing of the county. That suited him very well. He would do it soon.

He slurped his mint tea loudly – he was particularly looking forward to it.

Chapter Six

Detective Inspector Andy Ramsden had moved to the Kent Police Force out of pure pique. An opportunity for promotion had arisen in Chelmsford and he knew he was in the frame along with a couple of other local officers. They were interviewed and the best man won; it wasn't Ramsden. Despite the decision, his superiors were at pains to tell him that it was merely a matter of time. They thought that he was a reliable and dedicated copper of the highest calibre – if somewhat driven at times – and they thought that he should wait just a little longer and the next rank would come along in quick time.

But this was not good enough for the egocentric Ramsden. He kept his own counsel for a while, but soon applied for and was accepted for a post with Kent CID. There were mixed feelings at the Chelmsford police station. He was not an easy man to work with. He was humourless with his team and unctuous with his superiors - he knew how to reel them in with expert clichés and adroit one-liners of the 'good old boy' style, avoiding too much detail and making too many promises that his team then had to fulfil. He read a political situation like no one else could and used it to his advantage. His nickname was Teflon. It was a nickname earned from his days as a detective sergeant when, unlike others in his team, he completely avoided blame during a particularly badly handled investigation; nothing ever stuck to Andy Ramsden.

But Kent was a long way from his home is Essex. His marriage was already under considerable strain and the daily travelling coupled with long hours – as usual – cut down his family time. This was why he was doubly grateful for the informal and 'off the record' call from the Essex Chief Constable. He attended a hastily convened interview and then shortly afterwards accepted the promotion to Detective Superintendent and the responsibility of leading the major crime incident team – known as the MCIT - to investigate two local murders.

Ramsden was pleased with this success and considered it more of a victory over local sceptics.

It would be good to get back to Essex – especially with his new rank.

Angie sat in her lounge and read the newspaper cuttings that lay in front of her again and again. They were scattered over her couch and some had fallen to the floor. She wondered what to do next, without even considering the reasons why. Her head was beginning to clear. She hated herself one minute then loathed the evildoers described in the newspaper cuttings the next. She knew it was wrong to act the way she was and it went against all her training, but now it was all so different. She felt let down by the system, then a thug killed her lovely mother and she was impelled to do something about it. Nevertheless, she put her hand to her head and rubbed her brow. It was all so confusing and frightening. She felt as though she was a different person. How could she do the things she was doing? It was almost as though she was standing to one side, watching herself do terrible things; she had lost all sense of right and wrong, even the ownership of her actions.

Several times she had flashbacks of the feverish hammering of nails into flesh, the cutting and slashing of flesh, the screams and the ringing in her ears; Ackroyd and Stevens' wide eyes, appealing for mercy and none being given. She drank more alcohol to block out the memory and to reinforce the fact that her mother was always right. She had let her down before and she would not do so again. No, no, not ever again, never, never, never.

As she began to lose consciousness and an alcoholic mist clouded her mind, she wondered where her mother had been since she had hacked at the rapist's body with a carving-knife? She desperately needed her mother to tell her that it was all right and she had done the right thing.

Why hadn't she come back to see her?

Perhaps she would come tonight?

Angie sat motionless, listening to the radio playing a soulful piece of jazz. It was at that point, she remembered that her mother had pointed to a cutting that described a drunken spree by two teenage male car thieves that ended the lives of a young family. No insurance. No tax. No driving licence. No sign of any contrition. Merely smirking faces given short prison sentences – so short they were already out of prison. The punishment, not for murder, but the lesser motoring offences was derisory. The judge had been at pains to point out that it was not a criminal charge, as if excusing the lack of a custodial sentence. This did no more than inflame the family and friends of the victims and gave the media an opportunity to excite its readership.

Her head buzzed and she rolled it backwards and forwards as she reached for a bottle of single malt on the nearby coffee table, swigging it without bothering to put it in a glass. She imagined the smiling young family, doing no harm, out for a drive, laughing and having fun. Then she sucked in her breath and her chest knotted as she saw their squashed and bloodied bodies, innocent victims, and the misery of their relatives who were left to grieve and memories of the smirking faces of the two teenage boys responsible.

Perhaps the message pumped out by the media was not far from the mark: the popular claim being that the courts are designed to protect the perpetrators, not the victims. It wasn't right. Her hand clutched the whisky bottle tightly.

Just then, far in the recess of her mind she was sure she heard her mother's voice, softly saying something like, "that young family didn't deserve to die like that. Those boys will do it again, I just know it and you know it too. You've got to stop them, Angie, it's for everyone's good – for everyone's good, Angie," but the sound of it was so soft, that she almost thought she had said it to herself. She shook her head and swigged the bottle again. She couldn't be sure.

Angie sat motionless in her chair for hours and hours in a trance-like state. She awoke early the next morning disturbed from her slumber by the sun as it rose in the light blue sky and shone through the crack in her curtains, burning her face. She felt the nagging pain of an alcohol-induced headache. Apart from that she was crystal clear about her next move and the planning that would be needed.

She knew exactly what she was going to do – and to whom she was going to do it.

Detective Inspector Jack Rollo and Detective Sergeant Jenny Ellis sat at the morning briefing in Chelmsford Police Station and a strange tingle ran down their spines. The duty inspector's words rang in their ears.

"Last night at about midnight, two local lads were parked in a car up on the A414, a couple of miles outside Chelmsford, near the wildlife and Picnic Park. They had been drinking heavily and had taken drugs. We know that from the discarded spirit and beer bottles and early blood tests. Anyway, how I do not know, the car had been covered in strong industrial binding tape to make it impossible to escape. Then a hole had been made in the side window and petrol poured inside and ignited: then 'pouf' goodbye, two young men."

This caused a gasp of revulsion around the room and the inspector straightened up as if enjoying the chance to brief the assembled company on something as gory as this.

Jack Rollo was the first to speak, "Christ, what did they do to deserve that?"

"Well, that's just it Jack. Someone thought they did something. More to the point, they even left evidence to that fact," said the inspector.

The officers looked at each other.

"Go on then, guv, what's that?" said Jenny.

The duty inspector held their attention for a few moments longer. It wasn't every day that briefings took such a turn and he was going to milk this one for all its worth.

"Ah, yes, er, evidence was found. Let me see, yes here it is, a press cutting was discarded some yards away. It was about these two young chaps and a court case that was held three months ago. It would seem that just under two years ago they stole a car, let me see now, a yes, a Ford Mondeo," he ponderously peered at his papers as if checking this minor detail.

Jack made a sign to his colleagues that resembled a wind up motion.

The duty inspector continued, "yes, that's it, a Ford Mondeo Ghia, nice car those are. Anyway, they then proceeded to get high on cocaine and booze, then motored around the county at high speed. The inevitable happened. They crashed into another car which burst into flames and the whole family travelling in it was killed."

He referred to his notes again, the silence infuriating his audience.

"A Mr and Mrs Olsen, both in their mid thirties and two young children died."

Jack looked up, "This could be a revenge attack then?"

"Yes, Jack, and don't get so excited, we're interviewing the remaining teenage son of the couple who were killed in that incident, some time this morning. He was on a scout holiday when it happened and is now an accountant and works in Colchester. He has agreed to visit the station to talk to us."

One of the police officers at the back commented loudly, "Nice one. You lose your mum, dad and siblings to a couple of hooligans high on drugs, booze and in a stolen car. Then almost a year or so later you get interviewed as a revenge suspect. I bet we'll be popular?"

Loud mumbling followed and the duty inspector did his best to quell the noise and resume his briefing about traffic diversions, petty crime and the pending visit by the Chief Constable. No one was listening. They were already comparing the seriousness of this strange and violent action with two other incidents: the crucifixion of a thug and emasculation of a local man released on a rape charge. There had to be a connection; all the crimes were weird and well planned. But it wasn't only the local force that was beginning to think this way.

On the way out of the briefing room Jack walked behind Jenny, at first keeping a small distance from her and so allowing him a view of her curvaceous rear. Jack enjoyed a happy marriage and wasn't the type to stray or behave stupidly, besides his age and shape narrowed down that possibility. But he convinced himself that he could enjoy the view as well as a disgusting imagination – he felt it kept him sane. Working with a vivacious and bubbly young woman like Jenny was a bonus and he was the envy of half the male staff at the station; it greatly amused him. For all that, he was particularly careful not to give in to the temptation to touch or leer; he actually hated that tendency in some of his younger colleagues. But he had to admit that working with Jenny sometimes made even him come close to the line. In fact on some occasions he thought he knew her better than he did his wife.

He caught up with her and bending forward slightly, taking in her soft perfume, said in her ear, "I've got some gossip for you."

That tone in Jack's voice usually meant trouble. Jenny knew every one his foibles, they had worked with each other for long time, and Jack was most definitely a 'rumour merchant'. His biggest fault was that he was the resentful 'older male' policeman who hated working with graduates, especially female graduates.

He had a supercilious look on his face.

"I got a call from my mate in the admin' office. You know the other murders, the thug and the rapist? Well, the elastic in the Home Secretary's knickers has finally broken and he taking a personal interest in the situation. He's called the Chief Constable to book on this one and almost bypassed Her Majesty's Inspector of Constabulary, the HMI, which apparently set everyone's teeth chattering. Anyway, there's going to be a lot of effort put into reforming the MCIT that was set up to investigate the crimes. It's also going to be larger and led by a big hitter. This is going to be high-profile stuff."

"Oh my sainted aunt," she said, "just as I get the chance to work on something really juicy it's likely to be taken away from me. They'll draft in outsiders, won't they?"

She idly kicked a plastic bin and it fell over.

Jack laughed at her reaction.

"Take heart dear girl. The request was followed up by, guess what? The recognition that predominantly local officers should man the team – and my contact tells me that because we got involved early on, it means us!"

Jenny beamed. She wanted excitement and challenge, not vandalised trade premises or graffiti crime.

"Oh, okay, great, all is not lost then, that's something at least," she said.

"Yeah, and there's more. The MCIT will be located at Chelmsford police station, on the third floor. And wait for the other news. Detective Superintendent, yes Superintendent, Andy Ramsden will head it. Now, my dear," he placed a fatherly hand on her shoulder, "I have a couple of local investigations to follow up in Danberry on the A12, so why don't we go to The Bull pub there and let my favourite greyhound, Frankie, lick me to death. We'll have a swift half and a sandwich and I'll tell you all about the infamous Andy Ramsden."

Ralph Hardacre, the Home Secretary, had taken post in difficult circumstances. His predecessor resigned due to ill health and poor attention to key matters during the last months in post, were evident for all to see. As every man and his dog knew, the Home Office was enormous. It was difficult being the 'virtual' chief executive of one of the largest enterprises in the UK, or Europe for that matter, and being a politician as well; it was a popular, frequent criticism of the way governments work. Some more able and well-educated critics said that these were the ingredients that spelled almost inevitable failure for all governments, no matter what colour of politics.

The notion was that you were neither a businessman, nor even your own man; you were a party member, a politician, doing the bidding of your political masters, despite the needs of the task or, for that matter, the people that needed any one of the multifarious services. A bit simplistic perhaps, but given the performance of some of his theatrical predecessors with their personality-driven adventures and the magnetic appeal of dogma dominated-politics, he secretly agreed with that view. For his part, he felt strongly that he was his own man.

Today, he was justifiably fed up with the amount of work that he had to contend with, a cancelled holiday in South Africa and vindictive speculation in the press that he might not be the right man for the job. No one wanted to listen to his difficulties or excuses – he simply had to survive for as long as he could before succumbing to large doses of Valium and a final wave goodbye when it was his turn to 'spend more time with his family'. He playfully wondered if he could apply now.

He heard a knock on the door and his PA put her head around it. "Sir Peter Robinson, Her Majesty's Inspector of Constabulary for you, sir."

Rosemary Jenkins, his mature PA, was the only person to be able to break his attention when he least wanted anyone to, or guide his thinking during difficult times. Hardacre looked over his reading spectacles and half smiled. He had nominated Elizabeth Curtis MP to take the first political steps to quell discontent due to the murders in Essex, and now he wanted to chance his arm with the man to whom the UK Police Forces answered to professionally. Sir Peter was enormously respected, himself the ex-Chief Constable of Herefordshire.

"Thank you, Rosemary, show him in please."

Sir Peter entered the room and was shown to a seat on the right-hand side of Ralph Hardacre's desk. He was an imposing man who dressed remarkably well and today wore a chalk-striped suit, light blue shirt and maroon silk tie. A reputation for 'no nonsense' had seen him the clear candidate for the job two years ago and he was a very popular choice with the rank and file police force. But Hardacre was equal to him and they sat facing each other ready to joust.

"Essex," said Hardacre, without even the nicety of a welcome or hello, "they tell me that there have been three terrible murders in the region of Chelmsford that are moving people's thoughts towards an Essex Ripper or something of that sort. There's also evidence of widespread dissent throughout the UK on the government's performance on the criminal justice agenda. What do you say to that Sir Peter?"

Sir Peter Robinson knew where the Home Secretary was coming from and was well practised at the political 'put-down,' but wasn't likely to use this technique on the Home Secretary. He relied on the safety of the independence of his office and instead offered a polite reminder.

"Yes, it is worrying, Home Secretary. But you are not surely stepping over the boundaries between politics and policing to get involved in the investigations now are you, Ralph?"

The Home Secretary knew only too well that he should not attempt to influence or intervene in local policing; it was taboo. That was the task of the Local Police Authority, comprised of local politicians, magistrates and lay members. He harrumphed loudly.

Sir Peter continued. "The Essex Chief Constable is keeping me informed on this one. A rum do, I must say. Very confusing."

Hardacre's gaze hardened. "So what are you doing about it?"

Sir Peter's hackles began to rise, but he contained himself, recognising that this was a political crisis and Hardacre could be forgiven for being more than a tad anxious.

"As I understand it, the Chief Constable has nominated some of his best CID people in Essex to form a major crime investigation team, and MCIT, the usual stuff, you know. There's not much more I can say at this stage. But what they mustn't do is to panic into believing that this is any more than a rather unusual spate of violent crimes over a short space of time. I grant you it is unusual though, very unusual. But it I think it would be quite wrong to overreact."

Hardacre appeared mollified, but reflected on and valued the tip-off from his political contact in Essex, which was that this could be one more nail in the government's criminal justice coffin lid if it got out of hand. The incidents had been anything but unusual; everyone knew that, they had been violent and premeditated. He allowed a silence to form in order to encourage Sir Peter to say something silly to fill the gap. He obliged.

"I must say that it is more likely to be the work of drug gangs meting out punishments to recalcitrant agents…"

Hardacre banged his fist against the desk. "Crap Sir Peter, sheer crap!"

A brief silence followed.

Hardacre's PA had been round the block a few times with various masters and with impeccable judgement she knocked on the door and entered without being summoned. She carried a tray of tea and biscuits. Without a word she put it on the table and said, "I thought you might both appreciate some lubrication." Then she left as quietly and quickly as she had come in.

Such moments are rare and always have the desired effect.

Sir Peter was used to rolling with the fire and took the initiative offered by the PA.

"Remarkable lady, she could probably stop World War Three with a cup of Earl Grey and a Rich Tea biscuit!" he said with a smile.

Even Hardacre half smiled. "Yes," he gruffed, "remarkable."

When the tea had been poured and politely sipped, Hardacre looked squarely at Sir Peter.

"I am not blaming you, I am sorry if it seemed that way. I meant that you are getting the wrong intelligence. There are signs that this could get really nasty. It naturally has possible political ramifications for the police force as well as the government. I hope the investigation team that is forming in Chelmsford is a good one? Anyway, I have a nasty feeling about it all. Besides, I have so much to clear up in this post that I wouldn't be surprised if Lady Luck has one or two more gems to foist on me yet. I don't want us to fall out, Sir Peter. I understand that I must keep policing at arm's length I'm not that stupid. It's just that it always bounces back on the government whichever way the ball is kicked."

He let out a loud harrumph.

"Frankly, I am already in bad odour with almost everyone I know except the PM; so if we should fall out you would simply join an extremely long queue. Let's therefore say no more other than for me to wish you good luck and thank you for coming to see me."

Sir Peter appreciated the Home Secretary's candour and knew the precarious position he was in. He saw no further use for protracted conversation. He bade him goodbye and left the office. As he walked down the corridor he resolved to call the Chief Constable of Essex – it seemed to him that some encouraging words of support would be needed.

The MCIT would need to be really good.

Detective Superintendent Andy Ramsden stood six foot four inches in his stocking feet and weighed fourteen and a half stone. He had wide square shoulders, strong chiselled facial features and dark hair cut in a slightly old-fashioned way, which made him appear oddly aloof. He dressed impeccably, but his bland choice of shirts and ties did not mark him out as a man of style. Nevertheless, he was an imposing character who got noticed wherever he was.

Andy Ramsden was one of those who, psychologists would say, never ever got to reconcile today's person with tomorrow's person. That is to say, they act on impulse, usually enticed by some kind of stimulant, for example, sex, food, alcohol, sporting prowess or perhaps the need to buy something, without considering the consequences. Then having made their choice, today, tomorrow's person regrets what has been selected, done, or even said, but of course by then it's too late to turn back.

This was how it was with his career. He was ambitious and he knew it. Not a natural copper, Ramsden worked hard, stood back and studied the formbook. He knew how to please his superiors by accepting almost any task that he was given without demur; most of all, he was adept at getting the maximum amount of credit for every job that he did.

The tomorrow's person in Andy Ramsden was a man who loved his family. It was only that his ambitious nature never allowed him to turn down an assignment or make enough room in his life for them. If a task was offered it had to be grabbed. Family issues never came into any decision-making. Now it was almost second nature for him to work late, turn in at weekends or accept a task over an anniversary or school event. He would of course bitterly regret it the next day and make all kinds of apologies and overtures to those most affected. In denial, he would accept their generous responses, but deep down he knew it did matter to them and they only capitulated easily because they didn't want to create a fuss.

In the early years his wife Sue had been loyal and supportive. She entertained his bosses at home; even with two toddlers to look after, attended all Police Force events and put up with his erratic and lengthy work patterns. But slowly, as time went on, it all wore thin, when their two children got older and she was left to make almost every major decision for the family. He was never around long enough to talk to. Sue remonstrated with him and sometimes this led to a row. Sure he was contrite, but that didn't last long; he had a man's attention span – that is to say full concentration, until the next deer needed to be hunted. Consequently, as the children grew she concentrated on a life for herself as a teacher and she was very successful at it. Almost inevitably, her personal needs surfaced as she focussed on her promotion ladder at school and where she wanted her life to go.

Ramsden, typical of some of his gender, failed to spot the signals and laboured under the misapprehension that as long as there was cash in the bank and a secure future ahead their relationship would remain sound. But he was soon brought down to earth with a bump. He remembered sitting behind a pile of files one night not so long ago in the local station, sifting for some clue or another in a drug bust. He reflected on a number of comments recently made by Sue, such as, "Hello, children, can I introduce this man, he's your father." That hurt. He began to notice the change in her and slowly it dawned on him that his crown jewels, his very reason for being, were slipping away from his grasp. It worried him a lot.

They had also had a big row recently. Not an enormous one, but one of those where home truths uttered softly and gently have greater cutting power than a chain saw. Sue had reminded him of his childhood and the issues he had with his father. It was not that his father was a bad man, far from it. Once roused, he could be amusing and the centre of attention. Otherwise, he had a lazy, indolent nature and tended to be maudlin, morose and often took to the television, as if wanting to enter into another world and not be responsible for anything except the remote control. Sue was convinced that her father-in-law would look at the television screen so long as there was a light shining from it – even the red on/off switch.

Several times his father had turned up to see Andy at school. But it was always as the art class was closing and his work was already put away, or long after he had thrown the best javelin distance in the school sports day. He forgave him, because it was just good having his dad with him at school – but he really wanted more.

Now Sue was accusing him of being the same as his father. He was facing the truth and he didn't like it. It was ironic, because she ignored his return to Essex which cut his travelling by eighty per cent and focussed on the enormous task he now faced to head up the team to investigate the gruesome murders that had taken place in the county. He couldn't see that she had become so burdened with the expectations that he would never be there for her that she was unable to think rationally about anything he did.

He remonstrated with her, because he felt that she simply did not understand that this was the best chance he would ever have to establish his career, he wanted to get one more promotion, after that they could settle back as he worked towards early retirement. It was perhaps understandable that she thought this an unlikely outcome, because he didn't talk to her about his plans.

It had all been fraught and he felt deflated that this recent posting and promotion hadn't received the glowing praise and applause he really wanted from Sue. He was reconciled to another night at home that could be compared to the Ice Age. Despite his misgivings about his personal life he knew he had to put this to one side and retain his demeanour as he arrived at the Chelmsford police station to take up his new post in his new rank. He had his detractors and was prepared to deal with them.

As he parked his car outside the station, tomorrow's person in him was beginning to question his judgement and for once in his life his stomach nerves were in turmoil. For all his bravado, he was trying hard to review his home and work life and realised that he wanted everything: a successful career, promotion, a good marriage, a happy family and a comfortable life. He had been on a cushy number in Kent, where, even in a short time, he was respected, doing work that he knew well and progressing steadily up the promotion ladder. And now his ego had made him accept a job, albeit closer to home, just so that he could stick two fingers up to his critics, which could be a poisoned chalice and lead to more endless long shifts.

So why take the bloody job in Essex?

Chapter Seven

Detective Sergeant Hannah Sinclair's foot caught the kerb just as she was getting out of the police Panda car and as she lurched forward to catch her step the files under her arm slid out and fell to the ground scattering papers, file covers and dividers over the path. She knew that it was going to happen as soon as she caught her foot on the edge and experienced that sick feeling you get when you see something happening in slow motion and you can do little to stop it. That wasn't the worst of it though; looking up as she bent down to pick up the papers she saw a window full of smiling young faces, some still adjusting their police uniforms and could just hear the faint sound of a cheer.

Hannah smiled up at them and gave a 'V' sign – this produced an even louder cheer.

It was good to receive that kind of banter, but it hadn't always been that way. When she first arrived at Chelmsford Police Station eight years ago it was a haven for male chauvinists. They hadn't meant to be that way. It was part of the social makeup and learned behaviour. Bad habits, racial and anti-feminine comments abounded; silly boys attached labels to situation and accepted things at face value and didn't know any better. But it was bad. Her female predecessor left the station suffering from work-related stress and ended up taking the Force to a tribunal; it was all settled out of court. That was of course the worst possible result, because no one got to know who wais in the wrong and little could be done to put things right.

Hannah was a different person to her predecessor, the shy and slightly introverted PC Juliet Gooding. She was neither a prude nor a tart; not physically strong, but would never shirk a fight. However, she was intellectually very bright and a good problem solver. These qualities ensured her distinguished pass in her sergeant's examination and move to the criminal investigation department, known as CID. But those early days as a probationer constable had not been easy and the experiences stayed with her.

When she arrived at the station, the Force bully made a move on her as soon as she arrived. At first it was silly remarks about rape being an assault with a friendly weapon, and then it moved to sly sexual asides. Inevitably, he went through the touching ritual; a sequence of moves men make that leads from hands and arms eventually to somewhere else – all in the name of fun.

Thankfully her father had been a wise man, with years of army experience behind him. He schooled his daughter well and she knew that she should not feel guilty in standing up for herself. In particular, that the only way to deal with a bully was to fight back, hard and quickly, otherwise the bullying would go on. She had done this as a school prefect, but never expected to have to do it in the Police Force.

It was Constable John Biggins who more than adequately filled the role of Force bully and it wasn't only Jane who suffered. Biggins, many times passed over for promotion and several times disciplined for bad behaviour, brought his rugby club antics into the work arena to antagonise and hector his colleagues, male or female.

On one fateful day, for him, he came up behind Hannah as she was using the photocopier. She saw his reflection in a glass-fronted picture on the wall; he was leering and gesticulating to those in the office behind her back, making a skiing movement of his hips. He moved up close to her, putting one knee between her rear thighs then put his hands round the front of her chest. She spun around immediately and shouted, "stop that, Biggins, you're a pervert!"

He was taken aback, but determined not to let it faze him he playfully recoiled and sneered, "Oh, your majesty, I do apologise, you are too haughty to be touched by a mere mortal like myself?"

Then he playfully bowed.

"You damned fool," she said, walking towards him, a script already forming in her mind, "how would you like me to grab your parts in front of all your friends, eh? That would be terrible, so how do you think I feel?"

Hannah was a chess player. She stood there, hands splayed outwards with an innocent look on her face knowing how he would answer and precisely how she would reply.

He bellowed with laughter, his overweight frame rippling as he did so, and faced her front on.

"I would be so delighted your majesty – go ahead, it's all yours."
He thrust his pelvis forward.

That was Hannah's cue and she reached forward with both hands and grabbed his testicles in a vice-like grip. This was enough to wipe the smile off his face, which went suddenly red. She squeezed harder and harder, and he could do no more than mumble and move his hands to hers.

"Get those hands away or I swear to God, Biggins, I'll rip your balls off right now you bastard!" she barked loudly.

Biggins moved his hands away quickly and looked straight at him. Then she spoke clearly and coolly.

"Get this straight. Nobody likes being fondled, man or woman and nobody likes being bullied. I am not PC Juliet Gooding, I am PC Hannah Sinclair and you better believe that if you keep trying to make me look stupid I will win the day, I promise you I will. Now shall I let go and will you please leave me alone?" She glared at him and tightened her grip.

"Okay, okay," he said and before he could go on Hannah squeezed some more, "Aargh, yes, bloody yes, I was only joking just let go will you?"

Biggins' voice was by now showing evidence of the pain he was in and he looked visibly pale.

Hannah let him go and without a word went straight back to the photocopier and carried on working as though nothing had happened. Biggins left the office and was heard retching in the men's room. There was a nervous, embarrassed silence in the office. No one said a word and she knew that she had to do something. She finished her copying then turned on her heels and faced the room. Everyone was pretending to be busy.

"Okay, I know you are pretending to work. Just let me know Guys," she splayed her arms out wide, "numbers out of ten?"

At first no one said anything, after a few moments, one of the younger detectives who had suffered Biggins' attention put up his hand and shouted, "Eight point five."

Colleagues then joined in."

"Six." "Nine." "Eight."

"Nine point nine," said one wag and then the laughter started. She had burst the bubble and after that, she was one of the team. The station sergeant heard about the fracas and Biggins was quickly moved to another station; not long after that he left the Force and became a security guard. After the incident, things began to look up not just for Hannah, but for everyone.

Hannah gained valuable experience that day and often had to call on her strength of character in similar situations in the future. If it wasn't arresting, then later investigating the work of mindless thugs, it was dealing with the awful outcome of rape or paedophilia. She was asked to work on the paedophile unit, but after only two weeks in the job she applied to be transferred back to the station. Everyone understood. It was the only team you could move out of quickly if your stomach couldn't stand the work. She wasn't used to failing in anything – but in this case sensibly accepted that there has to be exceptions.

Hannah gathered her fallen papers from the pavement, keeping her knees quite close together having been informed by her fellow PCs that there were frequent bets on as to the colour of her underwear – bullies may go, but boys will be boys! Then she straightened and walked into the station, through the security gate, along a corridor smelling of disinfectant and upstairs to the main CID office.

"Nice one, sarge," said a young cheerful new male recruit, "if that's the Williams case then you might have left it in the gutter."

"Thanks James, but no it wasn't, more's the pity!" she replied.

Just then her boss, CID Detective Superintendent, Pete Swanley, put his head outside his office, "Hannah, just the person, step inside if you please?"

Hannah put the files on her desk and looking a little perplexed said, "Yes guv' right away."

As she closed the Inspector's office door she studied his face. He was serious, which was par for the course with this friendly but dour man, and his forehead was wrinkled as he frowned at a letter on his desk. He steepled his hands and looked at her.

"Am I in the poo, boss, and if so I'll make a run for it now?" She said.

He smiled, which was a rare occurrence.

"No Hannah, not at all. In fact that's just it. You are rarely 'in the poo' as you put it. You are a good operator. No it's recognition of just that fact I suppose. You are to be promoted to Inspector and seconded to a major crime investigation team, MCIT, being set up to deal with these grisly murders, you know, the Ackroyd boy crucified to a barn door and the mutilation of the rapist. It's also causing a wee problem and some anxiety for our politicians – bless their hearts! Anyway, the upshot is that you will be seconded from Monday to the MCIT that will be located on the third floor. Your new boss will be Detective Superintendent, Andy Ramsden. Now, Hannah, I always keep my own counsel and rarely talk about my peers, but be warned, Andy is a driven man. He is very ambitious and comes with a health warning. You might have of heard of him he was here not so long back, but in a different capacity and section to you though?"

Hannah shook her head not really taking in what her boss was saying about Ramsden – the good news was slowly sinking in.

He went on. "He's not stupid mind you, but he does have a reputation for burying people he doesn't like. You are good Hannah and I don't want to see you fall foul of a singularly ambitious officer. So roll with the fire and remember that expediency often rules the day. Eh?"

Hannah stood up, non-plussed for a few moments, but elated, she felt as though she was walking on air.

"Guv, this is a great chance, I don't know what to say?"

"Maybe you don't – and for the record in your case that's a first, young lady! It is a well-deserved promotion and will be popular with the Force. Very well done and congratulations."

She smiled broadly.

"But take it from me this is a difficult case to crack and I have to admit it seems beyond us so far. I'm just glad I'm not in the chair. Someone is committing a series of murders and at first it was considered that they were not connected, but now we have a very strong suspicion that they are. But, there are no clues whatsoever. The ground is as dry as a bone. This is not going to be easy. I don't want to keep repeating myself, Hannah, remember this, will you? When the going gets tough, clever and ambitious men see the writing on the wall and start to blame others. But of course I didn't say that and you won't quote me?"

He reached into his desk drawer.

"I know you are a bit of a puritan when it comes to this kind of male behaviour, but let's have a quiet drink now, to celebrate your career move. What do you say?"

Hannah had in the past been critical of boozy sessions in work time, but she readily agreed and soon they were sipping good whisky and reminiscing about her rise through the uniform branch to Detective Sergeant in the CID. She was feeling very warm inside and only just able to contain her excitement. At the same time she was slightly apprehensive about her new job.

They laughed a lot as the barrier between employee and boss lowered with each glass of whisky and Hannah suddenly realised just what she had achieved in such a short time in the Police Force.

It was a great feeling.

Detective Superintendent Andy Ramsden stood ominously in at the front of the MCIT briefing room. Everyone had introduced themselves and only four outsiders had been drafted in from other forces. Everyone was made aware that some work had already been done to investigate the murders and Jack Rollo was nominated the second in command position and briefed the team on the action taken to date. Ramsden stiffened and waited for him to finish. Then he addressed the team.

"Well now. Thanks for that Jack. I need to say something straight away. Investigating murders is, as you all know both interesting and yet hazardous – to us that is!"

There was a ripple of surprised laughter at the early and unexpected injection of humour.

"This particular case is no exception. So far there has been little evidence available for us to get our teeth into. Even our poor old Home Office, Holmes database, is sucking at a piece of blotting paper, but there are signs of information dribbling in and we must make the most of that. That said, I must say that I have been a little disappointed at the depth of some of the investigations."

He paused and let this remark sink in.

"To that end, I want us to start again – and I mean again, from the beginning. Don't take anything for granted, get every ounce of information you can and plot it on Holmes. It's a good system and now has plenty of credibility with UK police forces. Let it work for you by noting all the information correctly on the incident sheets, then leave it to the tasking team – the names of officers on that central administration team are on the briefing sheets in front of you by the way – they will schedule tasks for the two main investigation teams each day."

He paused again and surveyed the room, looking at each and every person present and continued.

"I can tell you at the outset that this is going to be a difficult case to crack. The only way we can do it is to act and work as a team. I will, I promise you, crack the whip hard – if you don't like that then don't stay. Leave – I really don't care and won't hold it against you. I have a small list of things that I have personally unearthed and will give it to the team leaders. Now listen, if I can find this sort of stuff out then I ask myself why professionals were unable to do so before."

He handed the sheets of paper to Jack Rollo and Hannah Sinclair and they skim read the contents – the brief was clear and hard hitting, he was correct in his observations, right on the button; they looked up surprised.

Then Ramsden concluded his brief."Okay, refer to the briefing sheet regarding the schedule of work and the way we will go about sharing the day's tasks with each other. Each day will have a strict format. Get to know it, prepare for it and don't ever be late for a briefing – if you are then it may be your last. That's it now. Let's get some work done."

For some people, being directed tightly, without ambiguity is just what they want, they almost enjoy being harangued, but at least they know where they stand. For others it is a painful experience and they want a little more personality, freedom and flair in their lives. With the mixture of team leaders, led by the redoubtable Ramsden there was something for everyone.

He finished his brief with more motivation and a description of the core task processes. Afterwards, there was a buzz as the officers reviewed the handouts and swapped information about who was on what team. Most of the officers wanted to carry out the investigations and work on tasks; no one wanted to work in the administration team. There were twenty-five officers on the MCIT, Detective Superintendent Ramsden, headed it up, three detective inspectors ran the administration and two investigation teams and they were: Detective Inspectors Jack Rollo, Jim Barrell and Hannah Sinclair respectively. Ramsden had got the right mix of junior and senior ranks – that was important. Too many chiefs and not enough Indians, or too many hotshots and not enough disciplined plodders always led to internal politics and personality conflicts. The MCIT had to be manned by people who were given responsibility and knew that doing well would get them noticed. Jim Barrell was of the old school and his experience and precision in terms of procedures and protocol, would keep them well managed and administered.

Detective Inspector Jack Rollo was sitting with his colleague Hannah Sinclair and they both read the sheets of paper they had been given. He winced.

"How in God's name did Ramsden find out that we had listed the late Robert Ackroyd's alleged victim, Alice McNulty as childless when she in fact had a young stepdaughter called Angie MacPherson? It was something to do with the names being different, because the child was from a previous marriage, or some such crap. How does he do it? This means that some snitch here knew we had rushed this and hadn't said anything at the time. What bollocks – if I find the person concerned…"

His voice tailed off as Hannah raised her fingers to his mouth.

"Jack, no more. Get mad, get it right and move on. My list is twice as long as yours. A friend of mine told me that it was his style to tightly audit every task undertaken before he starts any new job, to sort out inaccuracies and show everyone he's on the ball. Be fair old chum, the leads were overlooked. He's not getting at anyone, but is just asking us to get it right."

Jack grinned like the man who has walked-the-walk a long time and said, "I do like newly promoted detective inspectors."

Then he stood up. "Right then, let's dig out young Ellis and give her a job to do. Where is she?"

Hannah watched him look for Jenny Ellis, his big frame gently barging his contemporaries right and left. He wasn't a fat man, just big. He seemed to use up all the available space wherever he went and someone playfully suggested that when he sat in a Panda car it was as though the passenger air bag had inflated and filled the compartment. There was much sympathy for his diminutive partner Detective Sergeant Jenny Ellis, but she really didn't need it, she could look after herself very well indeed.

Angie MacPherson drove her grey Volkswagen Polo through the Essex countryside. She had tidied up her flat in Welwyn Garden City and locked it safely. It wasn't so far to her new down-market semi-detached house in Steeple, a few miles from Southminster, on the B1021, where her family home had been.

It was a pleasant day. The sky was bright blue and white puffy clouds were racing along the skyline, driven by a moderate breeze. She never tired of the Essex countryside and had long considered it to be quite under rated. It wasn't hilly, but on the other hand although it was flat. The almost constant breeze always felt good. That was why there were so many very high hedges, to stop the wind eroding the soil. It was certainly quiet and peaceful, not at all like Hertfordshire, which was getting more built up by the day. That's why her mother had stayed in Essex; to be at peace – not to be killed.

The car windows were open and she felt the warm breeze on her face. Several cars came up behind her so she let them overtake and move on. Her addled mind told her they were, of course, following her and so she slowed sufficiently so that they had to overtake her and move on; only then did she feel safe. She knew she had to remain calm. On several occasions she had nearly lost her composure and knew this would not help her cause: the cause of right. The cause that puts bad people just where they should be: six feet under, with other criminals shivering in the shadows, regretting they ever did anything bad to anyone. Her hands gripped the steering wheel tightly as she quietly repeated her mission.

Whilst she was deep in thought she failed to give enough room to a cyclist she was passing and he swerved and turned into a ditch shouting, "Stupid bastard!"

Angie merely took this to confirm that she was, after all, being watched by everyone and had to be ever vigilant. But all that mattered little; she could cope with that. She was certain that her new personae had been firmly established, firstly at the hospital, the registrar's office and then locally. And so she left life in the Hertfordshire CID, suitably camouflaged and out of reach. In fact she quite liked frumpy, dumpy MacPherson; no more dodging unwelcome advances. It was also easy to observe the world around her; no one took any notice of a plain girl.

She drove up to her new semi-detached house and parked her car in the garage. After securing the garage door she unlocked her front door and kicked away the junk mail that had piled up in little more than a week. The house was one of four in a fairly isolated position outside Steeple and at the end of an unmade gravel road about a quarter of a mile long. It was square and boring, built during the soulless nineteen sixties, when owning a house was itself considered a lower middle class luxury; so a cheap square building with small windows was not to be sneezed at. It afforded her good views of the countryside as well as the quiet nearby main road into Steeple.

She put the kettle on then began to tidy her simply furnished lounge. As she did so she idly looked out of the window and saw a dust cloud thrown up by a vehicle driving up the gravel road towards the houses. She walked to the window and grabbed a pair of Zeiss binoculars and trained them on the vehicle. There were two passengers and her instinct immediately told her they were not local villagers. Adrenaline flowed and she ran into her bedroom.

She knew she must quickly look like the dowdy, slightly dumpy Angie and act as though she was not exactly 'Brain of Britain.' So she quickly reached into her wardrobe and brought out a bag of ill matching clothing, specially purchased from a local charity shop and put the items on the bed. But no sooner had she greased her hair, dulled her face with makeup and stripped to her bra and pants, when there was the sound of a car door slamming and knocking at the door. She knew the procedure. One knocks and the other goes round the back. There was only one thing for it. She opened the curtains to her bedroom window, took off her bra and pants and immediately turned round so that her naked back and bottom could be clearly seen whilst she fiddled with clothing she held in front of her.

She heard the unmistakable noise of feet crunching around the gravel path. Then the sound moved towards the window. All the time the knocking on the front door continued. Then the movement of footsteps stopped outside the window and she heard a young voice say, "Whoops!"

Angie turned around, exposing one breast and saw a startled young man looking at her. She screamed – loudly.

"Oh, goodness me. Sorry ma'am. Er, police, here look at my card, oh heck, where is it? Here ma'am, here it is. Don't be afraid. I'll go back round the front. So very sorry. Take your time. Please do excuse me."

As he hurried back to the front of the house, Angie permitted herself a smile and laughed to herself. Nothing fazed her. She could do anything. The clothing she held in her hands fell to the floor and she now turned to the window and faced it, her face flushed and her arms and legs wide open and laughed wildly.

"Come to me little police-boy. I'll suck you in and blow you out in bubbles," she said, then she laughed some more.

The knocking on the front door abruptly stopped; the young constable had obviously reached his partner.

She held the pose for a few minutes with her eyes closed. Her nakedness seemed to rejuvenate her and she felt the warm sunshine caressing her body. After just a minute she realised she had a job to do. They would wait a while after their embarrassment, but it wouldn't last forever. Suitably dressed she went to the door, opening it slowly.

"Hello. Sorry. I thought you was burglars. Lots of 'em around, y'know? If you's police you'd better come in now," she said and opened the door wider, beckoning them to follow her into the sparsely furnished lounge.

Detective Sergeant Jenny Ellis cursed her luck. It was bad enough that she was the one to have to revisit all the previous interview scenarios and this one was a classic cock-up of poor detail checking. All she needed now was a complaint from the member of the public about harassment and that would sink her in Ramsden's eyes – without fail.

"I am so sorry," she said in a suitably apologetic tone. "We need to speak to you, and we were, er, well, we thought you might have had an accident. I hope you weren't too frightened?"

"Well, no. Just a little scared that's all. So, what can I do for you, er…" she craned her head forward as if asking for an introduction and cursed herself for doing that. It was almost as if she knew the drill and was prompting them.

"Oh, gosh, sorry. I forgot. This is Detective Constable Joe Grogan and I am Detective Sergeant Jenny Ellis, Essex CID. We want to ask you some questions about your mother Alice who was killed about six months ago."

Angie feigned tears and sat down abruptly in one of the worn armchairs.

"What for? Why do you want to talk about my mum dying'? Can't she rest in peace?"

"Miss MacPherson, we just want to check that you are all right, that's all, and to ask about any other brothers and sisters there may be. We missed you first time round, so let's be sure that there are no other relatives. It's because your name is MacPherson and your mother's is McNulty."

"Yes, well I am the product of a nasty man that mum married, you see. She married him because of me you know? She said she looked at me when I was a baby and thought me an angel that needed to be saved. Well, she soon kicked my dad out after she married him; he weren't no good. Then she took her old name back, but I kept mine for school and stuff. Simple as that. We ain't seen hide nor hair of him since the day of the divorce many years ago; I think she paid him some money, but can't be sure. Anyway, I ain't got no brothers, no sisters, no aunts or uncles, nephews or nieces. We were just the two of us. Happy until that little bastard killed her. Now there's just me."

Angie simulated some tears and anxiety and Jenny touched her arm.

"Can we make you a cup of tea or get you something?"

"No. You can just tell me what you want with me, and then fuck off."

Jenny was taken aback.

"Well, I'm sorry if we have upset you."

"Well you 'ave. I'd almost forgotten it all and now you've given me a bloody headache making me remember about mum and all."

"Okay, look, here's my card. If you remember anything at all about anyone you might have seen or anyone you know your mother had contact with who might have had a reason to hurt her, other than the young man who was charged with her murder just let me know. Remember that the case was never fully proven against Ackroyd.

But we are particularly interested in any friends or relatives who might want to seek revenge for her death. Angie, you do know that Robert Ackroyd, the boy charged with her murder, was killed in a particularly gruesome way. We want to talk to anybody who may be able to help us with our enquiries."

She handed Angie a card, "just call me on this number and I will gladly speak to you Angie."

Angie took the card and pretended to read it.

"Plenty of people liked and loved mum, what are you going to do, arrest the whole of east Essex? Besides, if that person is found then they'll probably get a medal."

"Not quite Angie. We just need to talk to those who think they may know something. It's a long shot really. Look, I think we'd better go now. You stay there, we'll see ourselves out. Thanks for talking to us and we really are sorry to have startled you."

Detective Sergeant Jenny Ellis and DC Joe Grogan left the house, got in their civilian registered Ford Mondeo and drove away.

"Phew. What a strange bird she was?" said Jenny. "Her pallor was so pale she seemed almost bloodless."

Joe smiled and scratched his chin.

"Yeah, you're not kidding, a strange lady indeed. I have to say though, for a woman who seems quite podgy up front, she had an amazingly pert and attractive arse!"

Jenny frowned.

Chapter Eight

The morning rush hour in the Ramsden house in How Green, Chelmsford, was something to be avoided by the faint hearted. The Ramsden's had two children, Becky who was fourteen going on twenty who hardly spoke and had to be guided like some kind of automaton: from sleeping station, to cleansing station, thence to feeding station and onward to school. Jason was a typical bright but hopeless twelve-year old boy, forgetful and forever in another world. He would announce, almost absent-mindedly at the breakfast table, five minutes before his mother was due to lever him into the car, that his class needed to discuss exotic fruit that had to be purchased and then cut into equal pieces, or perhaps, that there was an extra sports period and he needed his kit.

Andy Ramsden was of course already long gone by the time the family arrived to graze at the breakfast table; on the odd occasion that he was there, he failed to notice or even step in to put matters right. A stern word in the right direction might have helped.

Later that evening, as his wife Sue cooked a dinner that she was sure Ramsden would be home in time to eat, she regretted her recent outburst at him. She had reached the end of her tether and was never sure whether he really understood what her concerns were, about their work-life balance and the increasing pressures caused by his job. Getting violently upset rarely does any good, despite what some misguided counsellors might say; if you express yourself in anger you just learn to be an angry person. The trouble is, she knew her man and knew just how hard it was to gain his attention let alone train him in any of the tender arts of fatherhood or husbandly behaviour and it was getting worse. He hardly ever remembered to do the little kindnesses that had marked them out as a truly loving couple and bound their relationship. Valentine's Day was forgotten or considered a nuisance and small gifts or help in the home had long since disappeared. She knew he didn't mean it – it just happened. Sue remembered the phrase 'growing apart together' used by a French poet and was determined that their marriage would not follow that route. Her parents had done that. They entered their retirement years hardly exchanging a word, never arguing and yet never loving.

The sound of the front door opening and closing made her jump. It was only half past six. It was him – on time!

He came over to her and pecked her on the cheek.

Sue frowned and looked up at him and not wasting a minute said, "I'm sorry I went on at you the other day, but Andy I have to ram it up your backside to get you to understand. You know, sometimes I get the feeling that if I don't then I will end up ignoring you. In the end it would just become a habit, a bad habit. I'm not sure either of us wants that?"

Ramsden held her shoulders and looked straight into her eyes. He might be the Emperor at work, but at home, however difficult it might be, and democracy was the order of the day. Here, he had to compromise.

"Look, I promise I'll change. I really promise that I'll do no more special jobs other than what comes my way as a result of my daily work – throw of the dice and all that. Okay?"

"Other than the one you've taken on already that is?" she retorted.

Ramsden winced and she continued. "Anyway, do you really mean that? Do you want to know how many times you have let the kids and me down? Andy, maybe I should ask you to take aversion therapy – you know what I mean? Connecting ten thousand volts to your bollocks, so that every time you even think of putting work before family there's a sudden flash of pain to remind you just who we are."

She smiled at her own stupidity, but then realised that if she made a joke of it, it would simply reduce the impact. Sue didn't want that to happen and so she drove her views home – hard.

"If this continues, then we are no longer a family Andy, we are just people who happen to live in the same house."

Ramsden pulled his wife towards him now and she nestled her head into his broad shoulders. He smelled her freshly washed hair and felt her soft body against him. The very last thing he wanted to do in his life was hurt his wife and family. It wasn't worth trying to make any excuses. Even he knew he had no more platitudes left. He also knew just how hard it would be for him to change.

But he would try.

Professor Gary Randle put the phone down, kept his hand gently on the unit and smiled to himself. It was enormously flattering to have a younger woman fancy you and with well over ten years separating their respective ages he considered himself to be a lucky man. Not just lucky, but incredibly fortunate. His life had been at low ebb for about five years following the death of his wife Abigail. It was true, you never really know anyone, not even the person who you live with and love the most. But then that's obvious – who can easily share the worst nightmares or feelings of inner fear or failure? Abigail had been suffering from severe depression for some time after her doctor had confirmed that she could not have children.

The years before her suicide were horrendous and he lived in a state of almost constant tension, convinced that he was growing an enormous rock in his chest. He wondered how he would get through each day and thanked his lucky stars that he was a lecturer and writer on criminal profiling; he only had to keep his persona focussed for brief periods so no one ever noticed his pain. But the chaos at home continued. One moment Abigail was up and the next she was down. Gary was convinced that she was suffering from some kind of bi-polar condition, but this was never diagnosed. Each day brought a new issue for her to rant about. But things reached the lowest ebb, when she physically attacked him with a knife and he had to have her temporarily sectioned, for her own safety, not his. It broke his heart.

The doctors thought that the nine months of treatment she underwent at a specialist clinic had been successful and she had turned the corner. There was a slight suspicion that she was sometimes focussed obsessively and intensely on daily tasks that needed to be done, but otherwise she was considered to be quite normal. On the day she died she seemed cheerful and full of life.

But when Gary returned from lecturing at the Kings College in London at around six in the evening, he found her dead body in the living room.

She had done a good job – a mixture of sleeping tablets and Paracetamol ensured a swift exit from this world to the next. Her note didn't really explain anything, not that Gary expected to find any sense or clues in the text. He knew very well that clinical depression makes an individual see the world in an entirely different way to everyone else and no appeal to the sufferer based on normalcy ever really worked.

Gary was devastated and inevitably blamed himself. He needed counselling for quite some time afterwards.

Two years later the successful publication of his book that outlined the key components of criminal profiling lifted his spirits. It had taken quite some time to find an agent willing to take him on, but the contract proved to be quite lucrative. The trouble was that Abigail's erratic behaviour had landed him with a number of enormous debts and most of the money was used to clear them off. His subsequent books were taking a long time to sell. As if that wasn't bad enough, he was now part of a burgeoning industry of criminal profilers, all of whom being enticed into the profession once they had watched the increasing number of television series and films where profilers were the heroes or heroines.

He met Hannah Sinclair, a police detective sergeant, at a university lecture, funded on the course by the Essex Police Force. She had been the most interesting of his students. He remembered how her titian hair glinted even in the poor light of the lecture room and how she had an uncanny way of unsettling him as he delivered his lectures. Perhaps it was her almond eyes, or just that she was so bloody attractive? But equally attractive was the fact that her questions had depth and she showed a talent for understanding how and why crimes are committed.

After a long period bereft of emotional or sexual gratification, Gary quickly fell under her spell. Very soon they formed a close friendship and did what close friends do: they talked about everything from art to criminal behaviour, to favourite foods, to sport, in fact, to everything. They were happy in each other's company and filled their hours until they could meet again. It didn't take long for them to sleep together. Hannah seemed totally happy with their relationship and did not appear to mind the ten years difference in their ages. Whilst they stayed at each other's flats, hers in Chelmsford and his in Maldon, they reserved judgement on permanent cohabitation, preferring at this stage to maintain their independence. With that arrangement, came a beautiful sense of courtship and seduction. Sex didn't just happen because they lived together; it was always subject to some kind of planning, preparation and joyous anticipation.

He repeated to himself that he was truly a lucky man indeed. She had just telephoned to say that she would be around for dinner and his mind turned to plans for a special dinner – nothing too heavy of course.

Elizabeth Curtis MP had fought her way up the political ladder the hard way. She worked for years as a party supporter, researching, delivering leaflets, making coffee and acting as a general factotum for the old school in her party, many of whom never ever stood a chance of winning anything let alone a constituency seat. Then she mixed with the intellectual, red brick university candidates who publicly drank draft bitter and ate ham sandwiches with the trades unions, but privately preferred Merlot and Chateaubriand. She was an active and successful researcher, then a local councillor before finally being singled out for possible grooming. She responded to the challenge. Her private life was put on hold, which was no real problem because her husband was a successful business consultant who often worked away from home. They made an odd pair; many of their friends were confused as to who followed whose politics and playful wags suggested that during sexual gratification they politically insulted each other to get turned on. Elizabeth was used to being lampooned.

She rose steadily through the ranks and was nominated as the local MP for Dagenham. This coincided with the dying days of the dominant political party of the time and a chance of working in government with the incoming party. Right place, right time. Two years of hard work later and she was promoted as Parliamentary under Secretary to the Department of Work and Pensions. Never really a popular MP within her party, she was at least functional and what she lacked in intellect she made up for in work output and loyalty, always ready to change direction as soon as her masters told her to do so.

When the Prime Minister himself spoke to the Home Secretary and asked for her to set up a local, but well publicised meeting on law and order in Chelmsford, she readily agreed – it wouldn't have occurred to her to refuse or side-step the issue.

But it was a curious choice. Controversy always dogged her private and her working life. Her husband's advice to a multinational company to close large factories and outsource work to Asia was not popular in her party. That was bad enough, but not quite as damning as a failure of judgement to penalise two men working for a local authority in a nearby county of which she was the past leader. The allegation was that they abused two young girls whilst they had been in temporary residential care. Because the incident might have hampered her relentless climb up the political ladder, she personally intervened and had the investigation toned down and the two men were eventually exonerated. They were moved on; sadly, one of the girls committed suicide.

Nevertheless, she weathered the storm and made up for the incident by working twenty-four hours a day to impress her masters. She ran a cruel campaign that pilloried the local political opposition and openly abused her privileged position by 'outing' a gay MP who had wanted to keep his sexuality as his own affair. Her ruthless, tactical and strategic thinking was beginning to get noticed at the highest levels; she was just what the party wanted.

She was now a successful MP and tipped for even higher things. As she looked in the mirror and was pleased with her looks and attire; she felt unassailable.

But as most politicians know this is when the trouble usually starts.

Elizabeth Curtis was aware from the outset that the meeting she had instigated on crime and policing in the community, to be held in the Guildhall Council Chamber was not going to go well. Despite the fact that it was a pleasant early summer evening she was experienced enough to know that things just did not feel right; she felt the brittle tension in the air as people entered the chamber.

The audience was mixed, comprising elderly people as well as a large number of middle aged business types and lots of younger parents. There was something about some of their expressions and the way they leaned against each other to talk and pointed at the podium with their agendas. Others had that, 'here we go again' look.

Elizabeth was undeterred, because she had calmed bigger and tougher audiences than this. That is why the Home Secretary had asked her to do something. Her only concern was the reporters from the red topped newspapers who had been tipped off by her staff should all be present; she wanted to make absolutely sure that her speech received the widest possible coverage.

She was joined on the dais by the Chief Constable of Essex, Alasdair Blackley, two county councillors and a magistrate from the Local Police Authority, a member of the Chelmsford and District Resident's Association and the local political party representative. The attendance was good, the Chamber was now quite full and the chairman leaned forward to tell her all was ready and she agreed to his introduction. He did this faultlessly, unctuously and then put his arm out as though welcoming royalty; Elizabeth stood up to begin her homily.

"Ladies and gentlemen, I really am glad to be here tonight to talk to you on a subject that I know is giving you all grave cause for concern, especially with some rather nasty murders that have taken place recently. Firstly, I want to say that the murders are clearly the work of a psychopath and we should not let this colour our views of law and order generally in Essex or elsewhere in the country."

"That's a relief!" shouted a member of the audience and there was sarcastic laughter.

Elizabeth smiled condescendingly and continued.

"As you know, this government is tough on crime and the causes of crime, and…"

That was perhaps the worst thing she could have said. It was a classic government platitude, now consigned to the 'disused cliché pile' and to use it to this angry audience was more akin to an early 'own goal'. A little reconnoitre by her research assistants would have paid dividends. Chelmsford had the highest number of burglaries and street crime in the UK and as if that wasn't bad enough, boasted the highest number of pensioners sent to prison for non-payment of the community charge in protest at local services. There was also a local campaign being pursued in criticism of the Essex Police Force.

"No they're not," shouted a middle-aged man, "there's more consideration for the bloody criminal than honest people in the community."

The audience murmured and shouted encouragement. Elizabeth gathered her spirits. This was almost like a political set up – she knew only too well how easy it was to organise those - but it couldn't be because this was of her own making. She was confused. There were some pre-positioned party supporters in the audience, she could see them; they stood out because they were so few and looked less volatile than those around them were. Her local party officials had done a very poor job. They were outnumbered and poorly positioned. The local party chairman looked worried, stood up and called for calm, which came after a few minutes.

Elizabeth maintained her composure, smiled wanly and continued, this time her voice was higher pitched and a little too strident.

"What everyone fails to see is that this is a local problem it is none of the government's making. Our record is a good one with more crimes solved per head in the last five years than any other government in the past."

There was more murmuring and shuffling of agendas and she continued.

"I know how difficult it must be for you, but you must understand that the whole reason I am here is to listen to your problems and take them back to Westminster. The Prime Minister himself has directed me to come here and personally find out what needs to be done."

There were howls of laughter from several people. One man dressed in a jacket, open necked shirt and cavalry twills, made his point eloquently.

"We are all I am sure grateful for your intervention," there were more murmurs, "but the fact of life is quite simple and you do not need to come to Essex to find that out. This Human Rights stuff gets in the way of dealing with criminals who seem to use it to their advantage. In addition, it appears to us, the law abiding rate-payers, that it is easier to punish an elderly resident for non-payment of council tax, with a fairly long period in the clink I understand," he looked around and got nods of approval, "than it is to deal with delinquents who frankly end up with crime sheets as long as your arm and countless hours community service, painting fences."

He got a round of enthusiastic applause and someone shouting about the uselessness of community service was completely drowned out.

Elizabeth had something prepared about the Human Rights Act and smiled patronisingly at her questioner. But as she positioned herself to respond, she visibly paled. Standing staring at her from the back of the Guildhall was her Nemesis. Beryl Grant, the mother of one of the girl's sexually abused when she was leader of a local council was walking slowly down the centre aisle. Her daughter had committed suicide and she was determined to one day seek retribution. Today was that day.

The audience became aware of her slow walk down the centre between the rows of seats and a slow hush fell; it was almost hypnotic. She reached the middle of the seating area and stopped. Then she spoke in a very clear, calm and measured way.

"How can you tell me you want to uphold the law after what you did to fend off charges of sexual abuse against men in your county residential homes, when you were chairman of Dagenham council? My daughter killed herself because she felt that nobody believed her, nobody listened and nobody cared. Politics was all that was important; your bloody career against my daughter's wellbeing."

Elizabeth could hardly control her throat and tried to respond, her lips moved, but no sound came out. Beryl Grant continued.

"The Prime Minister has the cheek to send someone like you, to tell all these people that the government is in control of law and order? You're here to make a name for yourself. Shame on you. Shame on you."

She finished by pointing her finger at Elizabeth and repeating the words over and over again. Then the audience took up the chant: "Shame on you. Shame on you."

Even when the Chief Constable stood up and appealed for calm they continued.

Then it had to happen. Some fool threw a rolled up agenda, then others followed. After that, it was chairs and anything else that came to hand. Elizabeth was hastily withdrawn from the podium and taken to a room at the back of the Council Chamber. Soon, the sirens of a large number of police vans could be heard and they arrived to calm the situation and take away one or two of those considered responsible for the melee.

At the back of the hall there were two people, each oblivious of each other. One dressed in dark sombre clothing, standing in the shadows, quietly laughing at the outcome of the meeting. The other was Chips Johnson, independent reporter for a large number of local and national newspapers. He was scribbling in a notepad, furiously describing the scene that unfolded around him – the Beryl Grant idea had been a real gem.

It had been two days since the Chelmsford debacle and Elizabeth Curtis had worked hard to convince her masters that it was a set up and she was looking into the cause. But the damage was done and she was aware that the Home Secretary was furious and on record saying that he regretted that he had placed someone with so much 'baggage' in such an important situation. Her mood further soured when her aides gave her cuttings from the national and local Essex newspapers. It all looked and sounded twenty times worse than it was and naturally, the national newspapers hostile to the government had a heyday using the situation as a springboard to other issues.

For once in her confident life, Elizabeth Curtis felt truly miserable. But there was more to come to put fear into her belly.

The telephone rang and she answered it.

"Hello, Elizabeth Curtis MP."

"Hello Elizabeth," said a familiar female voice, "I have a question for you, don't interrupt me. Wait for it Elizabeth. Do you know where your daughter is?" There was a long pause and the voice said, "Goodbye Elizabeth," and all she could hear was the eerie sound of the dial tone.

She stood there with the telephone in her hand, her mind numb, and her body frozen and almost motionless with a sudden pain in her chest. The adrenaline flow drained her stomach and she felt real gripping fear. Her head throbbed with instant pain and she almost lost her balance.

"Oh God no," she cried as she tapped out the police emergency telephone number for use by members of parliament.

When an MP is in trouble, it would be fair to say their needs are seen to a little quicker than the rest of the herd. Very soon the police were at her daughter's school and questions were flying like loose grit off a newly prepared road.

It had taken Beryl Grant many hours of observation, but in the end it paid dividends. Elizabeth Curtis's daughter did not like cross-country running. Her school, a more progressive and less liberal private education establishment made all the boys and girls take part. But fourteen year old Christina was a schemer like her mother and was determined to avoid the slog around five miles of farmland.

Every two weeks, when the cross-country run was scheduled, she and a friend would deliberately fall back and divert via a local farm. They would spend a pleasant hour smoking and talking about things that girls talk about, at the back of a large barn. Then they would creep through the woods and tag on behind the last of the runners back to the school. They had it off to a fine art.

All Beryl had to do was make her call about ten minutes before the girls reached their diversion point. By the time the hue and cry went up they would be smoking behind the barn. The school children would be gathered up quickly and after a roll call the Curtis girl and her friend would be discovered to be missing. The ensuing hour would be the most frightening that Elizabeth Curtis had ever experienced in her whole life and she would never fully recover from it.

She then drove to the school car park to watch the fun and sat back waiting to be arrested. It would be worth it – to see the pain on Curtis' face.

Elizabeth Curtis embraced her daughter and held her really tight. Her mind had gone through a hundred scenarios involving kidnap, rape and murder, and she was physically and mentally exhausted. Beryl Granger was arrested and interviewed. She was contrite and admitted everything, she didn't care at all – she had had her day.

The real problem was that the incident stoked up the fire surrounding the issue of law and order. Grant actually became a heroine rather than a villain. The person who had put the idea into her head told her not to reveal any clue whatsoever that would lead to an identity; she was so grateful for the chance to hurt Curtis that she wouldn't let the person down. She would never ever let on that she had been put up to it. Beryl owed the person that much.

The catch phrase the local and national newspapers used the next day was based on her words when arrested and would soon be applied to all politicians.

'Now she knows what it's like to really suffer!'

Chapter Nine

The prostitute stood in a dark corner of Lead Alley, just off the High Street in Chelmsford and four streets away from the main public houses watching people going about their business. She wore a loose fitting belted ivory raincoat over a short mini-skirt and white blouse. Her blonde hair caught the light from the street lamps and this gave her face a somewhat shaded look. There were sounds of music and laughter. Everyone seemed to be having fun, except her of course, stuck in this dank and dim alley littered with used syringes, piles of rubbish in black plastic bags and the occasional rat for company. Thankfully the night wasn't too cold, but she felt miserable as usual, wondering why she didn't have a comfortable, stable, warm and loving life to lead just like everyone else. The simple answer was that there wasn't one available for her.

She had been taking drugs to keep her happy and help her survive. It also made her a little less miserable. But the drugs blurred her vision and made her less alert. This left her vulnerable to abuse, especially when she was high, to groups of young men who would rob or sexually molest her. This wasn't the best way to make a living, but for her it was probably the only one. She leant against the wall and licked her lips to make them shiny. She wasn't unattractive and her body was in good shape, but she was no fool and knew that this wouldn't last long. There was really no way out. The more she plied her trade, the more drugs she took, the worse it became for her and her life spiralled out of control.

As the darkening evening wore on, she had an awful feeling that someone was watching her. She thought that it was one of those pervy customers who liked to come and look at her walk around and teased her to try to get her to drop her price. She never did. Nor did she care. But tonight she was very edgy.

As she walked up and down to loosen her limbs, a man dressed in a grey raincoat with the collar turned up approached her. It was too dark to see his face and he kept looking around to see if anybody had seen him; another nervous punter wanting to retain his anonymity.

Without a word he offered her money – it was at least ten pounds more than she normally asked and she took it quickly, but then hoped that he wouldn't ask for too many 'extras'. Some 'extras' were so vile that no amount of money could buy them – unless of course you are heavy into drugs and then anything would be done for a fix; absolutely anything.

It took her a few moments to loosen her panties and pull them down to her knees then find a niche in which she could lean. When she was settled with her skirt held high, her pearl white tummy almost shone from the reflection of the distant street light and made it seem almost florescent.

The man opened his raincoat, fumbled with his trousers then got down to work. He tried to kiss her, but she moved her head left and right, it was the prostitute's rule never to kiss the punter. He didn't seem that concerned.

After about three or four minutes of thrusting she looked over his shoulder. She was horrified to see another figure close by; was this by arrangement or what? She stopped wiggling her bottom. The man stopped thrusting for a moment, conscious that something was wrong and he looked over his shoulder. As he did so, they both let out a startled gasp as the figure moved towards them and raised a hand holding a knife, its silver blade glistening as it caught the light of the street lamp at the end of the alley.

The figure brought the blade down in a straight-arm motion on the man, but it was parried with the man's right hand; it cut him and he yelped. He quickly moved backwards, several paces away. The girl screamed loudly and the figure moved towards her slashing wildly; it was almost as though it didn't have any particular plan of action or didn't really know what to do next except impale her in some way. The prostitute was frozen with fear and couldn't move a finger to defend herself.

Then the figure plunged the knife deep into her chest just below the heart. Her eyes opened wide like saucers and she looked as if to scream, but no sound came out. Her body slumped backwards, and then slowly slid down the wall to the ground.

Without adjusting his clothing the man held his bleeding hand and ran for the entrance to the alleyway, where some people had gathered across at the adjacent road – he was fast, he knew he was running for his life.

A group of middle aged revellers about to get into a taxi heard the girl's scream and one of them frantically called to a police car that was parked some fifty metres away.

The police car windows were open and the driver saw the people waving like crazy. He wasted no time, revved the engine, turned the car and drove up to the group screeching to a halt by the taxi stand. As it did so its blue flashing light intermittently lit up the alleyway; blue light then darkness, and then repeated again, just enough to highlight a crumpled figure on the ground together with another one nearby. The police car then slowly turned and directed its headlights down the alley. About halfway down, they saw the body of a young woman being cradled by a man who held a knife in his hands. On approaching him, the constables noticed he was wearing a clerical collar.

One of the constables said, "all right, stay where you are, don't move."

The man looked up. He was about forty years old, dark haired and had a kind looking, round face.

He looked straight at them and said, "Well, one of us is not going to move that's for sure. I'm afraid this poor young lady is dead."

The young policeman was confused. "And you are, sir?"

"I'm Reverend Alex Allan, that's my church just down far end of the alley towards the road; it's in the converted Quaker Reading Rooms. It's called The People's Church. I was putting some bags out and I heard screams."

"Did you see anything, sir?"

"I thought I heard a figure running down the alleyway, but I saw nothing constable."

The constable maintained his distance and said, "can I ask you to put the knife down sir?"

The vicar looked startled. "Oh, yes, I'm sorry. I automatically picked it out of her chest. It was just, well, kind of hanging there and looked so awful. I guess that was the wrong this to do wasn't it?

"Yes, perhaps it was sir, but don't let's worry about that now."

The knife clattered to the ground and the vicar gently lay the girl's head down beside it and moved away.

The police constable walked towards the body, then stopped and looked down on the lifeless shape. He winced. He spent years on traffic duties and had never seen a body contorted like this before.

"Okay. Let's get this young lady seen to. Jim, radio for an ambulance will you," he said to his partner.

The vicar interjected. "It's too late officer, she's quite dead. I felt her jugular and pulse and there is nothing. She was alive for a few moments then it all sort of faded."

"Did she say anything?"

"No. Nothing at all. She was barely alive, but I think I caught her and was able to bless her and commend God to receive her into his forgiving hands."

The vicar put his hands to his eyes, unintentionally smearing his face with her blood.

Within fifteen minutes a squad car had arrived, together with an ambulance. The area was cordoned off with blue and white tape a white tent was erected. The vicar got into the car and was taken to the local police station. He was isolated in an interview room for a few minutes then a young policewoman detective sergeant came in and closed the door.

"Reverend Allan, I am Detective Sergeant Jacqueline Wilson, I'm sorry to keep you, but we have some things to do. I need to interview you."

"Are you going to interview me or question me?" He said.

She looked at him squarely, "I'm sorry, but I suppose we have to question you, because you were there, you did have a knife in your hand and, er, well..." she stumbled slightly, but he smiled and interjected.

"Yes, of course, how stupid of me. Please don't feel awkward. I am the silly tyke that picked up the knife. I was there and I am therefore a suspect. That doesn't need any explanation at all. How silly of me."

As a precautionary measure she read him his rights and he refused a solicitor.

"Really, I just don't want one. I have nothing to hide and want to tell you all I can so that you are able to catch the evil person that carried out this crime. So please just do what you need to do."

No amount of persuasion would lead to a solicitor being present, so the detective constable gave up.

She looked sheepish.

"Er, there is one other thing, Reverend. The girl was either having sex or was raped. That means we need to test your clothing, you know, for DNA and so on. You will also be medically examined. So you need you to take all your clothes off and put them into this plastic bag. Then put this blue one-piece suit on. The room is quite private and I will wait outside. I'm sorry sir, wrong place, wrong time, I guess. If nothing else then it will eliminate you from enquiries, won't it?"

The Reverend smiled, shrugged and began unbuttoning his shirt as she left the room.

Angie lay in crisp, clean white sheets and felt very calm at long last. "Drugs are indeed a fine thing for a troubled mind," she thought. But was that all she really had, a troubled mind? The headaches were less frequent and she didn't she feel so frantic and disturbed. Her mother wasn't with her in the evenings now, in fact she hadn't seen her for some time. She slept, sometimes deeply and sometimes lightly, on and off for days. It enabled her to call up happy childhood memories.

Alice McNulty had been a good Christian lady. It was her religion and her happy and determined nature that enabled her to work her way through a failed relationship with Angie's violent and feckless father and, despite not having much money, to ensure that Angie had everything a young girl would need as she grew up. Their relationship was as solid as the Rock of Gibraltar. Although Angie was not a practising Christian, she had been well schooled by her mother who had chosen to attend St Thomas's church in Bradwell-on-Sea, not far from her small house in Southminster. She preferred that to the rather ugly and austere looking St Leonard Church down the road from her house. She never really minded Angie's religious scepticism, but always hoped that her daughter would find peace some day and return to the church.

What was so remarkable about Alice was her ability to relate to her daughter as a friend as well as a mother figure. They talked about everything, friendships, cookery, politics and even sex. She was no prude at all, despite her sombre exterior and very religious outlook on life. In fact they enjoyed a lively and open sense of humour and Angie loved the way her mother would use naughty words, all the time knowing the meaning, and yet pretending not to. She would use expressions so that it appeared to be in reported speech rather than her own words.

"Darling, the bank manager is, what did that chap say in the bar last night, a wanker, or whatever that is?" She would say, and Angie would feign surprise and embarrassment; they would fall about laughing. The best days had been in her late teens before she went to university, and their frequent walks to the Celtic chapel, St Peter on the Wall, a mile outside Bradwell-on-Sea. Angie and her mother talked and talked, and a strong bond had been cemented for life. Alice felt particularly close to the area, but didn't know why. She almost revered anything to do with Celtic history and filled her house with artefacts and books on the subject.

But then Angie left home and went to Kings College University in London. She inevitably spent less time with her mother, which Alice understood, but then redressed the balance by getting a job in the Hertfordshire Police Force after she had completed her degree and police academy training. Whilst this was some distance from Southminster, it was in a neighbouring county and not far to drive from her flat in Welwyn Garden City. Her mother was pleased for her – that's why she was so worried when Angie's resigned.

To Angie's great shame and sadness, she had been too busy to visit her mother as often as she should. She selfishly withdrew into herself after leaving the police force in a fit of pique and consequently wasn't there to help her mother move to Bradwell-on-Sea to be closer to her church and her favourite places.

She hadn't been there for her mother when she needed her. So the temptation to ask a local layabout like Ackroyd to help, a chance encounter, had led to her death. It was her fault. In her dreams and her waking hours she cried from pain and guilt, her chest heaving and her breath coming in short sobs. It was almost too much to bear.

The effect of drugs made her feel drowsy and she was able to feel comfortable at last. Would this be momentary; would it last, would she ever be free of what she had done or was about to do? At this moment in time she simply did not care. She needed rest and lots of it. It was all so complicated and her head was woolly. Angie would think about this later.

For the moment, she just wanted 'later' to be a long way off.

Reverend Alex Allan sat impassively waiting for his interrogators to arrive. It was a typical Spartan interview room, furnished with red plastic chairs and scruffy grey metal table and cream fabric covered walls. Some of the fabric came away in the corners providing irritating little curls that cried out to be pulled. On top of the table was the obligatory tape machine and a jug of water with several plastic cups. The blue overall felt warm and light against his skin and was so soft and thin that it felt as though he were naked; only the Velcro strips which irritated his skin at the ankles and wrists reminded him he had some kind of body covering.

Two officers came into the room and he stood up and said hello.

One was the policewoman who spoke to him earlier, and the other a male colleague Detective Sergeant Jack Rollo.

"This won't take too long sir," said Jack, who sat down and did the introductions for the tape. With the tape running, he asked him again about arranging a lawyer.

"I would urge you to ask for a lawyer to be present, sir, it is in your own interest."

The vicar smiled and shook his head, "And more cost to someone more like? No, please don't worry. I am not a Jack the Ripper and want to help you all I can. I want to tell the truth. So, no more please, let's just get on with it."

Detective Constable Wilson pressed the button on the tape recorder and it whirred silently.

"I am Detective Inspector Jack Rollo and this is Detective Constable Jacqueline Wilson. We are at Chelmsford Police Station in Interview Room Three." Jack gave the date and time and coughed and had to take some water, he continued, "I have advised you to seek legal representation and you declined. Would you please confirm your name and date of birth, and that you declined a solicitor."

Reverend Alex Allan looked serious and confirmed his name, his birthday as the second of February nineteen fifty nine, and that he had indeed declined legal representation because he wanted to tell the truth and had nothing to hide.

Jack coughed again, and then began the interview.

"Okay. Can you please describe the events that took place this evening which led up to the murder of a young girl called Kelly Golding in Lead Alley, Chelmsford," said Jenny Ellis, "we want to know everything."

"Oh dear, that was her name was it? Poor girl. Well, I was tidying up the church and had a number of bags to put out for the morning. As I was putting them out, and I must confess my mind was on other things so I didn't immediately notice anything. I'm a bit of a daydreamer I'm afraid. Anyway, no sooner had I dropped the bags but there was a huge scream or should I say a howl, really, full of fear and well, er, so awful."

He looked down at his hands and continued, "I looked up and saw a man running off in the direction of the front of the alleyway. Inspector, to my eternal shame, and I mean that, I feel so awful, I got scared and ran inside my door. My heart was pumping. I am not a violent man you understand. Then I chastised myself, quickly prayed for strength and less than a couple of minutes later I ventured through the door again and back into the alleyway. I called out several times but there was no sound. I crept down the alleyway and saw the poor girl. She had this knife sticking out of her chest. It was just dangling there, awkwardly, with blood oozing all over the place. It looked vile, it was horrible."

He gulped and reached for a plastic cup and Jack filled it with water. He downed it in one.

"Leaving the knife like that, sticking in her flesh, just seemed, well, awful. So I took it out. Whilst I was doing so, I noticed she was fading fast and blessed her while I could. Then I could feel no pulse or sign of life and concluded that she had died. She was so young and so lovely. It's such a pity she lived the life she did. At least she is now in a better place"

He poured some more water.

Jack looked at the notes, but didn't say anything.

Jenny looked straight at the vicar and said, "Let me see, you said you saw a shadowy figure when you spoke to the police constable attending the scene, can you explain more?"

"Oh, yes. Well I suppose it was nothing, my mind was in a whirl. It really frightened me to think that whilst I was cuddling the girl someone was still there, you know what I mean?"

"I understand how you must feel, but can you say more than that?" said Jack, looking up from his notes, slightly irritated.

Reverend Allan paused and thought for a moment before replying.

"No, actually, I am not really sure whether I saw anything, or if it was my imagination. Perhaps the man who ran away earlier came back to finish the job, I really don't know. As I said, my mind was in a whirl, Inspector, I was terrified. Sorry, I'm not very good at this sort of thing."

"Really sir, please don't be upset," said Jack, "you've been most helpful, just a couple more questions. You said you blessed the girl," he referred to his notes, "and 'passed her into, quote, 'God's forgiving hands', what did you mean by that?"

The vicar looked non-plussed, but then gathered himself.

"Inspector, when we go to God we all need to be forgiven something."

Jack continued, "Yes, I know, or at least I think I know. It's just that the girl was a prostitute and I wondered how you knew this."

The vicar sat back in the chair and paused before he spoke. "I rather thought that she was a prostitute and that may have been uncharitable. It's just that I have seen all sorts of girls in Lead Alley. In fact I have been able to encourage one or two to come to the church and they have changed their lives because of it. But not this girl."

"You mean you knew her, she turned down your offer of salvation?"

The vicar looked annoyed and his eyes narrowed.

"No, I do not know her, at all, as it happens. I'm merely making an observation that some manage to turn their back on this kind of work and some cannot, or will not. But even so, I bless them all; my blessing on her was based on a simple premise; God forgives all. I know that there is a strong chance that you are an atheist, but believe you me, He forgives – I believe in this, it's my stock in trade."

Jack smiled in agreement. "Well that's a relief to heathens like me sir! Just one more question if I may. Can you account for your movements on twenty first of March, the twenty seventh of March and the tenth of April this year, between about ten in the evening until three in the morning?"

A slow smile crossed the vicar's face.

"Ah, of course, the grisly murders. Oh dear me, am I lumped in with that lot?"

"Not necessarily," countered Jack, "but I do have to ask you."

"Yes, I suppose you do. Well let's see, I have no recollection whatsoever about my whereabouts on the first date you gave me. But I suspect that I was painting the church, as usual, and that afterwards I fell into bed and slept soundly. Now the other two are easier. I was in Devon helping a friend on a religious retreat. It was just outside Totnes."

"That's fine, Reverend, can you establish that for me?" said Jack.

"I'd be glad to. I have the details and will give them to you. Now, is there anything else you need?"

Jack sat back and folded the papers in front of him.

"No more for now sir. Thank you for your trouble. That will be all for today. Can we arrange a lift home for you?"

"Yes that would be kind of you. I don't want to get arrested for being on the streets in a blue baby grow now do I?"

Jack smiled, officially gave the time and date and ended the taped interview. Jenny switched off the machine and took out three tapes, sealing and signing them, keeping two and handing one to Reverend Alex Allan.

A police Panda car dropped the vicar at his church where he lived in a flat on the premises. He was assured that his clothes would be returned as soon as possible and seemed quite unconcerned, joking that they were worn out anyway.

Jack and Jenny said goodbye, then got out of their vehicle and walked back down the alleyway to review the murder scene again.

Jenny felt the closeness of the alley walls and its muck and smell. She tried to imagine what it was like to have to sell your body for sex in conditions like this. What drove girls like Kelly to do this? What was it like to have to have sex with any man who was willing to pay you, no matter how they looked, or smelled or behaved? She shuddered. Jenny cherished her independence and in particular her sex life which she controlled with precision. The late young Kelly had none of this – she shuddered involuntarily. Standing over the sight of the killing and turned to her companion.

"This was a particularly senseless killing Jack. At the moment at least, it seems motiveless. What about the man running away? Well there's a stupid thing, he's hardly going to knife a girl he is the throes of shagging?"

Jack laughed, "I've been in this job for many a year my girl, and I can tell you, you never really know."

Jenny was lost in her thoughts.

"Jack, Reverend Allan said he heard her scream, but no one else did, or did they? We need to talk to more witnesses and review more of the statements."

Jack Rollo tilted his head. He would make a successful detective out of this young lady, if it was the last thing he did.

Hannah and the team sifted through endless records on the first three victims and all possible links with family, friends and work-mates. They created model after model until the Holmes police computer system groaned at the different permutations that it was being asked to perform.

The mood was grave after the killing of the young prostitute. The fourth murder had been a kind of wild affair and there were two men in the frame: a hapless vicar intent on getting the victim into God's grace as quickly as possible and a man in a raincoat seen running from the crime scene.

The records showed that the girl, Kelly Golding, was a well-known prostitute who had been subject to a number of minor convictions, ranging from soliciting to possession of class C drugs. She had been involved in a sexual encounter before she died and there was no indication that this had been forced, and she had also recently taken drugs. There was no semen DNA evidence, but a number of pubic hairs belonging to her last customer were retrieved and tested. Other than that, the poor girl had no other injuries and died almost instantly from a knife blow to the heart.

Detective Inspector Jack Rollo and Detective Sergeant Jenny Ellis talked to the other girls working that particular area of Chelmsford and they all said that they felt that there was a presence in the shadows often watching them. They ranted as all prostitutes do, about the way the trade is treated.

The most outspoken said, "Everybody needs us, and that's the truth! But nobody wants to protect us or even legislate and legalise what we do, like other bleedin' countries," she leaned towards Jenny mockingly, "if more wives gave their husband blow-jobs at home, they wouldn't engage us to do it, now would they?" The girls all laughed but Jenny failed to acknowledge the remark.

There was a degree of consistency in the prostitutes' remarks that highlighted the fact that they all felt that they had been watched from time to time. Otherwise, the dead girl, Kelly, had kept herself to herself and no one knew anything much about her.

Two Detectives were sent to see her parents in Stoke. They said all the right things, but the trained interrogators were quick to notice the scruffiness of the family home and the lack of photographs or childhood memorabilia in the house. They feigned surprise at her activities and claimed to have talked to her recently, but could not even remember her mobile telephone number. Sickened, the officers left the house and journeyed back to Essex.

Hannah sat in the incident room office and sombrely read the reports. She was perplexed.

Why a prostitute?

The team sat sombrely awaiting their new boss. Detective Superintendent Andy Ramsden called an early meeting for all members of the MCIT. Just when they thought he would be late, the door crashed open and he strode into the room followed by Detective Inspector Jim Barrell who looked harassed and nervous. He carried a video case in his hand and comically was almost in step with his boss.

"Right now. Good morning. I hope that we are all awake. I am and what's more I'm bloody fed up. Fed up with evidence not being recorded properly, fed up with a complete lack of intelligence in some of the MCIT and frankly, fed up with work half done or done shoddily. As from today, any sign of that and there will be a cull. I did say you could leave if you wanted to and no one did. But I promise you if you are asked to leave now then it will be with a black mark against you."

Hannah watched his performance closely. It wasn't her style, but in her heart of hearts she knew that some, not all, but some of the team needed that kind of treatment. He dealt it out so effortlessly and without a trace of weakness or condescension. Ramsden continued.

"I know you all sit watching your televisions avidly and you may have seen this, but let's go through some newsreels."

Jim Barrell inserted the video into the player and pressed the start button. The resulting local and national news that covered the debacle resulting from the attempted spin on law and order by Elizabeth Curtis MP was covered in various ways. But the underlying message was of police forces and the government in crisis. Then after the video stopped Jim displayed on a screen, using an overhead projector, copies of articles in newspapers and magazines. The lights went up and there was complete silence.

Ramsden stood up and put his hands on his hips.

"The man in the street is worried, so are our masters. The fact of the matter is that a lot of good work is being done in most areas of the country, but there are some places that are in a bad state. We are not. I am not an apologist for the Criminal Justice System; I just do my duty. What hurts me, and it should hurt you, is the implication that we are slack at our job. That's why I have to drive you hard. I know it's difficult and I know I can be a hard bastard – you don't think I don't know that? But if I wasn't then things would slip and we cannot allow that to happen. That's why I am dealing today with key advisers on the subject of public relations so as to ensure we are not always reacting to headlines, we are feeding them ourselves."

He let the matter settle and then turned to Jim Barrell.

"Jim here is gong to be your first port of call when you get any, and I mean any, inkling that matters are getting out of hand locally. So, keep your heads up and be aware of situations around you throughout the investigation of this case, be careful what you say to anyone, let alone the press, be careful what you ask and how you present yourself; above all give the public the impression that you are upbeat and determined that we will catch the killer. Okay that's it, get back to work."

His dismissal without questions was typical of him. 'Now hear the word Ramsden,' as his co-students were to nickname him on his senior management course. In some situations it was just what was called for.

But was it right for Chelmsford?

Chapter Ten

Detective Inspector Hannah Sinclair sat with her colleague Jack Rollo and Detective Sergeant Jenny Ellis, and together they ran through the short statement made by Reverend Alex Allan.

"Jack, it all seems quite plausible, the Reverend has alibis for two of the murders – what's your gut feeling?" said Hannah.

"Just that Hannah: reasonable, plausible and no little cracks. I am always surprised when people want to co-operate fully with the enquiries and refuse a brief. But I must say if I had been found in the same position as our dear Reverend, I would've engaged Max Clifford. But there you go, funny old world."

Jack laughed to himself and sat back in his chair, his arms above his head, stretching his corpulent frame so as to cause the shirt button by his trouser line to come undone, exposing a small area of hirsute flesh.

Jenny looked anxious as if about to say something.

"Go on Jen' what's on your mind," said jack, "all views gratefully received."

"Well, he's a bit naïve isn't he? Pulling the knife out, sitting cradling the girl in his arms, her blood spilling all over him. He could be using this as an excuse for his innocence?"

Jack nodded sagely. "Yeah, but then if he was really guilty he would've made a run for his church, locked himself inside, then removed his clothes and popped them into the washing machine, then into a shower and we would've been none the wiser?"

Jenny looked deflated. "Oh, yeah, I suppose so, guv."

Jack leaned over to her in a kind of fatherly way.

"Jen' you may have a point, but so do I. You've got to learn not to feel deflated just because someone else counters what you say. Let's let the pendulum swing your way shall we? You see I am a bit bothered by the way he seemed to know that young Kelly was a prostitute and why did he commend her to 'God's forgiving hands?' that's a bit presumptuous isn't it? We need to take a view on this Jen', do we pull him in for further questioning, and if so what the hell do we ask him? We also need to consider getting a warrant to search his church and home."

Hannah liked the way that Jack and Jenny interacted, they made a good team: Jack's experience and Jenny's youth and keenness. She sat back in her chair and tapped her shiny black shoes with a pencil.

"Let's think about this," she said "Why don't I take his clothes back to him when forensic have finished with them, and I'll have a casual chat with him, you know, find out a bit more about him? Then we let things lie for a bit. We can carry out a full search of premises a little later. If there is anything slightly odd or worth following up then this will slip under his guard, especially if I indicate that there probably won't be any further questions."

They talked some more, poring over the transcript of the interview and the notes on the murder scene, reviewing the links on the Holmes printout. Several cups of coffee later they all agreed that was the best tactic. Even though the vicar had been found in a very compromising position, his alibi was reasonably solid and they could not yet establish a motive. It was all a bit thin.

Hannah would take the vicar's clothes back to him and see what came out of the conversation.

Detective Superintendent Andy Ramsden was quite clear in his brief to Detective Constable Jenny Ellis. Local journalist Chips Johnson was a menace. He had been tipped off by a contact that the journalist was whipping up the local press and there were fears that he would soon do so with the nationals. UK Police Forces were under immense pressure already and this case, with the mystery killer, had stirred up a frenzy of criticism. It had the potential to get as political and critical as the Yorkshire Ripper case.

He told her that she should make a date to talk to Johnson and get him on their side, rather than have him as a continual critic of police methods. She was to use her experience, such as it was, and if necessary, her feminine wiles; Jenny bristled at that comment but let it go. She understood it was an important assignment to try and reduce the stress on the team and was content to do what she could.

Jenny was keen to succeed and quickly contacted Chips Johnson to arrange a meeting just before lunch on the coming Wednesday. The venue was the Lunar Café in the Chelmsford high street. Jenny arrived early but didn't order anything. She saw two men arrive and recognised Chips from a description of him and waved to get his attention. He waved back and she was surprised to see that he had brought a blind man with him. After shaking hands he introduced the man as Andrew Carter. He was a good looking, tall and well built young man with pleasant features. They settled down at the table, Andrew folded his collapsible white cane and after ordering three coffees, Chips brought out a notebook.

"Whoa, Chips, no notes. I want us to share information in the hunt for the killer in our midst and I want to discuss local incidents and so on, I'm not having you quote me or the Police Force in any way, they would fry my backside," said Jenny.

"Jenny my love, I'm not taking notes I'm referring to 'em. Don't get so sensitive. Anyway, if you weren't desperate you wouldn't be talkin' to me babes, true?"

Jenny huffed, "Not quite Chips, I just want to know what you know and see if we can work together on a few things, that's all."

"Well, I'll take that with a pinch of salt. For what it's worth my next independent piece of journalism will feature on parental control and the lack of respect and discipline in life today. Not exactly controversial, but people just love to read what is so obvious, you know that? That's why I brought our Andrew 'ere. He was done over, if that's the expression, in his own home by a bunch of teenage girls. Girls, but thugs nonetheless. You 'appy to tell 'er Andrew?"

Andrew straightened up, his blind eyeballs flicking left and right indicating some agitation as he prepared to tell Jenny about his experiences.

"Yes, I suppose so, the embarrassment has faded now, it happened about a month ago. The girls must have seen me leave the local shop in town and followed me as I tapped my way home; it's a well known route for me and I have no trouble in going to and from the local shops. I knew there was something going on because I heard sounds, but well, without sight there's not much you can do. Anyway, as I unlocked my door, several pairs of hands propelled me inside my flat. I yelled at them, but the weight of several teenagers is more muscle than one fit man."

Jenny saw that he was a little pink around the cheeks and let him go on.

"They tied me to a chair and kept hitting me in the face and stomach, demanding money and the like. I told them where I kept my cash and this seemed to satisfy them. But a brighter member of the group asked for my credit card and PIN number. At first I resisted, but it's amazing what gentle pressure to the throat will encourage you to accede to."

Chips winced and his face stayed in a frown as he sipped his coffee loudly.

"Not content with raiding my savings, they then began drinking my whisky and vodka."

Jenny followed the story and said, "What age group do you think they were Andrew?"

"Oh, thirteen to sixteen years old, I think. They didn't talk like young women, but like, well, schoolgirls, I suppose, that's how I know. That didn't stop them enjoying the power they held over someone vulnerable. They really seemed to enjoy that. I think they would've done this to a pensioner or other disabled person for sure. In my case it didn't end there."

"What do you mean?"

"They decided to tie me up and have some fun. At first they began cutting my clothes away and made rude remarks about what they were going to do. They were quite drunk and giggled as they did so, each girl urging the other on. Eventually, I was naked. As I said, they really enjoyed the power they had over me. I think some of them had either been abused or been subjected to some kind of male sex by force. It was just the way they seemed to see me, you know, the focus of their attention, someone to use as a target – someone to suffer in the way one or two of them had or perhaps along the lines of some scummy magazine or television show? Anyway, what followed may be in some men's fantasies, but not mine. My only regret is that a man cannot control his body in all situations - if you know what I mean. After they had finished it was another playful beating and off they went."

"What happened afterwards?" said Jenny.

"Well, miraculously they had been spotted leaving the flat by some local people who later identified them. Although it was twenty-four hours after my housekeeper released me, they were quickly caught and charged. The situation was explained in court, but when it came to mitigation, you should've heard the rubbish that their lawyers spouted. It was unreal. Issues such as broken homes, parents on income support, poor life chances and feelings of failure in a competitive society were trotted out. What crap!"

He shifted uneasily in his chair and Jenny recognised the script.

"The upshot was they all got bound over and given some kind of community service, despite having quite a record of offences. One of the parents even blamed me. She said that I had provoked the kids, then, half in jest, that they had given me the time of my life and I shouldn't complain. It was all just a big laugh to them. Needless to say I didn't get any money back."

Chips flicked through his notes.

"And we have several more cases in my notes and they all indicate that the great British public is made up of parents with very little respect or control over their brats. Not very nice at all is it?"

"What's this got to do with the killer?" she said.

"Easy really," Chips replied with a broad smile, "the next victim is going to be a wayward child criminal. I will lay odds of five to one on that. The killer thinks your policing borders on the comic my dear Detective Sergeant. In short, it's bloody useless."

He smiled – a large fake, irritating smile that made Jenny feel angry. The trouble was Jenny knew that the general public felt this way too. It was the everyday stuff that seemed so difficult to police. Jenny felt confident that they would nail the killer, British police forces were good at the big stuff, but the damage done in everyday society was what caused the biggest problems in terms of image. She could only sit there and let Chips have his say.

Chips continued, "there will soon be a war conducted against all criminals in our society Jenny, people are fed up with a complacent and hopeless Criminal Justice System, full of Human Rights rubbish that is designed more to be nice to the criminal than help the victims. It's interesting, dear heart, that those murdered were, how shall we say, the dregs of society?"

She noticed his face reddening as he spoke – and thought to herself that this man was 'off the wall' for sure. Chips paused for a few seconds to let the message settle in and then resumed his tirade, arrogantly leaning back in the seat.

"And guess what, people are talking about vigilante groups, self help groups, and taking the law into their own hands. It's spreading like wildfire Jenny and there is nothing you can do about it – except catch the killer of course. It looks to provide me with a lucrative number of contracts, especially given my already jaundiced view of the Police Force. Is that what you wanted to hear?"

Jenny's throat tightened. "No, not really. I was kind of hoping that you might work with instead of against the police and that you might have some clues that we could follow up. Look Chips, if you are not careful, what you write will stir people up in all the wrong ways. You know very well that some people with febrile minds take what's in newspapers and use it to justify their own ends. You can see how dangerous this would be, surely you can?"

"Oh, deary me. The Police Force want you to persuade me to be a good boy and not to let the already fed up and frightened British public know how absolutely useless you and the government really are? You want to know something, they also believe that even if you managed to catch the perpetrator the system would probably be kind to him anyway? No sweetie, you've got the wrong hack!"

He smiled like a benevolent football referee sending a player off with a red card, indicating this was something he simply had to do, but of course didn't like doing it.

Their meeting had not been a success. Jenny tried hard to move him away from confrontation journalism, but failed. More galling was her failure to get any information out of Chips about anything at all useful, although Chips seemed to have something up his sleeve and teased her that the mucky stuff would soon hit the fan. She didn't know what he meant and he wouldn't say any more. They argued after that with Jenny accusing him of double standards, then the meeting came to an abrupt halt; unsuccessful and bruised she said goodbye to Chips and Andrew and left the Lunar café.

Chips had been described as a loose cannon and she now understood why. He was tuned in to the populist view of law and order and fanned the flames with a fury. But was he doing it because he felt strongly about protecting the community, or to earn money from his journalism? She was also perplexed: how could he purport to speak confidently on the killer's raison detre, or even guess at the next murder victim? More worrying to her was the story of the teenage girls and the blind man. When was it, that society lost its respect and dignity?

Jenny felt a little bruised and knew that the meeting had been and abject failure; she even had to pay for the coffee.

Andy Ramsden was driven to the school in a squad car; it was the only way to beat the traffic. The driver did things that ordinary motorists could not and halved the journey time. When he got there he asked the driver to stay and ran up the path to the main entrance. Jason's project classroom was on the first floor of the tall red brick comprehensive school, he knew where it was and went straight there. Jason was just clearing up. He was the last in the classroom.

"Jason, good grief son, I'm sorry. I suppose I've missed the chance to see your computer project?"

Jason looked up and half-smiled. Mature, well beyond his years he said. "Well dad, I guess you have. But don't flake out, I'm cool about it. Mum won't be if I tell her, which I'm not going to. Here take this," he said.

"What is it?"

"Dad, read this folder. Let's be honest, you either tell mum that you missed seeing my computer project, or you take this and digest the notes carefully. It is all about the project, how it works and how successful it is. Your choice, but frankly, if I were you I would take the notes," he smiled and sat on a desk, his legs swinging to and fro.

"Jason, I don't deserve you. I'll make it up to you I promise you. And don't blame your Mum you see…" said Ramsden, but Jason cut in.

"Dad, you don't have to explain about mum. Look I know how it is between you two. She doesn't seem to appreciate that almost every other kid in the class has a dad who works late or can't make school events. I'd love you to be here, but that's life."

Ramsden's throat tightened and he recalled Sue's words about his own father. He put his hand on his son's shoulder. He knew that he didn't deserve such maturity from one so young, but the boy summed it all up so succinctly. But he hated lying to Sue as well – but for the sake of avoiding another row and to achieve peace and harmony, expediency rules. They chatted for about thirty minutes and

Ramsden suddenly felt that he was really beginning to get to know his son. Just then a teacher, Mrs Rydell, came into the classroom.

"Oh, Mr Ramsden, nice to see you, such a pity you missed Jason's demonstration," she said.

Jason stood up and walked towards her.

"No Miss, my dad was here all the time. He was in the loo when you walked about earlier. It was my fault for not introducing you."

"Well, I must say I…"

Miss Rydell was cut short by Jason.

"Definitely here all the time Miss. It's been great getting his advice, really great."

Miss Rydell was used to parents being difficult but the situation seemed relaxed to her. She cocked an eyebrow at Jason and then looked at Ramsden. If this is what the boy wanted then who was she to step in their way. She didn't speak for a few seconds.

"Yes of course, I'm so sorry," she turned to Andy Ramsden, "sometimes I forget my own mind. But then as Jason knows all us teachers are a little batty?"

Jason smiled at her as she left the classroom and said, "She often talks to mum outside the gates, they are quite friendly. That's settled that piece of evidence."

Ramsden grabbed his son by the shoulder and ruffled his hair.

From that day, he and Ramsden junior had a clear understanding of their lives and a father-son partnership.

Hannah sat with Gary Randle her boyfriend of some ten months in an up-market café in the centre of Chelmsford. They didn't mind paying over the odds for coffee and cake, because the décor was relaxing and the seating comfortable. Today they were pleased to secure two seats on the only large leather sofa by the window. She noticed that he was a little low and knew the reason.

"So the latest book didn't get off the ground, so what? But listen, it's not the book that's at fault, it's the lack of energy from your lacklustre agents. Threaten to change them, that will put a bullet up their arses?"

Gary laughed.

"You know, for an educated middle class young lady you come out with the most remarkable comments. What was it you said about me the other day? Oh yes, that's it." He reached for her hand and added, "When I asked whether or not you fancied me in the early days you said no, only in your 'fuckination'' – you add such an academic flavour to foul language you know that?"

Hannah laughed.

"That's not fair. Besides, a little fuck and imagination together is a good thing, hence my new word. That's better. You're smiling now."

"Yeah, you're right. Smile and the whole world smiles with you. Something will turn up."

"Perhaps it has already," said Hannah, "Look, I've been thinking, how about offering your criminal profiling services to the Essex police force in connection with the recent spate of murders in the county? My goodness, you are good at what you do, you are well known, you have had successes, albeit in the past and you lecture on the stuff."

Gary blanched at the word 'stuff'.

"That's not such a bad idea Hannah, but there is an approved Home Office list and I have never applied to be included on it."

"Yes, but it's only a recommended list and contains a lot of national contacts, you have the advantage of being local. If you feel happy about it, why not let me talk to my boss? You never know."

Gary smiled at her. Nothing much had gone his way recently, except meeting and forming a relationship with Hannah, so why not.

He surely wouldn't be the loser for it.

Later that day Hannah managed to corner Detective Superintendent Ramsden in the station coffee room. After getting him to sign an innocuous piece of paper on police overtime, she manoeuvred herself into discussion with him on the difficulties in dealing with a succession of apparently motiveless murders with few clues. He raised an eyebrow and she felt his gaze as she tried her very best to move the conversation around to the use of criminal profilers. She was certain he was asking himself what she was up to. But he listened to her.

She produced some articles from internet web sites and began to weigh up the pros and cons. He quickly reviewed the contents and nodded at one or two.

Hannah pulled a feigned serious face, pulling her eyebrows together and tapped her pen against her teeth.

"Y'know guv, I can't help thinking that we need an edge on this investigation. Some idea, any idea on the mind of the killer would be a start."

"What are you suggesting Hannah?" he said, tilting his head and frowning.

"Well, guv, I know this feller. I know him quite well in fact. He's a criminal profiler, but not just a practitioner, no; he's really quite smart. He has lectured at Kings College in London on criminal psychology and profiling. Oh, and he's written a couple of books on the subject. I don't mind betting he would agree to do some work with us."

"Have you asked him already Hannah?"

"Well, er, I kind of suggested it, but didn't make any promises, that's really not my style. I just think it's something we ought to consider that's all. I wanted to see what you thought."

She thought for a moment that she had blown it and he would turn down the idea. But he surprised her.

"Okay," he replied. "I'll think about it. I have to be convinced because we are effectively asking a non-policeman to do our job for us aren't we? Whatever – let me sleep on it."

Ramsden looked at his watch and excused himself, walking quickly out of the canteen. It was not his style to stay and chitchat with any of his staff let alone the detective inspectors.

Hannah was left thinking that this a positive move to solving the problems they were already experiencing. Unbeknown to her, Ramsden considered it a very reasonable tactical decision to take. It was quite simple. If the investigation took a turn for the worse then he could shift the blame to the profiler; if it were successful then he would take the credit.

With the dearth of evidence so far, it looked as though he should start to think of a scapegoat without delay; it was a wise precaution.

Chapter Eleven

The Essex Chief Constable, Alistair Blackley, attended the morning MCIT briefing and was given a full outline of the investigation process and ongoing work. His face was grim and he addressed the team. The events of the previous week where an MP was almost assaulted by an angry crowd in Chelmsford was an indication of the frustration felt by local people and left a disturbing taste in the mouth. He urged them to find the perpetrator of the murders and he would talk separately to the rest of the county Police Forces about a 'hearts and minds' approach to policing. He was candid about the difficulties faced by police forces locally and nation wide and spoke at length about the strains that the 'dead hand of government' put on them all.

Alistair Blackley wasn't the archetypal career Chief Constable and the county police force warmed to his leadership, because he unfailingly considered their interests, not in front of the community, but equal to it. He remembered his days of walking the beat and knew the pressures his officers' daily faced. He embraced new technology, but rued the day that policemen couldn't use their judgement any more; policing by the book simply meant more books, more rules and more procedures. He told his officers this and they respected his honesty and candour; he trusted them not to report his words. Then he went on at length about the difficulties of policing in Britain and acknowledged the difficult day-to-day problems they faced. This raised their spirits.

Andy Ramsden stepped in quickly and surprised everyone in the room.

"I quite agree with your sentiments, sir. And that's why I am going to give a lot of consideration to bringing in a criminal profiler to help with our investigations. I need to be convinced of course. I have one in mind and would value your thoughts on the matter."

Hannah was about to swallow some cool water. When she heard this she almost spat it out. What a man!

"Andrew, I would be happy to discuss this with you. I know that they have been used many times before. I have an open mind."

The first part of the briefing ended and the Chief Constable left after taking coffee with several senior police officers on the MCIT. He was an adroit motivator and his presence always filled his force with confidence.

The briefing resumed with results of some of the investigations ongoing, particularly concerning details of victim contacts and the very slim links being made on the Holmes system. He was aware of the range of talent available, but it was becoming increasingly obvious that the murderer was leaving no clues whatsoever.

Ramsden was a canny individual, with more than his fair share of nous when it came to survival. He needed something or someone else to take the blame for possible failure; this profiler chap that Hannah Sinclair knew was good, maybe not; either way he was in a position to manipulate the situation. It would also show that his style of investigation was progressive and innovative. He knew only too well that sometimes success was all about how you played the game rather than the final result. Besides, if the investigation started to flounder, he would sack the profiler.

He left the briefing and called Hannah into his office to make the necessary arrangements to meet Gary Randle.

Two days later, Detective Superintendents Andy Ramsden and Louise Wellbeloved, a colleague from a neighbouring Force, sat impassively as Gary Randle came into the committee room, introduced himself and sat down to one side of a large mahogany table with a highly polished surface ready to be questioned.

Detective Superintendent Louise Wellbeloved introduced herself and Andy Ramsden. Randle thought how canny Ramsden was to let another person take the lead in the interview.

"Welcome Gary. You have had an initial brief from Detective Inspector Hannah Sinclair I understand, and that brings you up to speed on the situation regarding the four murders that have taken place over the last two weeks. I am here to help my colleague and add an independent view. We want to hear about you and your skills and consider what you can bring to this difficult investigation. We just want to be sure that we are making the right decision – it's as simple as that."

Gary smiled, "I fully understand, I think I would do the same."

The initial questions, fairly general in nature, came quickly and he batted them away with ease. Louise Wellbeloved had already used criminal profilers before and was quite supportive of the idea. But she couldn't make out Ramsden's stance and he seemed a little edgy and standoffish. He was more reserved than normal, even for him, and asked very few deep questions. This surprised her, because she had known him for many years and expected him to be more forceful and inquisitive. He always wanted to know 'what was in it for him' and this approach was absent today. Despite being friends, she also knew that it was his style to place responsibilities onto other shoulders and was wary of this.

It was towards the end of the interview that Ramsden threw a punch below the belt.

"Randle," said Ramsden, Gary hated his use of the surname, "your last book, er, what was it, oh yes, 'Looking inside the Criminal Mind', well, it wasn't a very big seller was it?" Ramsden sat back arrogantly as if he was about to enjoy Gary's wriggling.

"No, of course you are correct. But it depends why you write and what you set out to achieve. I never meant it to be a best seller. Not everyone warms to criminal profiling. If perhaps I had made it gruesome and populist it would have sold more copies, but this is a reference book not a kid's comic. It gives an outline of serial killers and their habits. It also covers police incompetence during investigations that were eventually considered failures, or shall we say almost failures. Take for example, the Yorkshire Ripper, the Gloucestershire Fred and Rosemary West murders and the debacle of the Lawrence inquiry. No, Superintendent Ramsden, I did not write it for commercial or egocentric gain, it's just a reference book. However, I am pleased that copies are held in major universities dealing with criminology and some more enlightened police stations around the UK."

Louise Wellbeloved beamed at their foiling and considered that there was nothing wrong with a bit of creative tension. So far Randle was fifteen to love up. Ramsden put this rally to the back of his mind and he continued.

"So how would you go about your work?"

Gary thought for a few seconds. He knew what he wanted to say and could easily give a quick and in depth answer. But it was his style to make it look as though he thought carefully before responding weighing his answers carefully; he knew how sceptical the police could be and this was a sales mission, not a seminar. He held the pause for effect, looking up at the ceiling.

"Well, I would want to firstly brief the team on what criminal profiling was all about. I know all your officers will have received shed loads of training on this and other techniques, but it is important that they see my services," he shifted the emphasis to himself, "as being very much integrated into the work they do – not as something completely separate. Solving murders is a team effort. I think we are all aware how precious some police forces can get about sharing clues and this happens within specialist teams as well. I think it's great that you have already embraced the need for local knowledge and included predominantly local police in your team."

Ramsden blanched at the big examples, but accepted the compliment regarding the composition of his MCIT. Gary Randle was obviously a very well informed and perceptive individual. Gary continued.

"The briefing should allow them to question the myths about profiling and get to know me better. I have to get the team on side. Criminal profiling is not an infallible science. Because people are soaked in the images portrayed on the television they expect too much from us. Profiling depends on the accuracy of information presented to the team, and I mean 'the team', it is not to be considered as an outside exercise separate from the main investigation. It is important not to settle on the single view of any one investigator, or for that matter the profiler. Profiling focuses on four aspects: investigation, analysis, psychological assessment and cultural anthropology. There is no readily available evidence to support the success of profiling or otherwise. We profilers exist as a kind of alternative item in the police portfolio and are increasingly used, as I am sure you are aware, to provide an extra angle on investigations. We are the, how shall we say, oh yes, the homeopathy to oncology. In other words, give it a try, if it works then all well and good."

He smiled, confident that he had got his message across, and then added, "I am here and can help, but I don't want you to believe in the commercial view that crimes are solved solely on the basis of a criminal profiler in shining armour coming onto the scene."

Louise Wellbeloved was the first to speak and turning to Ramsden she said, "What you say interests me Gary. I am aware of the successful work done some years back to find the murderer of several girls in the Home Counties. The killings were all committed within a triangle. The criminal profiler was Professor David Cantor. It was about nineteen eighty-seven, or perhaps nineteen eighty-eight. One of the girls was I think called Tamboza; she was Dutch. There were lots of clues, but the killer's profile was spot on. The man had a mother fixation and was inadequate with women. That was enough to convince me then that profiling has its place in criminal investigations. I've certainly heard enough to convince me that Gary has the skills and sense of teamwork you need, Andy. You wanted me to help with this interview and I think that you should follow your suggestion and let Gary here give a presentation to the team. If he is accepted you should proceed. It is entirely in your hands now."

She stood up and proffered a hand to Gary and said, "Gary, thank you too, that was most interesting and enjoyable. I will now leave you two to it. I'm only too sorry I cannot attend the presentation. Good luck."

Then she stood up and left the office.

When they were alone Ramsden softened and his bravado dissipated. The barriers lowered slightly and they discussed the details of the case and set a date for Gary to brief the team. As Gary left the station he couldn't suppress an uncertain feeling about the case, unlike any other contract he had ever had with the police. But he needed the work and the kudos it might bring.

Time would tell.

The MCIT was in high spirits. They were looking forward to meeting Gary Randle and learning more about criminal profiling. The briefing room had been prepared and Gary arrived, took off his jacket and then sat on the table rather than a nearby chair. He began by getting them on side with a few jokes and remarks about deductive profiling being no more than a 'wild-assed guess'. He took them on a journey that made them think about their own powers of deduction which were quite naturally based on their experiences. Whilst they thought that through, he gave the example of a crime that he helped to solve many years ago as a fledgling profiler.

A young man had been found near some steps in a local park, apparently badly beaten and dead from a head wound. He was naked except for a loosely wrapped but open raincoat about his torso. The prevailing view was that he had been stripped and roughed up, then wrapped in the raincoat and dumped near the steps in the park. Gary thought otherwise. The boy was a young student, heterosexual, fit and well thought of in his college. His feet were cut and bleeding and he died from a head wound that caused a blood clot in his brain.

Gary said that he reached into his 'bag of experience' to help him solve the case and he feigned sheepishness.

"Look, we're all adults so I will embarrass myself by telling you of a game of dare that an old girlfriend and I played in my adolescence. After drinking a little too much, we dared each other to walk across town wearing only a raincoat and flip-flops. We had several close encounters, but made it back to our digs undiscovered. Well, except for the fact that my raincoat got caught in the stairwell railings and a couple of buttons ripped off revealing my crown jewels to the landlady."

There was a ripple of laughter.

"So, you see, I considered this boy as a possible 'dare' victim. Then the clues fell in thick and fast. His feet were cut in several places because he wore no shoes and he was at the bottom of the stairs, I believed, because he fell down the damned things, not because he was dumped there. Equally, his head and other wounds were caused when he fell down the roughly hewn steps in the park. Now look at it another way. My police colleague had other views, simply because he had been involved in investigating at least four 'body dumpings' for the want of a better expression. You see, he was rationalising what he saw with his experiences, and er, I suppose I was too. But we worked together and after interviewing his friends it transpired that he had indeed been dared to run round the park naked, but opted for a raincoat and nothing else, not even any shoes. Sadly, for the boy, it all went tragically wrong."

Joe Grogan a young detective constable piped up, "Gary, have you got your old girlfriend's address?"

The team laughed appreciatively.

"Yes, and she is a very respectable lawyer now, so no you cannot have it," he said, "but I do have my original raincoat for you to use any time you like."

The team turned and egged Joe on, until Ramsden quietened them down.

Gary handed out some papers. "Look guys, I'm not going to bother you, but here are some psychology notes that I give to students who study criminology as part of a Masters degree. Whilst you are putting those notes into your folders, let me dispel some myths about serial killers, because that's what we believe we are faced with here in Essex."

He had their full attention.

"Firstly, serial killers do not look like crazy, wild scientists or Neanderthal beings, and yes girls, a lot of them are male. Men tend to be vicious and are the 'run out of the shadows to deal the death blow' types. The image of those killers, who enjoy developing clever ideas to abduct their victims or hold them prisoner, overly complicating the kill is quite false. There are some infamous female serial killers, but they kill quietly and tend to focus on victims they know. Generally speaking, serial killers are more often than not, just as pretty as you and me. And for the record they don't always live with their mum, although it has to be said they do often need to feed emotionally off someone or something. That something may also be an abstract cause or belief that they have, whether rational or irrational."

As he wound up the presentation, Gary looked straight at Joe again.

"And before you ask Joe, serial killers are not bright or brilliant strategists. If they were then they wouldn't do what they do. They would live a normal life like you and I - without the raincoat perhaps?"

The team laughed and admired the way he could joke at himself.

Joe Grogan also smiled and enjoyed being singled out. He liked the attention.

"Any questions?"

Jenny Ellis was first. "Gary, do serial killers play cat and mouse with the police?"

Gary frowned, "It's Jenny isn't it? Well, Jenny, this really is unusual. Most just kill then go on with their normal lives, returning sometimes to do another dirty deed at a later date. Don't ask me what drives them – I don't know. There are some that do taunt the police, and I know that, again, the film industry makes a lot of money out of portraying this as being normal, but it is the exception rather than the rule. Remember, the more contact they make the more mistakes they make by giving away clues."

Jack Rollo sat up and gave Gary a look that said, 'I'm an experienced old hand' and loudly proclaimed, "Gary, I guess it really is all down to brilliant policing then?"

Gary returned the serve down the centre line, "Sorry old chap, that's not always the case. In my experience, many serial killers get caught through sheer carelessness and from a lot of luck. It's all about looking at every detail, sure, but you do need to be ready for that bit of luck or a clue that arrives to an open mind. So, yes, some ways I suppose it is down to clever policing, but never ignore Lady Luck."

Hannah was in awe of Gary's approach, she had never seen him at work; he was certainly winning the trust of the team. He answered questions about the frequency of serial killings, whether they tended to go on until they died and the collection of souvenirs and newspaper clippings. He spent a long time with them and they were obviously enjoying his presentation. She caught Ramsden's eye and they both left the team room quietly and went into the corridor.

"What do you think?"

Ramsden looked nonchalant. "He's certainly a clever chap. I'll take him on. We can't very well lose can we?" Then he turned on his heel and went to his office.

Hannah took his arrogance for granted these days.

At least she got her own way.

Gary Randle arrived back at his flat in Maldon completely exhausted. It was his haven. He sold the big house he and Abigail had lived in and downsized to a flat that was easy to maintain and serviced by a contract cleaner. He liked Malden. It was full of long streets with low buildings, there was hardly a building over two stories high in the town, it had a quay and its quaint shops were a joy to amble through and sold the widest variety of goods he had ever seen. He was also able to indulge himself in several male pursuits. He was a member of the Malden cricket club and a season ticket holder at the local soccer club. He deliberately kept himself busy. Until his relationship with Hannah he had been afraid of being alone.

The MCIT had sucked out of him all the information on criminal profiling and serial killers they could, he could hardly satisfy their appetite. But at least it had gone well and he was accepted into their ranks. The next task was to work closely with them, but not to get in the way. He knew he was good at this and that patience always won the day.

He fumbled with the keys to the door. It had been raining lightly and his jacket was damp and hands wet, so the keys kept slipping. Finally, he turned the lock and he almost fell into his hallway. Hannah had said that she would meet him later. She had a key to the flat. As he entered it felt warm and he heard a noise in the lounge.

"Hi, Hannah, are you there. I missed you at the station?"

"Yes, I'm in the lounge. I had things to do," she said.

He suppressed the male response which would have been 'what?' hung up his damp jacket, put his papers and briefcase in the third bedroom which acted as his study and went into the lounge.

His face was a picture as he took in the sight in front of him. On the large coffee table in the centre of the room was a wine bucket they used for champagne with a bottle of Moet and Chandon nestling on top of a pile of ice-cubes. Standing behind the table at the far end, flanked by two large white leather sofas stood Hannah looking freshly made up, hands on hips, wearing a grey raincoat.

"What the..." he said. But before he could finish the sentence, Hannah let the belt to the raincoat slip loose and she pulled the sides open and behind her – she was quite naked underneath.

Hannah pouted at him.

"Well now, Mr Smart Arse Doctor of Philosophy, before we drink some champagne to celebrate your new job, you wanna tell me some more about your kinky ways with raincoats?"

Smiling broadly, he walked towards her and took her in his arms. Her lips were soft and her tongue tasted sweet. He ran his hands over her body, and then put his hands under her armpits. When their lips parted he pretended to look serious.

"I have to go into the bedroom quickly," he said with a pained expression.

Hannah looked startled. "But why?"

His face broke into a big smile, "something just came up…"

Hannah squealed, let the raincoat slip to the floor and said, "Herr professor, you iz stayin' right 'ere!"

She grabbed his neck and they both fell onto the left-hand sofa.

Gary Randle lay with Hannah in his arms on the soft leather sofa, their naked bodies covered by her light raincoat. It wasn't just the sex he enjoyed. It was the whole process of loving someone, holding them and being part of their lives, frequently doing the little kindnesses that make such a difference in strong relationships. He looked at the empty champagne bottle and then at Hannah who was still asleep and purring gently.

He knew the case was not going to be easy, he could tell that from the briefing. His study would need to be converted a little, because although he was usually quite happy to work in the team when this was needed, he valued his own space in which he would review the case. Any thoughts of opening the files and briefing packages he had brought home from the station paled into momentary insignificance as Hannah began to wake up.

As she did so she straddled his right thigh and began moving against him and he felt the roughness of her prickly hair against his soft skin. He laughed out loud and she sleepily giggled.

He thought to himself, "I think somehow the files can wait."

Chapter Twelve

Rory Gatlin was sweating profusely. His heart beat like a steam hammer and his hands shook. He moved slowly towards his window and moved the cheap net curtains to one side by about a half an inch. That was enough to set the mob outside his house howling, jeering and screaming with rage.

"He's in there the bastard, let's get him."

The mob howled and someone picked up a small rock and threw it at the window. It was double-glazed and only cracked under the blow. This only served to annoy the mob and they all took up the challenge to break the glass and threw more rocks. Gatlin moved away from the window and ran to the back door. When he got there he froze. The shadows of figures trying to crowbar there way in to his house through the door and kitchen window could be seen framed eerily against the window and door blinds.

Gatlin's mind raced. What would they do? Hadn't it been enough punishment in prison, when the warders were directed to put him on Special Section solitary confinement and deliberately left him alone in his cell for an hour? Ten men dragged him out and beat him, and then they did unspeakable things to him, things he would never ever forget. They were animals and their actions were worse than his had ever been, yet they were considered normal, and the process of hurting and humiliating him considered reasonable in the eyes of his keepers.

Now it was happening all over again. Just because some arsey social worker decreed that it was his right to live back in the Portsmouth community which he belonged to, because he had been successfully treated and declared not to be dangerous to children any more. Abstract clap trap always sounds good coming out of the mouths of the chattering classes, the cruel reality was formed up outside his home. How the hell did people find out he was located near to his old haunts; who told them and why?

Just then the doors broke free of its hinges and two greasy youths looking for fun more than retribution stood there with a crowbar and shank of wood in their hands. Like medieval peasants that enjoyed watching the suffering of public hanging and flogging, they were here to taunt, injure and have some fun at someone else's expense.

A tall gangly, spotty youth with long greasy hair smiled evilly and said, "Hello pervy Gatlin. Nonce bastard. Have we got something for you or what?"

He was soon joined by others in the crowd, who yelled with equal vigour. Rory Gatlin was rooted to the spot with fear. After a few moments urine began to run down his leg and his lips trembled at the frightening scene unfolding in front of him. He was absolutely helpless and there was nowhere to hide.

It was the good sense of a nearby neighbour who telephoned the police and told them of the incident. She said she knew of the man's past, but didn't hold with mob violence. The police car left its present location, but took the very long route to the street where they knew Gatlin lived and the incident had been reported. When they got there they soon regretted their self-righteous delay which would eventually be difficult to explain to an inquiry and lead to disciplinary proceedings against at least three officers.

The naked body of Rory Gatlin, bruised and burned by cigarettes hung from a nearby telephone pole with the words, "Nonce" written on a card hanging around his neck. People talked about the horror; some said he got what he deserved, but many more were deeply upset and worried about where it would all go from here. Who would be next; would there be mob violence whenever people lost faith in the police?

Exhaustive investigation failed to identify those responsible for the killing. The local newspapers were in their element. Criticism of the police filled newspaper pages for a few days then, somewhat predictably, observations were made about the morals and standards of people in everyday life and the British tendency to ill-discipline and violence. Bad news sells copy.

National and local media couldn't lose.

It had been five days since the murder of the prostitute and the police forensic department wanted to keep Reverend Allan's clothes a lot longer. Hannah decided that she could not wait and would make an excuse to see him again and ask more questions.

She parked her car in the High Street in Chelmsford and made her way down Lead Alley, past the spot where the prostitute was murdered and tried to imagine the scene on that fateful night. Although it was daytime it was still a gloomy and revolting place to walk through. The police had thoroughly cleaned the ground so that the ghouls in the general public were prevented from visiting the exact murder site. Then she walked slowly up the narrowing alley towards the church, her feet crunching on the gravel and ground up rubbish. When she reached the alleyway door to the church at the far end of the alley, she noticed how rickety it was. She pushed it lightly with her hand and she could just see through the gap between door and door posts. It would have been easy enough to hear a scream. But moving out to see what was going on would've needed a noisy action in the old fashioned mortise lock. Suddenly, she heard a sound from behind the door and called out.

"Hello, is anyone there? Is that you Reverend Allan?"

There was a short silence and then a voice answered.

"Yes, who is it?"

"I'm so sorry Reverend, I'm Detective Inspector Hannah Sinclair, I'm just visiting the scene of the crime and thought that I would come and see you. I hope it's not inconvenient?"

The rickety door scraped open and Reverend Alex Allan stood smiling with his shirtsleeves rolled up and pink Marigold gloves on his hands.

"We do have a front door you know? It's clean up time – if I don't do it then the cleaning lady won't, she's drinking tea at the moment. I'm far too liberal, but please don't take the Mickey!"

"No I won't Reverend, I promise. Besides, my cleaning lady terrifies me," replied Hannah with a smile. "You sound a model thoughtful and undemanding employer to me."

"Indeed Inspector, I guess I am that. C'mon inside and let's see if she's left anything in the pot. I deserve a break."

Hannah followed the vicar into his church. The corridors at the back of the church were dark and small, and led past rooms that looked like stores or kitchens, used in days gone by. He opened a large double door into the main hall and Hannah had to catch her breath. It was almost all carved wood in plain typically Quaker pattern designs. In its Quaker days it would have been quite austere

104

in decoration, but now the old wood had been cleaned and polished and the windows replaced with white double glazed units that let the light burst in. Rows of simple plastic chairs were formed into a circle with a single round dais in the middle of the room.

Instead of paintings and plaster statues, the hall was decorated with large photographs that were particularly artistic, very professionally finished and all mounted on plasterboard, the large being about twelve by six feet. Some hung from the ceiling and others from the walls; they were either black and white or sepia. The pictures depicted people, adults and children, in various poses of grief, play and work, holding hands, dancing or smiling. Hannah found herself attracted to them and even energised. They seemed to call out from the frame and touch her very soul; they were so vibrant and caught moods of youth, celebration and happiness.

Around the room there was a profusion of Celtic designs, or Celtic knots as they are called. Some had bird or human shapes woven into the design, others were just knotted motifs.

"Good aren't they?" said the vicar, "and they are better than all the stone Virgin Mary or apostles that adorn other churches. I love these photographs. This is what life is about: people. People make the world, they shape it, they are the clay in our hands and all we have to do is to mould it. It has been that way for centuries and yet we have allowed ourselves to be seduced away from local tradition and values. For me the realisation came a little late, very late in fact, but it's the Celtic element that fascinates me. The Celts believed that the devil is frustrated by anything with no entrance, or put another way, no break in it. God has no break, Hannah, so the devil cannot have final victory. Hence the symbolic values of the Celtic knot. Look clearly at the shape," he ran his fingers softly around an elliptical design, "you see how all the ends meet up and don't leave any gaps or ends? To a large extent communities are like that, or at least they should be. These days, Christian values are daily under threat, but then I bet you see evidence of that quite often?"

Hannah smiled at his sincerity and enthusiasm and wished she could bottle some of it for later. He was right, the photographs were better than plaster saints any day.

"Lovely sentiment Reverend, I bet you're popular with your fellow theologians?" she said with a hint of irony.

He stared at her for a few seconds almost as though his dark eyes were examining her soul.

"Well, yes, but there are many like me you know. Setting up churches in places other than, well, churches. Reaching out in a very meaningful way to – well, to people. Not just those who consider the route to heaven being through the flower arranging or coffee making roster." He smiled and added, "But I wouldn't say it's been easy. You know, in all my years in the ministry of God I was never able to connect with, well, what is all around us. What I am trying to say Hannah, is that we should retain some local history and meaning alongside our religion. That's what I think we try to capture here in The People's Church of Chelmsford."

He splayed his arms wide and raised his head to a large picture of three smiling babies, with a border of Celtic knots around the edge, hanging in the eastern side of the church. Hannah looked at this face and thought that he was in a dream world of his own.

"I'm sorry, I suppose I get a bit boring about all this stuff- but then that's what He pays me for!"

"On the contrary it is fascinating stuff, sir. You make it sound so good I may even turn up one day. But I'm sorry to say that it's the murder of the young girl that has brought me to see you, much as I would rather it be something more heavenly. I really want to know if there is anything you want to add to your statement, have you for example thought of anything that you might have not told us? By the way, this is an informal chat, if there is anything substantial I would ask that you come back to the station with me and we talk under caution."

"No, that's perfectly all right, I understand, I keep kicking myself for behaving in such a stupid way the other night. It's amazing how silly the brain gets when under pressure. The answer to your question is no, I cannot think of anything else. Except to say that some of the girls that ply their trade have come to this church and I have managed to turn them away from that work. Young Kelly Golding that was her name wasn't it? Well she wasn't one of those who crossed the steps to church?"

"Do you know her then?" said Hannah.

"Oh, yes, I suppose I do, but not at all well. I did speak to her in the park along with some of her, how shall we say, work colleagues?

Anyway, I was racking my brains at the police station and it only came to me today that I had actually met her before. But I must repeat it was only briefly. She was very 'anti' everything I said and faded into the background whilst two or three others stayed to talk to me."

"Do you 'turn' many criminals?" said Hannah.

"Actually, Inspector, I do. We get a slow dribble of offenders, from all sorts of crimes, through our doors. When I say 'we' I mean me and about half a dozen lay volunteers. Yes, a few."

"Did you ever meet a young man called Ackroyd?"

He half smiled.

"No, and I do know why you ask. He was never in one of our groups. By the way, we're up to two hundred and fifty parishioners now; not bad eh? My church-bound colleagues are a little jealous. We choose the hymns we want to sing, sometimes make up our own and we talk to each other, we don't believe in sermons – what a pointless exercise that is. All that kind of stuff stemmed from the days when everyone feared the word of God and the local clergy had to be listened to because they were considered intellectual – they then preached and merely underpinned the establishment message, if you will, and gave society its protective fabric. Whereas our congregation is intelligent and enlightened, from all walks of life I hasten to add, yes even the wrongdoers, and we talk about the rights and wrongs in God's world and pray that it can be put right. Praying is important and so is personal contemplation; we make room for that."

"And what can you do to make things right?" said Hannah.

Just as the reverend was about to reply there was a rattling of buckets and mops and a young cleaner, cigarette drooping out of her mouth, shuffled into the hall and crossed behind a large photograph of a happy smiling baby hanging from the ceiling on two strong wires.

"Ah Christine, can you make two cups of tea please," he inclined his head to Hannah, "milk and sugar?"

"Just milk, thank you."

The cleaner huffed as if it were an enormous chore she had been given. After a few minutes she returned with two steaming mugs and handed them to the vicar and Hannah.

They moved into a small office that he called his 'den'. It was untidy and full of bric-a-brac, books and lots of files that would have been better off in a cabinet. There were some old black and white badly faded photographs of a village, Hannah surmised it was somewhere in Scotland because the men wore kilts. They looked a dour lot. She and the Reverend talked a lot more and Hannah got the impression that he was a bit of a rebel. He grew up in Scotland, near Glasgow, having moved there from the Isle of Stronsey, off the Northeast coast of Scotland. His mother brought him up, his father having died at sea in a fishing boat accident. She was, apparently, ultra religious and hammered the word of God into him. But he didn't seem to mind and joked about it. He accepted that she had her beliefs and he had his own way of seeing God. Going to Glasgow University was, he said, a sensible move and he studied Theology, but also took some arts courses. That's where he learned photography. After being ordained he tried to minister in a succession of churches, but couldn't stand the style of the Anglican religion or the people that frequented churches. He took his missionary zeal to Africa. When he recounted his life in Burundi, Nigeria, the Congo and Rwanda he had a sad look in his eyes. It was the kind of look that tells you that a person is visualising something awful as they talk to you, almost as though you aren't there. He regained his composure, and explained that after a few years he returned to the UK and started to practice in exactly the same way, but this time in inner city environments. He laughed out loud.

"Frankly, the problems were exactly the same, selfish, tribal and often violent. But definitely too many witch-doctors," he said and laughed again.

Somehow, Hannah knew exactly what he was getting at.

He went on to explain that after a few more years he moved to Chelmsford from Liverpool. There was more than enough work to do here.

"One of the most satisfying things I have ever done is to have set up this People's Church. You must come and meet some of the people who attend regularly."

"I'd like to," she said, trying to avoid an invitation, still mentally stuck with a view that all churches were rather odd places where you went to get christened, married and buried, and along the way gallons of coffee was produced and hymns sung out of key. "Sadly my job keeps me on irregular hours and long days."

Hannah felt bad about making excuses. In fact, she was in awe of him and his work. It was always inspiring talking to someone who selflessly gave of their time and energy for others.

She stared at a photograph on the wall of a woman in a dark Victorian dress, wearing her hair down to her shoulders and in long curls from halfway. The woman wore three necklaces of simple beads. She looked serious and there was a slight turn to the side of her mouth, almost like a half-smile that seemed to challenge the viewer to get to know her more.

"That's Elizabeth Browning," he said. "She is one of my heroines. Elizabeth Browning had some Creole blood in her you know? She was a stalwart for the protection of children, particularly those who were abused and used as labour in the mines and factories in England, and also the dispossessed. She was such a remarkable lady, who wasn't just a poet of the Romantic Movement, but a prolific writer on progressive social ideas. Her life is an interesting story that fascinated me since my university days. I'm sure you wouldn't want me to bore you with it all just now?"

Hannah nodded, she didn't have time to pursue it, he was right. But she leaned forward and looked at the picture and read the inscription, and the first four lines of a poem that appeared below it:

Unlike are we, unlike, O princely Heart!
Unlike our uses and our destinies.
Our ministering two angels look surprised
On one another, as they strike athwart.

Hannah was tempted to stay and reflect on the words, suspecting that they probably meant different things to different people, but she knew that she had to leave.

"No you are right, but sadly no time I'm afraid. Just one more question though: do you minister anywhere else Reverend?"

He looked at her and after a second said, "Well, I do some counselling work for the local authority, talk in various schools and sometimes go back to my roots in Scotland to speak about the emergence of 'new' churches and the renewed path to God, otherwise, not much else."

Hannah's eyes scanned his desk and the headings on top of several pieces of paper stuck in her mind: local authority community charge demand, T W Swanley Building Contractor, The Sacred Heart Sanctuary, Frobishers Provisions and a milk bill. Then with a gentle pressure on her arm she was guided out into the main hall. She took a last look at the décor and the almost hypnotic pictures around her and said goodbye and made her way out of the front door, this time directly into the High Street.

Elizabeth Browning's words swam around her mind; she warmed to Reverend Allan and might try worshipping there one day.

Chips Johnson was just finishing an article about Jan Van Der Klarten a local businessman who had been cheating people ever since his arrival in Essex from Rotterdam four years ago. He set up several businesses and they all went broke leaving employees out of pocket and suppliers without payment. Now he was trying to pressure people out of leasehold homes that he purchased from a local Lord in need of cash, so that they could be knocked down to provide land to develop social housing units. There was also considerable unease that he had vindictively sold a large stretch of land to a community of gypsies, because the local planners refused planning permission for one of his building projects. He was therefore the toast of the travellers and the scourge of the local council.

This was Chips second article on this 'Essex bad boy' and he was to earn good money from it. In addition, it pleased him to see this man pilloried. But he knew that Van Der Klarten had a thick skin and really would not care at all. It was these characteristics that made him the complete shit that he was. His stomach churned and his chest tightened; he hated men like this, the image of his father, a bully who got what he wanted out of life at everyone else's expense. Chips would see to this man as soon as he was able; Van Der Klarten would regret his actions.

But today it wasn't the Van Der Klarten situation that bothered him. He had other things on his mind, like what to do with the two letters sitting on his desk. He thought about his situation and the work that he was doing. One stupid move and it could all be brought to an end. Should he deliver the two letters to the police or shouldn't he? He looked at them over and over again, and could not help smiling. The letters were crafted to taunt – wordsmithing at its best. They were magic, sheer magic. It would at least allow him to get a little 'payback' for past wrongs he considered the local police had done to him. He daydreamed the heading on a leader article he could write for local and national newspapers.

Essex Murderer Savages Police for their Incompetence. What a great heading and this was going to be an article that he would enjoy writing. Dare he do that? If he did take them to the police there would surely be some retribution, he had no doubt about that whatsoever. But Chips cared little about their sensibilities. He hated the local police force with a passion. They had been over zealous in their approach to some work he had done on a couple of particularly nasty crooks and he narrowly escaped prosecution; some justice that was. The moral seemed to be to employ a good lawyer and rely on the crowded and cumbersome legislation to provide a loophole or two that could be exploited. He was bitter at the way he had been treated and would never forgive or forget.

Chips cleared his mind of pent up thoughts of baiting the police and returned to his article on Van Der Klartan. He tapped away on his ancient Brother word processor and when he was satisfied with it he printed a copy, read it in hard copy and then folded it into an envelope addressing it to the editor of the Essex Advertiser. Then he turned his attention to the other two letters in front of him.

They were certainly enigmatic and a little frightening, but they also made him laugh. He thought for a few moments longer, then after gazing out of his window came to a conclusion.

"Yes, why not send them – why not, why not, why not indeed?" He thought out loud and laughed to himself. His reputation would be doubted, criticised and insulted, but when wasn't it? But didn't he always win?

He took a while composing a short note and enclosed it and the two letters in an envelope and addressed it to the local Essex Police station.

But, aside from the police baiting, even Chips was afraid of the way that he enjoyed the text – even the threats of more violence to come. For a second or two, he didn't like himself.

Hannah knew that she needed a break and wanted to see her Dad again. He left the Army and ended up at Shotley Gate, on the tip of the Shotley peninsular which lies between Harwich and Felixstowe, after buying an ex-Ministry of Defence house there in the eighties. He bought one and settled reasonably well, only to sell it ten years later to move to and area just outside the small village of Chelmondiston, called Pin Hill, two miles away. It was a more secluded location where he could enjoy the solitude of the countryside and a view of the River Orwell with its wild birds and frequently dotted with sailing boats, most of which left from the sailing club, barely two hundred metres from his garden.

He had been very ill and the prognosis was not good for the long term, but his indomitable spirit kept him going. He was helped considerably by his new companion, Petronella Ngime, a South African lady, brought up in the hard township of Soweto and now long-since domiciled in England. They made the most unlikely partnership. Her Dad had spent decades in the British Army and that had been his whole life until he retired in the late nineteen eighties. But several tours of duty in inhospitable areas such as Kenya during the Mao Mao, Aden and Borneo has hardened his attitude to foreigners, especially where the colour of their skin was concerned. It had been a major source of disagreement between Hannah and her Dad, especially when she was at university and flirting with Socialist principles and righting the wrongs of past generations. But like all solid families, they didn't let the general issues in life get in the way of love and mutual respect.

After her mother died five years ago he withdrew into himself.

They had always been a close family. A baby brother arrived when Hannah was three years old, but he died in the severe heat and poor conditions of Steamer Point in Aden. Her mother never held the British Army or her father to account and her deeply held Christian beliefs helped her to cope with the tragedy and eventually move on. Hannah was a privileged child in that her parents spent a lot of time coaching her and of course loving her. They helped her to read more widely and her father was especially good at teaching her how to solve problems and understand people; this would hold her in good stead for the rest of her life. She was never a great academic and always achieved her goals through hard work, but her logic, common sense and clarity of thought were qualities that brought her many compliments.

Throughout his life, and then when he retired her father wrote poetry and continued with his major love, oil painting. But it was obvious that he had lost that edge that her mother brought out in him. She was his muse and his focus in life. Without her he was a ship without a rudder or even a course to navigate. Then his health worsened and he was diagnosed with a rare form of degenerative cancer. She had forgotten the name, but it wasn't really important; nothing could be done. He needed care on a daily basis.

She often mused that cancer is such a cruel disease. First, the frightening news, then the awful treatment, then hopes are raised, dashed, then raised and dashed again. It toys with some people and for others it is a quick slash of a guillotine. There are no rules, no predictions, just the eventual reasoning from those who are paid to treat the patient and give the bad news that one should, 'stay positive'. What a laugh? In her father's case it was more likely that if his cancer had a personality, then he would chase it right back in the box. But of course it didn't, it only sat there feeding on his healthy cells happy in its metastasis. She imagined it grey and amorphous and often visualised smashing it with her tennis racket. It was a useful visualisation exercise, but not a world-shattering cure. For her dad there wasn't one.

He had a succession of rather dull and slothful care assistants, whom he regularly sacked. Then along came, Petronella – she was loud and brassy, but very strict on diet and cleanliness. At first they clashed and it looked as though Social Services would have to find someone else. Then, after a particularly debilitating episode of diarrhoea and sickness, she stayed and cared for him, unpaid and sleeping on a couch, he began to warm to her caring nature and carefree personality. She often sang sweet low songs from the South African township that lulled him to sleep. They talked and talked, and talk being what it is, cemented their relationship.

Petronella gave up social care and moved in with her Dad and he loved her company. They were now quite inseparable.

As Hannah walked up the path towards the small stone cottage on the Shotley Gate peninsular in the Suffolk countryside, her feet crunched on the loose shale and she heard Petronnela singing one of her songs. It made her want to dance to the rhythm. She saw Hannah arrive and called out to her.

"Hannah, my child, how good to see you," she said and hugged her against her ample bosoms her eyes and smile as wide as could be. Then her face frowned a little, "Hannah, your Dad is getting' very tired these days. You know that you must expect the worst some day." She squeezed Hannah's hand and went on, "You are a sensible girl. I want to say something to you quickly. If something happens to your sweet Dad, I will move out Hannah, this is your cottage not mine. So have no fear."

She continued to hold Hannah's hand very tightly.

Hannah held her gaze. "No, Petronella. We will not talk about this again, but you will stay and you will see your time out here, so no more of that."

Petronella was about to speak, but Hannah put her fingers to her lips; Peronella gently grabbed her hands, kissed her fingers and smiled. They both walked into the drawing room which had been set up as a make-shift bed-sit, where her father could move from bed to the easel and then easily around downstairs facilities. It had two double doors that opened to an immaculately laid out garden

Her father was lying on a Queen size bed dressed in blue pyjamas and a loose fitting, old-fashioned dressing gown and smiled to see her, he raised himself on to one arm. He was an imposing man who, even in poor health, gained attention. His lined face was softened by an explosion of grey hair, still uncombed despite the hour, and blue grey eyes that sparkled with life, even though he suffered almost constant discomfort.

Petronella, was smiling too and, tilting her head towards Hannah she said, "You know Hannah, when I comes down in the mornin' I 'spects to see my lovely friend gone from me, but there he is every time, right there in front of me." She laughed in a lovely rich, raucous and almost musical way that seemed to fill the room.

Hannah's Dad, was equally cheerful, despite his condition. He took Petronella's hand, pulled her towards him and kissed her cheek. "That may be so, my dear, but the only thing that really makes me want to keep going, is the knowledge that every morning I will look up and see that lovely black face beaming down at me."

Despite the chuckling that remark caused, Hannah noticed that when Petronella went to make some tea her eyes were brimming with tears.

Her father watched Petronella leave the room, then folded his arms and contemplated his daughter.

"So, what brings you to see me during the week, my sweet pickle. Checking up on my stock of gin or do we need to talk about something?"

Hannah looked sheepish. She did visit him regularly, but usually at weekends. Dad was still as sharp as a button.

"Well, no fooling you then? Before you ask, it's not about men or money!" She said.

He laughed. "That's a relief since I know nothing about either of those topics."

Tea arrived and Petronella made an excuse that the housework needed to be done; she never crowded Hannah's visits to her Dad. They talked about this and that, and eventually discussed the latest case she was working on. It was of course not the professional thing to do, but in her mind she thought it hardly dangerous to be talking to someone in such bad health as her Dad. In any case, his experience in the Royal Military Police had often been invaluable to her. She used his counsel wisely. He had always been able to guide her in some way or another. She had never needed him more than now.

He listened intently. When she finished talking he put his hands together and pursed his lips.

"And, this profiler chappie? Your eyes glinted when you spoke about his experience and knowledge, you obviously like him?"

Hannah smiled, "Sharp as ever pops. Yes I do like him. He's older and wiser and…"

He finished her sentence, "…and, a bit like your Dad, eh?"

"No," she spluttered, "well, yes, in lots of ways, but…"

"Stop. Hannah, don't make excuses, it's got nothing to do with me. Besides, if he is good for you then that's all I care about. Now, I am not exactly in God's Waiting Room, but I am not as energetic as I used to be, so if you want me to listen, whatever, get to the point quickly my girl."

The truth of it was that Gary Randle was older and wiser and did have the same kind of temperament as her father. She knew that she had fallen for a kind of doppelganger, a younger replica of her Dad, after many failed attempts to form relationships with younger less committed men. Gary and her Dad possessed the same kind of intelligence and humour.

She focussed on the case again and explained the lack of clues and their search for a motive. The way the victims had been killed in a cruel and almost a frenzied fashion, but that each murder must have taken some considerable planning; except perhaps the murder of the prostitute. They took more tea and talked well into the afternoon. Her Dad was equally bemused, but gave her a few tips on how to handle an ambitious boss – he had experienced many in his Army days. Remembering to make him look good; feeding Ramsden's ego was perhaps not bad advice at all.

Eventually, she had to leave and reluctantly kissed him and Petronella goodbye. Just as she got to the door, her Dad called to her.

"Just a thought, my sweet pickle, the victims all seem to have been killed in such a frenzied way. This seems to be a kind of retribution, personal in some way. When your mother died I wanted to hit out at someone so I gave up God. If anyone hurt you, I don't know what I would do, but I certainly wouldn't show any mercy to the perpetrator, that's for sure. Just a thought."

Hannah had always hated it when her father talked about crime and punishment, usually based on his experiences in the Army and in vastly different scenarios to her world. But she understood everything he said, and logged it away in her memory.

"Thanks, Dad," she shouted back and walked down the shale path to her Saab. It was gently spitting with warm spring rain and she was pleased that she had left the convertible top closed. Moments later she was driving back down the A45 towards Ipswich to pick up the A12 to Chelmsford. It was mid-evening, but she wanted to get into the office and review some papers now that she was relaxed and in a receptive mood to find connections or clues. She thought carefully about what her Dad had said.

So, he thought it was retribution?

Chapter Thirteen

Hannah was having a bad day. The coffee machine had broken and without her daily dose of caffeine she was like a bear with a sore head. On top of that one of the Detective Sergeants and a Detective Constable had reported in sick and her team had more Holmes' tasking sheets than they knew what to do with. She remembered the God Kali from Hindu mythology, with several pairs of arms, and thought of ordering at least two for employment as administrators.

The telephone rang and she picked up. She waved at Ramsden who was nearby talking loudly to Detective Constable Les Baker who was congratulating himself on being allocated a pair of Wimbledon tickets – much to the annoyance of his lucky colleagues.

"Yes, yes, fine," she said as Ramsden caught her eye and her waving hand and sauntered over to her desk, stubbornly not wanting to make it seem as though he had been beckoned, "I'll be right down."

She put the phone down.

"Guv, it's the guy who ran away from the alleyway in Chelmsford after the prostitute was stabbed. He is a Mr," she looked down at her pad, "William Hawkes. He's a local lawyer. He has just arrived downstairs with his brief and wants to make a statement."

Hannah put the tape into the machine, switched it on and went through the procedure of identifying Hawkes and his solicitor, herself and Ramsden, and getting dates and times right. Then she got the questioning off the ground, whilst Ramsden sat back and watched the proceedings.

"Mr Hawkes, just tell us all you know about the situation that led to the fatal stabbing of Kelly Golden in Lead Alley, Chelmsford on the night of thirteenth of May this year?"

William Hawkes cleared his throat and despite being in the room of his own volition and looking nervous, was plainly indignant at the process.

"Look, I'm a professional man, you know that, but I'm no saint. I just happen to like prostitutes. That's all there is to it. I propositioned the girl and got down to business. We had no sooner, er, started, when she kind of froze on me. I was aware that she had seen something behind her, stopped and looked over my shoulder. I was frightened I can tell you. I saw this medium sized shadowy figure holding a knife shoulder high approaching us both. The first blow hit me on the hand as I defended myself, see the wound here," he rolled up his jacket cuff and revealed a raw flesh wound, "it was painful and I yelped and backed away. Anyway, as I moved away, the figure closed in on the girl, there was nothing I could do and as I tried to stem the blood from the wound I saw the blow that killed the girl. I was scared I can tell you. So I ran like hell, out into the street and away from the scene."

"So, why didn't you report the attack?" said Hannah.

"Look, I know it was awful, but I was afraid of revealing my identity. You know how it is."

"No, I don't know how it is sir, but it is not up to me to make judgements. Did you see anything significant after you began to run away towards the street?"

"No, nothing," he replied.

"Did you run before the girl was stabbed or afterwards?"

Hawkes blanched at the question.

"You mean did I desert her? Listen, I was injured myself Superintendent and whilst coming to terms with a knife wound which I was holding to stop the bleeding, she was stabbed, then I ran. It was bloody frightening I can tell you."

Then Ramsden sat upright suddenly and Hawkes jumped back in his chair. He glared at him, his eyes fixed on the sweating suspect and his body language threatening; it was covert bullying.

"Look, Mr Hawkes, you expect us to believe that some mystical, shadowy figure committed murder whilst you watched and that you ran away to save your skin, then you decided to keep the whole thing to yourself to protect your precious identity? You were seen, Mr Hawkes, running from the scene. You didn't stop to talk to anyone nor did you call for help. Refresh my memory: you are a lawyer and so you presumably understand the difference between right and wrong, and the importance of evidence and perverting the course of justice?"

Hawkes bristled and went red in the face; his lawyer nodded him on, "Yes I am and I do, you know that. Yes, I ran away that was stupid, but no, I am not the murderer."

"Interesting, sir," smiled Ramsden, "we weren't saying that you were. Now let's see," he referred to some papers, "you are a criminal lawyer so most of your, how shall we say, clients, have, coincidentally been prostitutes and other individuals with, rather shady backgrounds. Perhaps this young lady was one of your customers, you argued and it got out of hand?"

Hawkes' lawyer grasped his client's arm and intervened.

"Don't answer that." He turned to Ramsden and said sternly, "Detective Superintendent, this has gone far enough. My client has come to this station of his own accord so that you may eliminate him from the enquiries I don't think that you appreciate that. My advice is that he says nothing further."

Hawkes, nodded and looked relieved to be rescued.

There was a pregnant pause and Ramsden then nodded to Hannah to end the interview. Inwardly, she seethed. He was deliberately antagonising William Hawkes and she was convinced that he wanted an early end to the investigation by finding any suitable candidate for the murder. His intervention meant that she was unable to stroke Hawkes' memory into life to reveal any possible clues. This was simply not professional. Something was up.

As William Hawkes and the lawyer left the station, Hannah turned to Ramsden.

"What's up?" she said.

"What do you mean?"

"Look, guv, you're more professional that this. You shortened the interview by coming in far too early and endangered the gathering of information by antagonising the suspect. If I had done that you'd have flattened me!" She was fearless, but not rude.

Ramsden stared at her. He was aware that his family circumstances were getting to him, but couldn't share them with Hannah – he couldn't share this sort of thing with anyone. It just wasn't his way. Her courage, compared to other people he had worked with, was admirable; but he always had to have the last word.

"I'm sorry you felt that way, I was going for a quick win. There is a strong chance that our lawyer-friend who spends his life acting for the rogues of this world could well be the murderer. I judged it suitable to rattle his cage a little. But I appreciate your forthright views - even if you are wrong. Write up the report and let me have it by the end of the day will you."

Without waiting for a reply, he turned on his heel and walked away. Hannah felt her hands tighten on the papers she was holding.

She would never like this man – ever!

Gary Randle sat in front of a large magi-board in the Team Room. Even when he was on his own he radiated a kind of relaxed superiority. He leafed slowly through the notes in front of him and looked at the board on which he had drawn four circles, each with a victim's name in the centre. Attached, like spider's legs to the circles were key pieces of information, each spindly strand having keywords attached, like a name, a place or a situation. He also looked down at copies of two letters that Detective Inspector Jack Rollo had just passed him which had been sent to the station by the local investigative journalist Chips Johnson. Accompanying notes said that copies had been sent to the Home Secretary and Chips was hoping to get an interview with him.

Gary smiled at the audacity of that approach – it simply wouldn't be accepted. The Home Secretary would never agree to that. As if in confirmation of that, a 'flash' note had also been received from the Home Secretary on the subject of the letters and copy of this had been faxed to the team; it was also included in the file. It placed the responsibility for dealing with the letters firmly back with the MCIT.

The first letter appeared to have been written on expensive vellum paper because a kind of watermark was just visible and it was clearly written by someone who was used to expressing themselves in print. The use of a semi-colon was interesting, not many people used them these days and the grammar was good, even if the message was simple – too simple perhaps?

"Dear Chips Johnson,

You are the voice of reason and justice in this Godforsaken county; do something!

Tell the Local Police Authority and the government that the people are sick of their policies and they must punish those responsible for bad things.

If you don't then I will continue to avenge the weak and the vulnerable.

You will dread my letters – you have been warned."

There was no signature and no date, and each letter making up the words on the page had been cut out of newspaper text. Chips Johnson had apparently received the first one some time between the date that the rapist was murdered and then joy riders torched. The second was received two days after the murder of the prostitute. He kept them to one side because he thought they were from a 'nutter', he got a lot of those kinds of letters in his position as an investigative journalist. The second was really quite weird, as such letters go.

"Dear Chips,

It hurts my heart to have to punish silly boys and clean up the streets, but someone has to do it and it would seem that I am still being ignored. Silly boys cause great harm to innocent people in the community and filthy women degrade our society, spread disease and destroy weak men's minds.

If nothing is done then examples need to be made of bad people.

I told you that you would dread my letters. I warned you.

So get on with encouraging those in authority to change things."

It was written on the same expensive vellum paper, using cut out characters again. The letter to the Home Secretary was different; it rambled in a neurotic way, but seemed even more frightening because of its persistence.

"Dear Home Secretary,

How typical of a man in your shoes to put votes before the needs of vulnerable people in society? You should protect the people, rather than criminals – assigning them rights as though they deserved to be treated normally like the rest of us. Even your stupid ASBOs are useless and you had the effrontery to send a memorandum to your minions suggesting they should get warnings instead of prison sentences when they break even these pathetic statutory instruments.

You make me sick.
You make the people sick.
You are a pathetic apology for a human being.
Keep watching the television and reading my letters.
Vengeance will continue until you DO SOMETHING."

Gary looked up as Hannah entered the office, harrumphed loudly and threw her papers on to the desk.

"Oh dear," he said, "that bad huh?"

"Yeah, that bad."

"Well, very soon your very best buddy, 'monsieur Guv' Ramsden will start climbing up the wall. See these photocopies, they are copies of letters handed in to Jack Rollo only this morning."

Hannah read them and laughed, which surprised Gary.

"Well, well. He will be displeased," she handed them back to Gary, "he got it into his little head that the man who ran into the street after the prostitute murder is the key suspect. He spent less time on the interview than I spend on my nails."

She paused and thought a little, "I suppose the letters could be written by a dope trying to cash in on the situation?"

"Yes that is always the case. Except that the first letter seemed to naively want Chips to tell someone higher up to take some kind of action. Nothing happened so the killer simply went on with killing the next victim." Gary looked at his watch. "As it happens I am scheduled to give a profile briefing to the team at three o'clock so give me time to consider some of these facts will you?"

Hannah smiled and let him get on with planning his brief.

Ramsden sat to one side of the MCIT briefing room looking dark and moody. Hannah realised that his earlier performance was preying on his mind, despite his bravado. He must have realised with the arrival of the letters that the lawyer was looking less likely to be the suspect than he originally thought – although everyone remains a suspect until all angles are completely cleared. Gary cleared his throat and smiled broadly at the team.

"Okay folks. This is not a 'now hear the word' briefing. It's my way of dealing with the facts that are slowly emerging, from a profiler's perspective that is. Remember what I said the other day, we do our work based on experiences, and notice I am not wearing a raincoat," the Team laughed - Hannah blushed ever so slightly - "more importantly, I don't have any preconceptions. Let's just look at the victims shall we?"

He turned to the magi-board on which he had drawn four large circles with the victims' names in each.

"Firstly, all four victims have been murdered within a five mile radius of Chelmsford, so naturally the odds are that this is a local man, sorry, person. But I look for differences. In the first murder the thug's hands had been nailed to a barn door. The murderer did this in a frenzied way, because we know that the hammer blows frequently missed the nails smashing bones to smithereens in several areas. Look at these photographs," he pointed to some photographs on the adjacent notice board that showed swollen hands encrusted with blood and nails, some bent to one side but clearly hammered deep into the wood and several faces winced.

Then he pointed to the second circle.

"Our rapist friend had been savagely emasculated, not with precision, but untidily and again in a kind of frenzy. Both victims were awake during their suffering. So it would seem that perhaps the perpetrator wanted the victims to know what was happening to them. Were they taunted; were they asked to repent; or, perhaps they had to beg forgiveness? We don't know, but we must let our minds roam over all the possibilities. Both these incidents had been carefully planned. The two joy-riders died in a terrible conflagration, and this was also well planned, but there was no evidence of frenzy, although the forensic team did find several dents on the side of the car indicating that perhaps the perpetrator hammered the vehicle several times with something heavy. Was this done to wake them up? Were they awake when it happened? Did the murderer lose interest in this aspect of the punishment? Who knows?"

Gary paused to let the team think on their own.

"On the other hand, our prostitute was one of several girls who regularly worked Lead Alley," he looked at his notes, "and nearly all of them had experienced a feeling of being stalked. And yet this appeared to be a crime that was carried out in a kind of frenzied way, which makes a mockery of careful stalking. The murderer seems to have thrown caution to the wind. We also need to ask ourselves, was the 'customer' to be punished as well? That is of course if we believe that the man, er, Hawkes, is innocent. I'm not too happy with this one. Anyway, another minute or so and it could've been a violent case of coitus interruptus."

The team laughed, but Ramsden frowned at the humour; his briefings were rarely a bunch of laughs and he didn't see any reason to change his style just because he was making room for this intellectual entertainer. Gary calmed the team and continued.

"Before I continue I want to get 'all academic' on you." He raised a book above his head, "Honore de Balzac, a French novelist wrote this, Le Comedie Humane, unfinished as it happens, and in its many short stories, he describes human nature. He makes an assertion that I have cherished in my work for decades. This man fundamentally understood the primeval brutality of simple untamed emotion. In his writings, he shows how, again and again, minor resentments, when nursed carefully and accumulated over time can come to dominate and horribly distort the mental life of a human being. Is our killer distorted? Is it a life-time's accumulated resentments that drive the need to kill?"

The briefing team was silent. It was a treat to be talked to as though they were intellectual human beings and not just clue-sifting bureaucrats. It struck a chord and two dozen minds instantly began to search for meanings, not just leads.

Gary continued, "Okay, guys, hold on to that quotation and let's keep our minds open. Now on that note, have a look at these copies of letters that were sent to Chips Johnson our well-known local journalist and Rottweiler to local crooks and those in power and authority. They are written by the killer. But why write such letters? It seems to me, but I want you guys to consider it in more detail, that the murders were planned to have an effect."

One of the team, a young lady not long in CID blurted out,

"Yes, Gary, they seem to be almost political, sort of, well, far reaching."

"Yes, they do Wendy, they do. Let's follow that through. For example, in the last case it would have the effect of driving the girls off the streets. But what about the murders committed beforehand? Did the murderer really think that it would stop all the yobs on our streets from carrying out crimes or rapists from yielding to their urges? My dilemma is that the first three look like retribution, or vengeance, and the last one looks kind of political or designed to have some kind of effect on law-makers or police. What do you think?"

The team room erupted in chatter, but Joe Grogan's voice rose above the others.

"Regarding the prostitute killing, I don't know about 'weak men's minds' Gary, unless the murderer knows Dan over there."

The Team laughed again and unnoticed Ramsden left the room, he was in no mood for humour. Gary responded to Joe.

"Joe, I'm sure Dan wasn't who the writer of this letter was referring to, but as a policeman would say, I'll keep an open mind. Listen, seriously now, it's all about trying to build a picture of this person. What I see here is a kind of separation between the three murders and the last one. I see lots of messages. So let's please pay homage to the Frog intellectual, guys, and think about those possible resentments can we?"

Dan recovered from being the butt of Joe's jokes and said quickly, "yeah, but like the rest of us, nothing succeeds like success. Now that the murderer remains undetected, perhaps there is a sense of invincibility and what we are seeing is a change of purpose, or even a playful injection populist propaganda as the, er, game, to call it that, continues?"

Gary glowed at this response.

"Yes, you mean trying to get the public on side? Why Dan, yes, that's a good point, perhaps that's the case, who knows? Let's look at the letters. There is an implication that the writer wrote the letters through Chips Johnson, almost out of admiration for what he does. And what does he do? He sticks up for the underdog that's what. And he's very good at it and very well known locally. That perhaps makes the killer a local resident don't you think?"

125

Gary stopped talking and let the facts soak in.

Jenny Ellis was forthright.

"The murderer wants to tap into Chips success as a popular journalist, but I'm baffled, why after a number of murders and not from the beginning?"

Mark Grainger raised a concern and everyone blinked.

"Of course, Chips could've written them himself?"

There was a low groan, and someone shouted, "oh God, get a good lawyer quickly!"

After that remark a debate ensued and lasted for forty minutes. Ideas flowed like water about the motives of the killer, the change in emphasis, and the letters and so on. Gary furiously made notes and drew more lines on the magi-board with his marker pen as the team threw up different views. Finally, he stopped and addressed the team. The prevailing view was that once the killer had started then it was a case of 'make it up as you go along', but there was a strong sense that the murders were some kind of vengeance for all to see.

"Thanks guys, I must go and fiddle with these facts and see what I come up with. All the time it's a case of keeping a clear mind and letting a picture emerge. The copies of letters you have are to be kept absolutely confidential to the MCIT, because quite separate action needs to be considered on this evidence, so keep 'em in your desk files. Besides, as I understand it, our favourite journalist will probably be making some ground on this issue and the 'red top' newspapers will be making hay with this little lot tomorrow. So keep it confidential please. Okay, that's it. See you again some time."

The team got up and wandered around the magi-board talking about the possible profile of the killer. It certainly beat the daily grind dealing with daily task sheets.

The next day the anonymous letters hit the public domain. Almost every daily newspaper had copies, thanks to Chips Johnson the killer had earned the nickname: **The Avenger**. Each newspaper debated the situation in detail, raising the spectre that The Avenger was a new Yorkshire Ripper, that there was an element of possible mental instability, or it was a political plot to destabilise the government. But all of them put the stress on the Criminal Justice System and the need for urgent reform; clearly the government of the day was at fault. Dozens of examples of citizens being let down by magistrates, judges, the police and so on, filled the pages, with pictures of elderly ladies bruised and battered and others robbed or cheated. The hoary old chestnut, The Human Rights Act came under fire. It was abundantly clear that this story would run and run in the press and to the government's chagrin their opponents took every opportunity to wipe the floor with them.

Oddly, the whole phenomenon now surrounding The Avenger mirrored the prejudices of the general public in an era where they genuinely felt that political correctness had tilted the scales in favour of the perpetrator. A failure to deal with this lay at the heart of the government's problems. Now the image was of an individual, albeit a psychopath pitted against authority.

It was getting out of hand.

The Team room had long since quietened after the early morning buzz of activity as tasks were handed out by the Holmes team and duly scheduled to be performed by various members of the MCIT. Piles of computer printouts littered desks and two team members were marking additional details for amendment or further query, with a black marker pen. The day was drawing to a close and several officers were attempting to clear up before the cleaners arrived. Security was dubious in this respect and several officers had caught cleaners lifting covers on the magi-board or peeking at files and computer printouts. It was well known that this was often the prime source of leaks to the press.

Detective Constable Joe Grogan looked up from his computer screen and gave out a shout.

"Hey guys, you're not going to like this."

They all came over to his screen. "Some misguided soul has set up this web site. It's all about The Avenger's crimes, but look they have comments, articles from newspapers where punishment has not been deemed to fit the crime. And look here too, it's a notice board for people to post their views about The Avenger. Well I'll be damned, the general public are winding him up. They actually support the bastard?"

There was silence in the office as he scrolled down the web site notice board and read the comments. Several officers took the web reference back to their desks and called up the site. It was true. The site was bulging with comments from people in the UK and from some abroad that were now following the case with interest. Some mocked the British police and the criminal justice system. A few, very few, deplored the frenzy being displayed by what they had thought was a moderate and law abiding nation. Some were significantly more violent in their views.

"Hmmm," said one of the detective constables idly, "look at this one, maybe this guy's right, he says paedophiles should be castrated?"

Hannah overheard and moved away from the coffee machine and towards his desk, leaning over to him she said.

"My office, now."

He looked sheepish and followed her into the glass-fronted office. She closed the door.

"John, let's get this straight. Our job is law and order. I don't like paedo's any more than anyone else does, but if the cleaning lady, or someone outside this building hears you say that, it will be taken as a direct quote. Can you see that? Imagine," she spread her arms like a billboard, "you can see it now, 'key police investigation team stalking The Avenger concludes that he is right and advocate castrating paedophiles!' Have a care about what you say John. That was incautious and immature. If Ramsden had been in the office and heard you say that, you would be out of the MCIT with a black mark so big it would block out the sunshine, no second chances. Now get back to work, John, you're too good to let go over a silly incident."

John thanked her and knew that she was right. The team had been talking about her leadership and management style and she hadn't disappointed them. She was courageous, thoughtful and expedient, but above all she was honest with everyone. She knew the value of leading by example and they returned her leadership with loyalty and respect.

Hannah's thoughts turned back to the web page. It was all getting terribly out of hand. Graffiti had been evident in a large number of UK cities, lauding The Avenger's activities and a prosecution was pending against a small company for producing Avenger T-shirts.

But everyone knew that if the authorities won this case it would be a Pyrrhic victory; others would spring up and the case itself would simply attract even more unwelcome attention.

Hannah reflected on Jenny's brief to her about her failure to curb Chips Johnson's journalistic activities, and now this. She knew full well that media interest would eventually develop into a feeding frenzy and all comments made by the team would be retained, pored over, questioned and reported on. They had to be really careful about what they said and to whom.

She sat down and filled a paper cup with clear cool water – but oh, how she needed a long gin and tonic!

Detective Superintendent Ramsden, was still smouldering. He was mad that Jack Rollo had given copies of the letters to Gary Randle the criminal profiler, who had then used them in his briefing to the team. They should've been kept under wraps for a little longer. He also wanted to throttle Chips Johnson who had now clearly unleashed a witch-hunt and whipped up the general public and that would make the job even more difficult for the police. The Essex Chief Constable had telephoned and although he was sympathetic, even he was beginning to feel the heat and he left Ramsden in no doubt that he wanted early results. Her Majesty's Inspector of Constabulary had also called him to say that the Home Secretary was fuming at the failure to nail a suspect. To top it all, there had been a break out of graffiti in the Chelmsford schools and central areas in town. Spray-can enthusiasts were happy to create all sorts of characters to fit the Avenger mould. It was as if an industry had developed overnight, masks, capes, false rubber dark eyes, gauntlets and gloves and all manner of cheap tat was manufactured and sold at markets around the UK. The possibilities for making profit out of the now famous 'Avenger' were limitless. Especially since the victims were not the nice person next door, but crooks or people who offended and abused the community.

The words used in the graffiti, web blogs and elsewhere were none too delicate either, insulting the police and authority in general. The local police officers on the beat were becoming figures of fun and it didn't look as though it was getting any easier.

Ramsden cursed taking the job and the promotion it offered. Then he looked at his watch – to his horror he saw that he was already a half an hour over his planned time to leave for home this evening. He had promised Sue faithfully that he would be home for his favourite dish of spaghetti and meatballs and the family would all eat around the table for the first time in ages. He was simply not going to make it.

His mind whirled. He could do without another night of aggravation on top of all this irritation at work. Just then he heard Detective Constable Les Baker's voice extolling the virtue of real ale and an idea came to him.

He rushed for the door and called out.

"Les, over here, have you got a moment?"

"Yes, guv, coming now," said Baker, never one to keep a superior officer waiting. He knocked at the already open door and Ramsden called him in.

"Come in, come in, sit yourself down. Look, Les, I'm in a bit of a fix. I need your help."

The young constable looked eager to help.

"You see, well, between us chaps, I need to specially treat my wife, my long suffering wife, for all the late nights that I've had to spend on this case. I'm sure you know the score?"

Baker looked serious and nodded in agreement even though he was not married and didn't understand his own mother let alone a female partner.

"I'll cut to the chase. Can you sell me the Wimbledon tickets you have for, say a hundred and twenty quid? I will of course make it up to you in many other ways too – one favour deserves another doesn't it?"

Detective Constable Les Baker knew full well that to turn down the redoubtable Ramsden would be a pretty poor career move. On the other hand, he had wanted to go to Wimbledon for years. But common sense prevailed and in a micro-second he made his mind up.

"Guv, of course I will help. No problem, look here they are," he reached into his jacket pocket and pulled the two tickets out, "you take them and give me the money when you can. I make a profit of forty quid and help you out, sir, and you and your wife get to have a great day out. Sounds good to me."

Ramsden took the tickets and patted Baker on the shoulder.

"Thank you Les, I really am most grateful. Well, I have to go home right now. I will take these to 'she who must be obeyed' and

I know that she will be as pleased as punch. The cash will be ready for you tomorrow. Thanks again. You're a good lad."

Baker left the office without a backward glance. That wasn't arse kissing that was self-preservation.

Chapter Fourteen

Moira Harold MP had had just about enough. She was fuming about the treatment of Elizabeth Curtis MP, a long time friend, who had been relieved of her position and abandoned to the backbenches of politics. Moira tried several times to raise concerns about the Criminal Justice System through party channels, only to be met with either rebuffs or complete silence. Suggesting adjournment debates and other ways of tackling the problem facing the government, to show people that they cared and wanted to listen to concerns and do something about them, came to nothing. Something had to be done. Her constituents were agitated and wanted action; they were fed up with increasing violence and inadequate punishments of offenders. Friends on all sides of the political divide told her that everyone was hopping mad – and her party, she thought, simply hoped that the crisis would go away. Well it wouldn't.

Moira left her tiny office in Norman Shaw South ten minutes before eight o'clock, walked down the stairs and through the enclosed courtyard to Portcullis House, across the floor of the Atrium, then down the escalators and along the colonnade in the New Palace Yard. Then she scaled the narrow spiral staircase to the first floor of the House of Commons. The doorkeepers opened the door and welcomed her by name; it is a nice touch and she wondered how it was that they managed to remember so many identities. Despite her foul mood she smiled and walked through the double doors to the Commons Chamber, entering behind the Speaker's chair. As she walked in, her heart started to pound – could she do this? Should she do this?

Moira made her way to the second back row, on the benches farther away from the Speaker, but adjacent to the central aisle between two blocks of seats. The seats around the Speaker's chair and around the Prime Minister are occupied by those seeking or given preferment, and they would be crowded. Those of more independent views occupied benches farther away from the Speaker. Moira's choice was perfect, she reckoned this was the best place to get noticed and also the easiest seat to vacate and chase the Home Secretary after her question to the Prime Minister; if she was lucky enough to get selected that is. She then filled in her 'prayer' card, which ensured the seat was hers and put it on the seat. This meant that she had to turn up for prayers; not to do so forfeited the place.

The odds of her getting noticed were good. She had not put in a question for consideration a week beforehand in the customary manner, on a card marked with an 'E'. But she had indicated to the Speaker's Secretary that she had an important constituency issue to raise and was aware that she had left it late. The Secretary replied very formally that there were not many ministers expected to speak and that he was aware of the issue and would see what he could do. However, the issue she indicated, education, was not what she would ask a question about.

Moira knew that the Speaker had to balance questions in proportion to the MPs in the House and the Secretary's formula was crucial. She was known to be a loyal party member and recently spent quite some time being seen and helpfully commenting on this and that, especially within earshot of the Speaker – the odd smile to him helped. Today, she would jump up at every opportunity trying to catch the Speaker's eye. The protocol was that if the Speaker wanted to select an MP to speak, he would catch the person's eye beforehand to ensure the questioner is paying attention. This was where timing was crucial; to get called too early might be a mistake. She was duty bound under current protocol to stay for at least two questions after her own. If the Home Secretary chose to retreat early, she would be unable to catch him. Twenty minutes after twelve would be perfect and she would vacate some time after twelve twenty-five. What a fig – all because she found it impossible to pin him down and get him to face facts any other way!

Moira left the Chamber and went for a walk intending to then take a cup of tea in the Members' Tea Room before spending time in the Members' Library, rehearsing her question and her plan of campaign. Although her question was short and sweet, she was aware of the need to maintain eye contact wherever possible and not make it seem as though she was reading, even though most people did. The question was typed in large bold print. Many a fledgling

MP has perished through over confidence; asking a question in the House was a nerve-wracking experience for newcomers.

The sound of her leather shoes resounded as she click-clacked around the Central Lobby, trying to rid herself of nerves and to allow the statues and paintings of this great institution to remind her of her responsibilities to truth and reason, on behalf of her constituents.

Ralph Hardacre hated Prime Minister's Question Time. It was all so stage-managed he often felt that his master was no more than a circus entertainer. Every angle was rehearsed in minute detail by both sides; it was always the supplementary and 'filler' questions that got the most interest and for that matter the best laughs. That was just it, a perfectly good democratic system of question and debate had turned over the years into a spectacle rather than an example of good parliament.

He stirred his coffee slowly and relaxed. Despite the frustrations of the job, this was the pinnacle of his career and he knew it. It was well known that this post was responsible for some of the most important policy in the United Kingdom, but that, despite whatever good work was done on central policy-making, his position was also subject to the onslaught of 'events'. And it was events that inevitably aroused enormous public interest; the Essex murders were typical of the kind of fires he had to put out before they got out of hand. But nothing was impossible and his job was to keep the ship afloat and maintain a sense of balance, whilst loyal and hardworking Mandarins and department heads carved out policy and procedures behind the scenes. They would always be there, no matter what colour the political flag. Perhaps he was, as Robin Day the preeminent political interviewer in the seventies had said to Defence Secretary Sir John Knott during the Falklands campaign, 'a here today and gone tomorrow politician?'

The coffee was strong and he slurped it without fear of being overheard. His office was large and very private. In fact he did rather well for accommodation. It was a shock initially to move from a small MP's office in Portcullis House, to that of the Home Secretary in the Home Office itself. His personal assistant had been very sweet. She had seen Home Secretaries come and go. After behaving a little like Oliver Cromwell, advocating an austere approach to decoration and the like, she gently steered him to put pictures on the wall and books on the shelves. A few ornaments from home crept in too.

Then, after she had described how many of his predecessors put something in the office that represented what they stood for, where they came from, or perhaps what they liked most, for example their favourite sport or something funny, he conceded ground – gracefully. He couldn't produce a cricket bat, a miner's lamp or photographs of him shaking hands with Presidents or the great and good, so he brought in something really precious. It was a clay model of a man sitting on a bench under a tree looking at a gravestone. His daughter made it after a much-loved neighbour had died; it was her way of coping with the old man's death and it summed up her lovely personality. Besides, it always reminded him of both his daughters whom he loved dearly. And that is just what you want when under stress – to look to something and connect in a way that reminds you who you were and what you stand for – to help you bat away the anxieties and the demons that lurk ready to hop onto your back.

His personal assistant, Rosemary, buzzed through and reminded him that his Private Secretary, John, a grade seven fast track civil servant, was patiently waiting to accompany him to Prime Minister's questions in the Commons. He smiled to himself thinking of the scene in various offices in the vicinity, where MPs were being summoned, lurching like automatons from offices and hallways to their seats in the Commons Chamber. He stood up and playfully put his arms out in front of him like a robot and closed his eyes.

Just then his personal assistant came in. "Home Secretary, what are you doing, are you all right?"

"Ah! Yes, quite all right Rosemary, thank you. I was just, er, doing some Pilates, Tai Chi actually, I was stretching before battle commences. Anyway," he grabbed his papers quickly, "I'm off before I am late for school."

He strode off down the corridor thinking that one could spend hours alone in an office, but not until one scratched somewhere disgusting would someone suddenly burst in. His Private Secretary caught up with him and they walked slowly to his ministerial vehicle. It was a short drive to the House of Commons, and there they drove into New Palace Yard. He cursed not making enough time to mix with his colleagues over tea in between prayers and questions and resolved to do that next time. It didn't do to remain out of touch for long periods. As he walked into the Commons Chamber he looked at his watch. It was eleven fifty-five on the dot. Well done John, he could always rely on him to get him to where he needed to be without a hassle and on time. That was precisely what he had to do after questions.

At eleven fifty-eight the Speaker took the final question on Europe. The Prime Minister, as always, made it by the skin of his teeth and squeezed along the row to his place. He moved to the Home Secretary's right and towards the Chief Whip who occupied the seat next to the aisle. He coughed loudly to remind the minister speaking that he was there, thus avoiding the possible embarrassment of him sitting on his lap. It hadn't happened to any Prime Minister yet and he was not about to have it happen to him. He was in a good frame of mind today despite the fact that he was expecting a hard time on several issues. He casually looked around, pretending to nod to various supporters around his own bench.

The Chamber filled up slowly and the Prime Minister sat, briefing folder in hand and head arched towards his Chief Whip listening to directions and other tit-bits of information. Today was likely to be difficult, with questions on asylum seekers likely to hurt, but recent successes in stalling talks with the European Union on the vexing issue of the re-invented European Constitution were ready to be praised and applauded by his own side. Which would come first? He acknowledged Ralph with a nod towards his briefing folder and thumbs up; the brief must have been just what his leader wanted and this pleased Ralph. The asylum issue was a minefield, but all the questions had been researched and robust answers and 'lines to take' drafted. This was political pugilism at its best. His job wasn't so much to announce policy, but to respond to the challenges laid against him, as predicted from current events and knowledge of the questions identified to the Speaker. Unless the opposition framed a question really badly, he would be unable to point to their track record and launch into a list of government successes. So, it was all about survival. Let gladiatorial combat begin.

Ralph was aware of the usual buzz around the Chamber. He looked to his left and saw an array of aides ready to whisper information down the line to the Prime Minister should the need arise. It always reminded him of lines of firemen ready to pass buckets of water – perhaps that's just what the whole process was, some big fire-fight?

It wasn't long before combat began with a few mild questions from the opposition, easily batted away for a few cheap laughs. The subject of asylum seekers was expected and took up quite a bit of time. The heckling was loud and furious, but the Prime Minister was prepared and after reading his brief swatted the questions away like irritating flies. He told the House that he had ordered an urgent review of port and airline entry points, which then allowed him to slip into a comparison between his government's successes and the past failures of the opposition.

Moira and the other MPs seeking to ask questions, jumped up and down like Jack-in-the-boxes to gain attention; some where chosen, but not Moira. A party lackey congratulated the Prime Minister on his success in stalling the reintroduction of the European Constitution. This got a mighty cheer and the Prime Minister milked it for all his worth. By now he was almost home and dry.

More questions were needed and to Moira's surprise she saw the Speaker look directly at her, she looked at her watch – it was a shade too soon - too soon. She smiled, then grimaced and started to cough and splutter. Seeing this, the Speaker immediately turned his head and called a member of an opposition party, who raised an issue on Network Rail. To his credit the Speaker looked back to Moira who shrugged her shoulders and mouthed 'sorry'. He noted her obvious disappointment and nodded. She was in.

The previous questioner was dealt with swiftly and then Moira was called to her feet. She stood up, her heart beat like a machine gun and her throat began to close. She coughed then breathed deeply. The House was silent. Then she began.

"Will the Prime Minister agree that the terrible murders that have taken place in my constituency, East Chelmsford, Essex, have highlighted a national concern about the Criminal Justice System in this country? Daily, we are faced with crime and disorder on a level never seen before. It now transpires that an unknown psychopath has taken it on himself to kill alleged perpetrators of crimes, solely because he has no faith in the authorities to either catch criminals or when they are caught, dispense proper, fitting justice. What is this government going to do about it?"

There was a loud roar of approval that shocked everyone. It was obviously a key constituency issue for a large number of Members who had hitherto been unable to get any sense out of the government or their framed question through the Speaker's 'question formula'. The opposition guffawed and waved their order papers at the Prime Minister. Moira felt bad. She felt that she had been forced to put her own leader on a spot; but she had, and it was purely and simply because party officials weren't listening to her. It was her job to work for her constituents – and by God they came first – which is why she got elected!

The Prime Minister's jaw dropped and for a moment his mouth resembled that of a ventriloquist's dummy. Then he did his best to answer the question, using the best known platitudes in the game. He commiserated with the relatives of the victims, then, obviously flustered, he praised the Essex Police Force and acknowledged that it was a tricky case to solve. It was a difficult situation and he thought they did a great job, but his conviction was questionable. As he spoke, the Home Secretary was whispering from his left. This is a time-honoured method of briefing your master 'on the hoof' so to speak. Only the cleverest Prime Minister's can speak and listen at the same time. He cleverly covered his tracks by pretending to look in his folder.

Then, more fully briefed, he added that significant extra funding had been allocated to County Police Authorities. Projects were now ongoing around the country to allow Police Forces to more closely engage the local community so that they understood the problems being faced by citizens. This was a major initiative and would ensure transparency and a real connection with the general public.

On steadier ground now, he became more self-assured and added with a wry smile, that it was crucial not to knee-jerk into major reviews, amendments, or new policies, that would inevitably need further revision, or cause more problems later on. They had seen too much of that already under the previous government. This government was continually reviewing the Criminal Justice System and had a tight rein on issues of law and order.

He hardly noticed the shaking heads, worryingly, on all sides of the House.

The opposition was quickly on his case, but they too were caught short and the questions were not incisive enough to cause problems. Mostly, they jeered and ranted as the Prime Minister spoke.

On a roller now, and instead of ending his response neatly, he then promised to follow on from the local projects recently set up and would ensure that when criminals were caught, justice would be dispensed quickly and appropriately. His government was tough on crime – period.

It was a class act, but he fooled no one. The rumbles and jeers continued as he sat down.

The Speaker quickly came to his rescue and moved proceedings on to a different questioner. In less than a minute and to the discomfort of members of the House, a sycophant was called to his feet and began complimenting the government on its recent success in gaining concessions on fish quotas in the North Atlantic. But the rumbling and bad feeling was palpable. No one listened to the rest of the questions and the Speaker had to twice call for Members to stop talking and pay attention.

After a painful conclusion to questions, the Prime Minister stood and before making to leave he glanced along the row and up at Moira; she felt really bad. As he turned away, the Chief Whip, who was a perfect match as the female Russian agent, Kleb, in the James Bond movie 'Goldfinger', and not known for her generosity of spirit, turned around and glared at her.

Nevertheless, Moira had another job to do and turned her full attention to her rehearsed route to the rear of the Chamber and down behind the Speaker's chair to snare the Home Secretary. She reached the door quickly and had to elbow her way through. To her delight she got a number of pats on the back from MPs on both sides of the House; that made her feel better. As she moved into the drab corridor, she spotted the Home Secretary walking quickly away with his Private Secretary to towards the New Palace Yard where his ministerial vehicle was parked.

"Home Secretary, your attention please?" she shouted.

Ralph Hardacre stopped in his tracks. It was bad form to ignore any Member let alone one from your own party. Moira reached his side and put her diminutive figure in between him and his Private Secretary.

"Home Secretary, have you any idea how wound up my constituents are, and indeed others in various part of the country, about the Essex murders and this psychopath's challenges to the government regarding the ineffectual way we deal with crimes in this country? The Criminal Justice System is in dire need of reform. We are almost daily reading reports in the popular press about dangerous criminals being bailed, chaos in the community with gangs of youths rampaging in towns, joy-riding in stolen cars, burglaries and muggings. Police are accused of avoiding conflict and dealing with the 'easy to do' crimes instead of the more violent ones. What am I to say to my constituents when so much of what I have suggested regarding this whole sorry state has fallen on stony ground? And what about this person, the, what is it, oh yes, The Avenger, will I say that they shouldn't worry because they will come and save them because their government cannot?"

Ralph Hardacre looked at the ceiling then straight at her.

"Moira. Just what were you playing at? You are such a promising MP, but this kind of disloyalty will not help your career one little bit. You know first of all that the government cannot be seen to be meddling in local police issues, but off the record, I have tried to get some fire into the investigations. I really have. I do have to be extremely cautious; it is simply not constitutional for me to interfere. You aren't stupid and you know that."

Moira was about to break in, but he put his hand up,

"There are broader issues too. It's bad enough with the failed amalgamation of local Police Forces and calls to improve our investigation processes post Soham. But, you really should have tried harder to get to see me first rather than make this extraordinary outburst in the Chamber. Expediency is all Moira, something you are not used to at your level. The government has the responsibility to encourage Police Forces to balance budgets, seek reductions where they are appropriate and gain efficiencies. We don't have killers all over the place and there is a danger that this kind of hyperbole could be used to put the government under pressure to pump even more money into the Police Forces at a time when we have to balance budgets. If I am not careful there will be a sack full of budget requests every time there's a panic. Chief Constables are canny individuals you know? And what about loyalty? The kind of dissent you showed today was quite unforgivable, it does no more than weaken our position on other issues and give great delight to the opposition. Take today, the PM was ready to roll on his recent tough and successful stance with the European Union; well thanks to you that was given barely a few moments air time and we ended on a weak note, with the opposition cock-a-hoop at our discomfort."

He was angry now and showed it. But Moira stood her ground.

"So there it is then," said Moira, "local needs, real needs of people who are genuinely worried about law and order, put in second place to political expediency; to make our leader look good, to avoid the tricky issues. Is that what it's all about these days?"

Hardacre made to respond, but Moira was having none of it. She turned on her heel with the words, "You haven't heard the last of this Ralph Hardacre, not at all you haven't. I promise you."

He watched her stomp away towards the Commons Library and the Terrace side of the Commons and let out a loud harrumph. For all that, he quite admired her spirit and for a few moments knew exactly where she was coming from; the situation was dire and he knew it. Expediency was a politician's rule and guide – but he still had a conscience.

Gary Randle wearily climbed the steps to his flat. It had been a long day at the police station and he had done his best to stay out of the way of the emerging politics; although he knew that he had unwittingly been the cause of a few problems. The team officers' morale was beginning to drop. Local and national newspapers daily ridiculed their work and one of them irresponsibly suggested that, The Avenger, was turning into a kind of macabre Superman, putting right what the authorities could not. Cartoons provided more fun, some showed images of policemen carrying backpacks full of policies, procedures and copies the government's Criminal Justice System and the Human Rights Act, thereby unable to run after robbers dressed in striped jerseys, wearing black masks, carrying bags marked SWAG. The cartoon caption showed one policeman saying to another:

"Each year I find it difficult to run fast enough to catch these little buggers!"

He entered his flat and smelled coffee freshly brewed. The automatic timer had worked and he congratulated himself on this most sensible of purchases. A slow cooker also provided another aroma of beef stew fortified with red wine. It was the most efficient of bachelor pads.

It had been a hot and sticky day and within minutes he had shed his clothes, sorted out his washing and walked naked into the kitchen. The cool air around his loins was such a joy. Sitting down all day was hot and irritating – walking around in the buff for just a while let his body breath and freed his most sensitive parts. Thankfully, he remembered to keep the Venetian blinds half closed so that his elderly neighbours didn't get too much of a shock.

He looked down and contemplated his best friend.

"Well, there you go, Mister Midnight, mustn't frighten the horses or the old ladies across the street."

After pouring himself a decent Belgian coffee, quite unlike the creosote served up in the canteen at the police station, he moved into his study. In trying to drink his coffee and walk at the same time he spilled some down the centre of his body below his navel.

"Bloody ouch. Sorry, Midnight old chap, won't do that again!"

He sat down at his desk. Out of his briefcase he took some papers, newspaper cuttings, the copies of the letters sent to Chips Johnson and photographs of the victims. He knew that the removal of sensitive information or making copies of material was most definitely not approved, but he didn't really want to spend more time at the police station than he needed to. The atmosphere when Ramsden was around was at times poisonous and he could not concentrate. He wanted to replicate a lot of the information on his own notice boards so that he could sit and contemplate the evidence. He would need to fix up a kind of curtain to hide the information from houseguests or his cleaner, but that would be easy enough.

142

After about twenty minutes he had pinned a wide variety of items on the left-hand side of the notice board. He stepped back and looked at his work and after swapping several articles around seemed satisfied with the presentation. He then cut a large map of Essex and put it on the right hand side of the notice board. Soon red circles were drawn to show the area of the murders, then blue circles where the victims had allegedly carried out crimes – it the case of the prostitute it was difficult.

It was beginning to be what he wanted, a rich picture, and he would add evidence or thoughts as they came to him. He reached out and absentmindedly spilled a box of small plastic topped pins onto the floor. They were different colours, red, blue, white, green and yellow. Cursing, he carefully picked them up as best he could, put them back into the box, keeping a half a dozen for use, and then carefully put the box away in a drawer. Then he went to his spare room and collected a medium sized curtain. It was made of cotton and could be easily attached to the board. He then began to pin it along the top of the board so that it hung over the information hiding it from general view.

Halfway through the task he heard the door click. Hannah? He quickly smoothed the curtain over the notice board, but one pin remained in his hand; he reached out and stuck it in the map, not wanting to put it back in the box.

As he leaned against the desk his soft flesh rested against the cool surface. He smiled at the pleasant feeling and thought of Hannah and what she would say when she saw him in his study in the buff. He began to feel aroused at the thought. As footsteps approached and then reached his study he turned and said, "Get your kit off and get a load of this honey-bunch."

But his face dropped when he saw Mrs Fryer, his cleaner and he quickly grabbed his Filofax to cover his embarrassment; the A5 document was only just the right size.

"My goodness, Mrs Fryer, what are you doing here?"

She stood her ground, unabashed that she was where she should not be at a time she was not expected. What made it worse was the way she craned her head to one side. Then, as he grew more uncomfortable, inevitably the situation worsened as his embarrassment grew and a slight smile appeared on her face.

143

"I think you ought to go, I'm sorry to have embarrassed you. Perhaps we can discuss this some other time?" he said, almost plaintively.

Mrs Fryer was clearly in no hurry. She raised one eyebrow and said, "ah! My handbag." Then she walked two paces to the right of the study, reached down and picked it up. "I'll be off now then, Professor Randle."

She turned, smiled again and without a further word left the room.

After she closed the door and it was clear she was well out of hearing, he dropped the Filofax and burst out laughing.

He hadn't laughed like that for days.

Ramsden's car slid to a halt in his driveway and he raced up the steps and in through the door. He didn't even take his coat off; his stomach churned when he went to the dining room and saw the dirty plates where his family had eaten, a portion of meatballs and spaghetti now cold in a serving dish and his clean setting at the head of the table.

"Oh, shit!" he said softly.

As he came back out into the hallway his son and daughter were tiptoeing upstairs – they turned and shrugged their shoulders. Becky blew him a kiss. Ramsden gathered his strength, took his coat off then went into the lounge. Sue was sitting in an armchair, her eyes reddened with tears and her hands holding a paper handkerchief tightly on her lap.

She looked up at him. An immense surge of guilt made him feel sick. The kind of guilt that makes you want to abase yourself and plead for forgiveness – to do anything just to make things right. It could only be that way if the guilt was real. This time it was real and he wished he could turn the clock back.

"So," she said, through a choking voice, "all the promises you made the other day – just a sham as usual. A simple request and you couldn't even try to make it. I am trying so hard, so very hard to make our family life normal. I want us to have some stability, love and sharing. Every time I think things are right you let me down."

Sue put her head in her hands.

"I'm truly sorry, I really am. You must know something..."

"What?" she interjected, looking up with red eyes full of tears.

144

"Sue, I got deflected, stupidly deflected, well, because I saw an opportunity to plan a really nice day for us. An opportunity came up and I chased it, but sadly, for me, well for us all, it took me a long time to negotiate. Once into the negotiation I couldn't back out. Darling, I'm so sorry. It was for these."

Ramsden reached into his inside pocket and pulled out the two Wimbledon tickets.

Sue stared at them and said, "The dates. It's a weekday. You never take holidays let alone time off on a weekday? Is this kosher Andy, do tell me it is, because I cried my heart out tonight thinking that you'd ignored my simple request and hadn't even bothered to remember let alone telephone me?"

"Yes, it's Kosher. If I hadn't been chasing this bloke down for the tickets then I would've remembered to call you and tell you what I was doing. I just got caught up in, well, chasing the tickets that I forgot the time. I'm a chump. I fell at the first hurdle. Can you forgive me?"

Sue reached out to him – then burst into floods of tears. He took her in his arms and held her tight as she sobbed. This was his wife who only wanted more of him as a husband and a father and he wasn't delivering the goods. He hated to admit it to himself, but he was not pleased that he had saved his skin and perhaps his marriage by the slimmest of margins; but this was down to a lie and he didn't like it. He must do better – he knew that he simply must do better.

The mood in the team room was subdued and the officers busied themselves rather less productively than they should have been. The morning brief had been full of Ramsden's hectoring and they had received little thanks for the small number of clues that had been unearthed. The killer was an exemplary tactician.

There was a good reason for Ramsden's bilious nature. Early that morning he received a call from the Chief Constable. There was a strong chance that because of the number of murders, the MCIT may need to be split into two and increased in size. This would entail raising the top rank to Chief Inspector; there might even be two of them. He would no longer be in charge.

Ramsden did not work well under superior officers.

The team were advised that Detective Robin Oakley had been kicked off the team, supposedly for commenting that the work was being made more complicated than it ought to have been; sadly his views came to Ramsden's attention; end of story. But the cruellest and most inept piece of corporate management was the sarcasm shown to Detective Sergeant Jenny Ellis for failing to influence Chips Johnson or to get him 'on side' during the investigation. Many officers wondered just how it was expected that such a mercurial character as Johnson would be lured into becoming a 'police Patsy'. Jenny was a tough girl, but this unnecessary and unfair treatment affected her a lot. That's where her partner Jack Rollo came to her aid and assured her that everyone, including him, was behind her.

Ramsden had enormously thick skin. He knew the effect he had on his co-workers, but cared little. His mantra was, pour encourager les autres, and was often quoted as saying that he wasn't there to win popularity contests, but to get results: it was a good enough platitude to impress the hierarchy, but made him an unpopular leader. Moreover, it didn't always work.

Hannah looked up as he approached her. He was in an unusually bouncy mood today.

"I've been thinking," Hannah winced and wondered what next, "we don't have that many suspects. A few names have been thrown up by the dear old Holmes database, but no real contacts. Perhaps we should be thinking more laterally?"

He turned to one of his acolytes, Detective Constable Les Barker.

"Les, c'mon over here, and you Jack let's have a quick round table."

Hannah was pensive. She absolutely hated bosses who were interventionists and Ramsden was just that way inclined. They scrape the surface, disregard all the facts, many of which they don't have the patience to consider and then proceed to shoot from the hip. The first shot from that direction came quickly.

" Chips Johnson. Les, what do we know about him?"

Somewhat suspiciously to Hannah, and she caught Detective Inspector Jack Rollo's eye too, the information was altogether too deep to be that which is available in the hip pocket for use at a moment's notice. Ramsden had been brooding on Chips Johnson's actions and was about to use Barker as his mouthpiece.

"Well guv, it seems that our friend Chips was a communist agitator when he was working as a union convenor with Ford in the Dagenham works. He was by all accounts a nasty piece of work and always ready to influence the work-force to go out on strike, or cause general mayhem."

Jack Rollo intervened, "Yes, we know that, but let's not forget that he also did a lot of good. Many people would've been out of work in Essex had it not been for him. I'm local, young Les', and I can tell you he was well respected by both management and workers."

The constable continued as is he had heard nothing – fine qualities for a politician thought Hannah.

"He left and went into journalism. His penchant for tracking down injustice was well known, and he did work hard to get to the crux of some pretty interesting and nasty scams. On the other hand, he was interviewed on more than one occasion about cases that he had actually set up himself. By that I mean he had a habit of manufacturing some evidence, not always I grant you, but sometimes. After that he wrote his copy according to mythology rather than fact. In one case he came close to being arrested, but bought off the other party and narrowly missed prosecution, living to fight another day."

Hannah wondered where this was going.

Ramsden half folded his arms and scratched his chin whilst looking at the ceiling; it made him look school-masterly and imperious.

"So, he's good at planning and is a trained dissembler! What does this seem to indicate?" he said

Hannah's mind raced as she realised that Ramsden was leading the team's thoughts. This wasn't new information it had been deliberately researched and was now being delivered to the team in the guise of 'guess what?'

Unsurprisingly, Les Barker waded in. "Well, sir, he could be, just could be that is, manufacturing his own stories, young Grainger brought that up the other day. He's got form in that respect."

"He could be a suspect then?" said Ramsden.

Hannah blanched at this blatant coercion and said, "that's pretty slim stuff, guv. He's hardly likely to be sending himself letters, then passing them to the police now could he?"

Ramsden flushed, as he always did when he didn't get his own way. Hannah realised that she was beginning to read him like a book. He persisted.

"But he does plan everything he does and very well by all accounts. His assertion that he has been contacted by The Avenger with these letters is just so convenient isn't it? He's making a fistful of dosh now and will do for as long as this case goes on."

Jack Rollo knew what was coming.

"Let's bring him in for questioning?" said Ramsden, abruptly.

"God no," said Hannah without thinking, "the local then the national press would have a field day. Chips will milk it for all its worth. My recommendation is, don't do it guv."

Ramsden ignored her and addressed the rest of the team.

"Any comments from the rest of you?" He said.

There was silence. Hannah fumed. Ramsden was condescending.

"I know we will have to take a lot of heat from the wider environment, not just from Chips, but that's what we're paid for. Just remember, the Force is with you – if you'll forgive the phrase."

Acolytes smiled and laughed at this weak science fiction reference.

Hannah went to say something, but the look on Ramsden's face made it abundantly clear that she should desist. Detective Inspector Jack Rollo was allocated the task of interviewing Chips along with Ramsden. Jack did not look too pleased.

Hannah glanced at him and they both had expressions that said, "This should be interesting."

Angie lay in bed, wide-awake, looking at the ceiling; she loved this feeling. It was like her memories of being looked after as a child. Sunday night was bath night and she remembered freshly laundered bed linen and the paraffin heater in the bedroom that gave the room a warm, nose-filling aroma, shining a round flickering circle of light on the ceiling. She conjured up that feeling of being protected and in a safe environment.

But her mother hadn't been to see her for ages – absolutely ages. She was upset at this. But sedatives had helped her to stay steady – long live drugs. They actually made her think straight too. That's when she realised that she had been very bad indeed and desperately wanted to let the world know what had driven her to do such dreadful things. She momentarily broke from the relaxed and positive personae she had managed to return to and raised her hands to the top of her head, holding her hair tight as if she was wrenching it out by the roots.

"I bet no one will listen. It's all results you see. Politics and results. Tick here, tick there. Tick, tick, tock. No one cares about me, or you Mum, or the rest of the victims who have to suffer. Tick, tick, tock, tock, make it all sound all right, get by until another day, don't rock the boat."

She gripped her hands tighter until the feeling of helplessness passed and she was left sweating and gasping for breath.

He would understand – she knew that He would. She would tell Him everything. He would understand for sure.

Then the door opened and closed quietly and she looked up and smiled with joy and relief at the figure in front of her.

Chelmsford Police Station was packed with constables who just decided to call in and have a cup of tea in the canteen or check their mail. It was the day that the infamous Chips Johnson, journalist, was to be interviewed. Everyone knew Jack Rollo was uncertain about the interview, but that Ramsden looked forward to the dual. They didn't know who to feel sorry for, but wanted to know the outcome. Behind the scenes bets were placed and a 'sweep' organised based on the outcome.

Chips Johnson and his legal adviser entered the interview room and sat down. Chips had the look of an arrogant man ready for a fight and his lawyer looked sharp and tetchy. Chips leaned back in the chair and ran his hands over his paunch. His lawyer, reading glasses perched forward on his nose, laid out his notepaper and three pencils neatly in front of him and sat with his hands clasped in front of him, staring at Jack and Ramsden. That in itself was unnerving.

After the normal tape introductions Jack Rollo started the interview.

"I am Detective Inspector Jack Rollo and this is Detective Superintendent Andy Ramsden. Mr Johnson, what can you tell us about the letters you received recently concerning the murders of four people in the Chelmsford area?"

"Mr Johnson now is it? Call me Chips. We are after all old friends and this ill-judged action is going to make provision for my pension fund, so why don't we stay friends?"

Jack looked exasperated.

" Chips, I'm sorry this has inconvenienced you, but we are doing our duty. You have received letters and we merely want to ascertain how and when you received them and if you know who sent them?"

"If I knew who sent them Inspector I would've bloody told you, wouldn't I? Look I know that you will be embarrassed by the fact that they have been made public, but hard luck. This Avenger chappie, is obviously far happier dealin' with me than you lot. Perhaps he thinks you'll lose the letters in your filing system? I don't suppose the Home Secretary was that pleased either and I note that I didn't even get the courtesy of a reply. But I care not. I want this case to be closed as much as you do, dear hearts. Believe me I do."

Jack frowned, "And of course you stand to make some money out of the journalistic work?"

"You are correct. And some of you will hope to make promotion out of the investigation I presume?"

Jack winced. Ramsden leaned forward.

" Chips, you've been an agitator for years, and these letters fan the flames of public opinion, don't they? In fact they insinuate that the police and government are useless. Doesn't this fit your style? Isn't this what you are good at? Why shouldn't I consider that you might have written them yourself?"

Chips solicitor leaned almost nose to nose with Ramsden.

"My dear Detective Superintendent, that was out of order and you know it."

Chips laughed loudly.

"Good man my brief, one of the best. He was a boxer at university so he'll take you on Ramsden, with words or otherwise. But let's help you out shall we? Why should I write those letters? Anyway, I cannot prove that I didn't, any more than you can prove that I did. So it's a pointless stalemate, or perhaps what they call a Mexican Standoff, isn't it?"

Jack quickly took over and pursued the interview along different lines, asking about Chips wild days at Dagenham and his near miss with the law concerning some journalism that was set up to entrap various individuals. But at every juncture, Chips had the best of answers and moved deftly out of range. Nevertheless, the responses seemed strangely choreographed almost as though he expected to be interviewed by the police; here was a man who was either adroit at handling interviews or someone who had something to hide about his past.

To Jack's dismay, Ramsden lost interest and they took a break while it took time to find a replacement second interviewer. Jack was dismayed with Ramsden's lack of professionalism. It was his damned idea about the interview in the first place! Proceedings continued when a second interviewer was identified for the tape. Chips was then asked milder questions about possible contacts he might have who could be playing tricks on him, as well as some crooks he might know who may just be culpable in the murders. But there was nothing of interest or value that could be offered. He accepted his copy of the taped interview and smiled like a Cheshire Cat as he put it into his briefcase and bade them goodbye.

Chips Johnson was no fool. As he left the police station with his legal adviser, his first port of call was back to the company's legal offices to pick the bones out of the interview and to see what gain there might be to him following this debacle. He would make a lot of noise about other things that were so much more important than interviewing an innocent journalist who had been selected as a contact by The Avenger. He still had a few tricks up his sleeve. Local people daily suffered violence and deceit and the police hierarchy would indeed pay for their incompetence.

Detective Jack Rollo gathered up the tapes and papers. He was furious. That interview achieved absolutely nothing.

Gary Randle made very few mistakes in his life, but today he stepped in a big puddle that would soon get so deep it would engulf him. Although he was an independent agent, he was under a strict obligation not to release any information whatsoever concerning ongoing investigation. He didn't do that. What he did do was to speak to Chips Johnson, who got to hear about Randle's involvement as a criminal profiler working for the Essex police.

Chips was an experienced journalist and initially called Randle about the working style of the nation's profilers for a background article he was writing for a national magazine. The conversation meandered around and Chips feigned interest, oozing charm his questions easing into Gary's psyche like WD40 into a rusted nut and bolt. Then he moved the conversation to a description of the style of work itself and before Randle knew it he was talking freely about how his skills were being used to catch The Avenger. Even the best of us has a small amount of ego and Randle fell for this approach hook line and sinker.

The resulting article in the local and national newspapers, headed: "Criminal Profiler set to catch The Avenger" was to cause a stir within the MCIT as well as the Home Office.

The Home Secretary was heard bellowing four corridors away in the House of Commons.

Andy Ramsden had not seen the daily newspapers, because he had risen early and breakfasted with his wife Sue on scrambled eggs and bacon. The mood in the Ramsden house was good, very good. They then made their way slowly from the train station through London to Wimbledon, then out and into the queue for the double-decker bus that takes some of the crowds to the world famous tennis courts. Getting into the world-class tennis courts was a slow affair and Ramsden couldn't help looking at his watch several times. Sue forgave him. Even in their courting days he would take her to the cinema and playfully whisper that he could be in the office doing some useful paperwork. It took several rounds of snogging to get his attention back and by then they had missed the main action in the film. In those early days she never really minded at all.

Today there was one tough concession. Neither of them had taken mobile telephones. This was really difficult for Ramsden, but he was determined to cope with being out of communication with his work. For a natural interventionist it was torture leaving the team for a day and not being in contact.

The tennis was good. They saw a ladies' match where Sharapova beat an Israeli amusingly called Smashkova, who did not do what her name suggested. Then they saw Andy Roddick struggle to beat a Serbian called Tipsarovitch, who revelled in the audience attention as they called out 'come on Tipsey'. As the day wore on and they enjoyed a good lunch, then later, strawberries and cream, and Ramsden began to unwind for the first time in ages. He looked at his wife Sue and realised how much he loved her. She returned his gaze and for the first time in a long while he felt disconnected from work. It didn't feel so bad after all.

The journey home was equally slow. But now, full of Pimms that they had imbibed to the sound of a jazz quartet at the Champagne and Pimms bar outside Number One court, they felt as close to each other as they ever could be.

Becky Ramsden hated her father's job. She reckoned that next to being qualified in vivisection, being a police officer was the pits. It had made her parents argue and she hated that. Every cross word uttered, every silence or dumb stare, made her heart beat faster and she would feel sick; sometimes the effects of attitude could be so much more devastating physical actions. If only her parents understood how their behaviour towards each effected her. She thought that she was over sensitive; perhaps she was, but it still hurt. Becky promised herself that when she grew up she would never row with her husband in front of the children; never ever, no matter what the problem.

As she walked along the Chelmsford streets to her Comprehensive school her best friend Charlie Mould joined her.

"Hi, Becky, how's things? Hey, is it true your dad's heading up the team that is chasing that Avenger bloke?" she said, pulling a face that was half scared and half interested – the way television viewers look when they are watching a plastic surgery 'nose job' being undertaken on Channel Four television.

"No, it is not cool at all Charlie. In fact it's flippin' borin'. Dad's always at work and mum has a moody half the time. Only my younger brother, Jason, is my salvation."

"Yeah, he's a looker your bruvver, I quite fancy 'im even if he is two years younger. Anyway, being a police officer's better than being an insurance manager like my dad. The most exciting thing he ever does is to renew a life insurance then look for ways of not paying it."

They both laughed and talked, as girls of that age do, about the latest pop idol, clothes, make-up and boys. As they approached the school gates a small group of local boys standing outside turned and faced them. They included some from the seedier parts of the town and looked shifty.

"Lookout boys, here comes the daughter of the pig," said the smallest of the boys. They all laughed, it was the kind of laugh that young boys make when they feel they ought to, out of bravado rather than spontaneity. A tall gangly boy with straggly blonde hair, a hooked nose and spotty face forced his hands deep into his pockets and stood in her way.

"My brother was pulled in by your dad's bloody lot last weekend. I hate the filth. That means I hate you."

Becky was feisty and undeterred.

"Well for the record I'm not enamoured by your ugly, spotty mush either Wayne Prentice, so piss off and leave me alone."

Some of the boys laughed at this and the tall boy blushed. He stood in her way.

"You think your bloody dad will always be there to defend you. You think you're better than the rest of us, don't you?" His voice was menacing and he was shaking a little. Becky was worried that she had damaged his credibility with his friends and knew she had to make a hasty retreat.

"Let's just call it a day, Wayne, you go your way and I'll go mine, eh?"

She smiled, but mistakenly, probably because she was getting worried, it appeared sarcastic and arrogant.

"You'll go nowhere bitch," he said and drew out a medium size sharp pointed knife, jabbing it at her midriff, "not so clever now are we bitch? Wanna call in The Avenger to deal with me? Where is he, swooping down from the sky being chased by hoards of PC plods? There he is boys – whoosh, swish," and he waved the knife around and played to the crowd.

Becky yelped nervously and most of the boys backed off. But some of those whose intellect was considerably lower that the average laughed at his stupid remarks and egged him on.

"Stop it Wayne, put that knife away," shouted Charlie, but he just swiped it past her face and she screamed too. He was enjoying the power of it all. The power to create fear and control someone, just like his big brother and his dad did with him. He moved the knife closer to Becky who was by now very frightened.

"Shall I, shall I, what do you say pig-daughter, what do you say, eh?"

He moved the knife closer to her chest.

"Stick her Wayne," shouted one of the boys and with that he pushed him hard in the back.

Wayne was very close to Becky and the push propelled him into her and the knife into her side. For a moment there was complete silence. He stepped back, open-mouthed and dropped the now blood stained knife. Becky's eyes were wide and full of shock. She winced, as a girl would with a period pain; but this was no period. Then, within seconds, the boys scattered and Charlie screamed loudly, as Becky slumped to the ground with blood trickling through her fingers as she held her hand to her stomach.

Chapter Fifteen

The Ramsdens arrived home and the kiss on the doorstep had been sublime. But the horror that followed numbed them to the core. They entered their house and after a few minutes noticed that the answer-phone was blinking. It was the long message that made them freeze.

Becky. Stabbed. In hospital, St Georges, come quickly. Your son is being looked after by Gayle and Bill Best – the rest of the message was a blur. Their heads swam at the bolt from the blue. They were so shocked they hardly spoke a word to each other.

Ramsden was sensible enough not to drive because he knew he had a lot of alcohol in his blood and called for one of the nearest squad cars to call in and take them to the hospital. They arrived in minutes and with blues flashing lights they arrived at St George's Hospital within twenty minutes.

No one likes hospitals. Everything smells differently and it always seems a strange and busy world over which no outsider has any kind of control. Ramsden didn't like being out of control and now was no exception. His pulse raced and he focussed on the young doctor who was waiting for him in the Intensive Care Unit.

"Where is she, Becky Ramsden, this is my wife Sue, where is she we want to see her now?"

"Can we talk first sir?" said the doctor, waving his hand towards a small room that contained four cheap armchairs and a small coffee table above which was a familiar Woolworth print of an Asian woman with a blue face.

"Oh, God!" Sue spluttered and she put her hands to her mouth. She watched television enough to know that this was where bad news was imparted and her throat began to close over and her legs felt like jelly. Ramsden held her tight.

"Mrs Ramsden, Sue, please don't jump to conclusions. I am Doctor Brian Buxton, registrar and I am looking after Becky. Let me explain, but let's do it in here and with a cup of coffee. Nurse," he said to one of the young girls busying herself with a chart, "can we have two cups of coffee for the Ramsdens, they are Becky's parents."

He noticed the inference, 'Becky's parents', which he assumed explained everything, even when asking an expensively trained nurse to get some coffee. The nurse agreed without demur and smiled at them both.

They went into the small room and Sue Ramsden was guided to an armchair.

"Mr Ramsden, sorry, Detective Superintendent, Becky is hanging on like no other stab victim I have ever seen. That girl of yours has some inner strength I can tell you. There has been a major bleed in her chest wall. The blade missed her heart, but it is touch and go as to whether it caused any other damage, that bit is quite straightforward. Our major concern is that she fell to the ground and hit her head hard on the pavement. This caused swelling and we had to relieve the pressure. We don't know if it caused any lasting damage and we're waiting for the results of a scan we did an hour ago. That's all I can say for now."

Ramsden held his wife's hand tight. There was simply nothing else to say except, "Can we see her now?"

The doctor agreed and they went to her bedside. Becky had tubes connected all over the place, but despite this and her bandaged head, she looked young and beautiful and not at all like someone with a fifty-fifty chance to live.

They stood there for what seemed like hours, then went home, numb, empty and powerless.

Hannah Sinclair let herself into Gary Randle's flat. It was just before seven in the morning. She carried a bundle of newspapers under her arm and was fuming. The bedroom door responded to a kick from her right foot and Gary sat upright.

"Whoa! Am I late or what?" he said.

"No, you're not late, but you are 'or what'! Get up now. I'll make some coffee. You're going to need it Mr World Famous Criminal Profiler."

Gary was confused.

Without waiting for further comments Hannah made her way to the kitchen, dumping the newspapers onto the coffee table on her way. Gary stumbled out of bed and cleaned his teeth. He was curious as to the fuss and thought that he would shower later. His towelling bathrobe would also do for the moment. The coffee percolator gurgled and the smell revived him as he went into the lounge and sat down. Then his face went taught and he caught his breath. The headline on a national red topped newspaper shouted out:

World Renowned Criminal Profiler Leads Essex Police to Catch The Avenger.

Gary exhaled, "Oh, my God."
The text lived up to the hyperbole of the heading. Gary was described as saying that profiling would lead to a successful conviction – when what he had said was that there had been many successful convictions through the use of profilers and it was hoped that his work would assist the police investigations. He also did not say he led the Essex police force; he always maintained that he was a member of a team and as a profiler was very much a privileged outsider. The article went on to describe various attributes of profilers and past successes around the world. That much was true; he had described the work of many renowned profilers. But then sadly it lapsed back into headline grabbing with claims that the Avenger may be a sad, sick individual seeking a thrill because of a damaged childhood, and so on. He threw the paper down in disgust and put his head in his hands.

Hannah came in with a steaming mug of coffee and put it down in front of him.

"Now then, let's think clearly. We need to discuss just what you say to the team and the Super' to get yourself out of this hole. We also need to review what you should've been aware of already; that talking to any member of the press comes with a massive health warning." She paused and sipped her coffee. "What's more, we need to know how to handle the influx of calls that we are going to receive from every nutter in the county, who believes that his neighbour is a psychotic sicko who murdered his cat or his goldfish, whatever, in a fit of rage about the Community Charge."

"Oh, my goodness. How stupid of me. It was that prat, Chips Johnson, I suppose. I was in such a good mood and had a couple of drinks under my belt. He asked me about profiling world wide, then turned to the UK and before I knew it I was sliding down the shoot and talking about its application closer to home. But I never, and I mean never, linked anything to the cases we are investigating. He has done that, I promise you Hannah, I am not that stupid. He has taken my general responses and overlaid his own comments to misquote and even fabricate an article."

Gary picked up his coffee and tried to take a gulp, burning his lips in the process.

Hannah felt sorry for him and said, "Yes, he's a class act all right. I suppose it didn't help that our great leader hauled him in for questioning the other day."

"Oh, did he now, that's interesting," said Gary, "it might've helped if someone had briefed me that this had taken place?"

"Yes, that's true Gary. Anyway, what's done is done. But let me assure you revenge is better served cold, as they say," said Hannah wryly. "Okay, let's get down to work. Read all the newspapers, make notes on what was said and we can then put something out ourselves. But let me tell you Gary, if there is nothing substantial that we can pin a rebuttal on, it's best to let sleeping dogs lie. Yesterday's news always dies quickly, remember that and we are dealing with the need to solve murders not deal with your precious feelings."

Gary looked at her, smiled and said, "well, I deserved that!"

She was of course quite right and he admired her for her straightforward approach and the way she didn't let their personal relationship allow their close relationship to get in the way – she was the consummate professional. She hadn't allowed it to blunt her judgement of what needed to be done.

He picked up the remainder of the newspapers and was soon spluttering words better suited to the football terraces.

Police Constable Colin Robbins enjoyed bowling. He had a wide circle of friends, mostly policemen, but he was always very clear with them all that his family was the centre of his life. Evenings out like tonight were a rarity even though his wife Trish urged him to get plenty of male bonding. She was aware that without it a man can become a shallow creature. It was perhaps because he had led a laddish life before he met his wife and settled down that he felt he really didn't need to prolong it any further. He dealt with those early lonely bachelor nights in a bed-sit by joining a rugby club and making a wide circle of friends.

Unsurprisingly, he was popular and after marrying his wife Trish it was a difficult process for him to disentangle himself from his networks and concentrate on family life. Now that he was a father of two young girls it all seemed irrelevant anyway. It was a clear moonlit night and the air smelled fresh after a short shower of rain. He decided that since he had imbibed 'one or two over the limit' it was better to walk home than be apprehended by his own police force colleagues. That would cause more laughs and embarrassment than he could handle. It was quiet and there wasn't much traffic about and he set out for home with his characteristic long strides.

After about ten minutes, he became aware of the sound of a soft purr of a car engine some distance behind him. He wasn't drunk, but he was merry and his judgement was poor. In his right mind he would've taken evasive action or called up local police on his mobile phone. But he didn't.

Seconds later the car accelerated and then pulled in, in front of him. Four big lads got out and each one had a baseball bat. His blood froze. He knew perfectly well what was coming and could do nothing about it. Running was impossible, he was not as fit as he used to be and the alcohol in his blood would slow him down.

He tried bluffing.

"Okay boys, what's going on now, you don't want to…"

He wasn't able to finish. Blows from the baseball bats rained down on his head, arms and legs and he fell to the ground like a sack of potatoes. He screamed in pain, but still the blows fell, great arching swings of the bats coupled with shorter stabbing jabs. Two minutes later he lost consciousness. Just before he did so, one of the young men bent down and raised his head, speaking into his ear; it was the easily recognisable voice of young Alfie Bishop the traveller.

"You had this coming pig, filth. Walking the beat is gonna be a little painful for you in the future. Goodnight Mr Pig!"

His head was released and it hit the ground with a thud. The four men laughed and Alfie let him have one more blow with his bat for luck.

Then the men got into their car and drove off laughing.

Detective Superintendent Andy Ramsden got out of his car and his whole body felt heavy; it was hard to move and his mind seemed to be wrapped in cotton wool. He walked past the reception without a word and several officers busied themselves rather than ask him how Becky was. Scaling the stairs to the first floor briefing room took all his energy. His head throbbed and for once, he didn't care about the work ahead of him. He was totally absorbed in the family tragedy. Unseen, he went to the side of the MCIT briefing room and sat quietly at a vacant desk.

A half an hour later, Gary Randle came in and stood in front of the team with his arms out wide. The room went quiet.

"What a prize prat I have been guys. I needed this chance to tell you that the stuff printed in the local newspaper and later syndicated to other nationals was a pile of tosh! The infamous Chips Johnson called me up to discuss the process, I promise you the process, of profiling. Then he exploited my ego, which is a little bigger than most. My answers were at best incautious and at worst suicidal. Anyway, the end product is what you saw. I need to retain your confidence, because if I don't then I cannot command your respect as a colleague and adviser. Frankly, guys, I was stuffed!"

The team was sympathetic and there were shouts of support, but it was obvious that he still felt vulnerable.

Gary's blushes were then spared when a uniformed Sergeant came up to Detective Superintendent Ramsden and whispered in his ear. He stood up straight away.

He sighed and addressed Gary directly. He looked weary.

"Look, Gary, we don't need to drag you through the mire by your balls, you know what you did wrong, so let's close this now shall we? We've all been through enough and I guess we will learn from this. Traps tightly shut boys and girls – that's the lesson to be learned. Now get back to work."

Hannah could hardly contain her surprise. She thought that he would wipe the floor with Gary in public, but he didn't. Perhaps it was because his daughter Becky was in intensive care? As these thoughts raced through her head, Ramsden looked over at her and beckoned with a sideways nod. She got up and joined him.

"What's up guv?"

"The rape victim, you know, the one that was allegedly raped by Carl Stevens, the third murder? She's downstairs and says she murdered him," Ramsden put his thumbs either side of his belt and looked up at the ceiling. "Silly bitch. Oh well, let's go and give her a good listening to. Will you please help me interview her?"

"No problem, guv." Hannah closed her briefing folder and followed him down to the interview room.

A duty solicitor had been called and the girl had accepted this representation, she was a well-known solicitor, used many times in rape cases. She had a warm friendly face and was well respected by everyone at the station.

Hannah started the tapes and went through the normal process of identification.

Ramsden then started the interview. "Miss Janet Anderson, thank you for coming to see us of your own volition. I believe that you have something to say concerning the murder of Carl Stevens?"

The girl put both her hands to her eyes and said, "yes, yes. I did him. I cut him and he died. It was me."

She paused and Ramsden and Hannah didn't interject, they let her settle down and continue at her own speed.

"He came onto me some weeks before, well before the murder. He was a handsome, strong guy. But I didn't fancy being taken for granted – he did that with all the girls you know. Anyway, I was havin' none of it and he got really nasty and ridiculed me in front of everyone in the disco. He said I was ugly, I had small breasts or tits he called them and I had a saggy arse. He was quite drunk anyway and that's why I think that he didn't remember me when he, er, raped me in the park. Look I know it wasn't proved, but take it from me he raped me."

Her eyes filled with tears.

"You wanna know how that makes me feel. To be ridiculed like that, then raped later? Then when everyone says that he will be brought to justice, the case collapses and I am cast aside like a lying slag."

She broke into a sob and the solicitor comforted her. Hannah looked at Ramsden who had gone quite white. She turned to the girl and said, "Janet you re a very brave girl. But we do need to consider what you say very carefully indeed. Can you go on?"

The girl sniffed and blew her nose. Then sipped some water from a plastic cup in front of her.

"Yeah, I'm okay. I did get over his ridiculing. I went for a jog in the park, like I did most days. He was waiting there, behind a large bush. I suppose I am bein' a bit paranoid, he didn't know me from Eve and I was just another victim. You see, that boy had had so many women that he couldn't remember who, where or when. Anyway, so there I am jogging along, to get rid of my saggy arse as it happens, and the next thing I know is this strong arm has me by the neck and I'm forced to breath something really awful that almost knocks me out. Then I began to come round and realised he was stripping me, but I was too weak to resist. Then he rapes me."

Then as if it were too much for her she burst into tears, the angry kind and she shook her head left and right as if to shake them off. She let out a small animal like cry then glared at Ramsden.

"So, imagine mister big man, two other big men grab and strip you then they rape you. How would you bloody feel? To top it all, you know what he did then? He kicked me in the arse and laughed. Yup, that's it. He laughed. So it's no wonder I hated him so much. That's why I lured him into the park and castrated him."

She made a slashing movement.

"Whoosh. Just like that. Then I ran and left him to bleed to death."

The room was silent and Hannah felt her heart beating.

"I did him proper, and I tell you I felt good, really good, can you understand that?"

Tears flowed again and her head fell forward, her breathing coming in short gasps.

"Janet, that was a very quick resume," said Ramsden softly, more softly than Hannah had ever known. "Are you saying that you castrated him?"

"Yes, yes, yes. How many more times you bastard. I did him. I hurt him. Now he's dead and bloody good riddance."

"He was tied up Janet, how did you do that?" Ramsden continued. Janet raised her hands to her head angrily.

"What on earth do you wanna know that for? He got tied up and cut up. For God's sake, charge me. I did it I tell you."

By now her face was bright red and she had shed as many tears as her body could possibly produce. Her eyes were glazed and face was all puffy.

Hannah went to stop the interview, but he held up his hand. Then, astonishingly Ramsden broke all the rules. He reached out slowly and took the girl's hand.

"Janet, you didn't do it. We always withhold some information about a crime and, well, Stevens was completely emasculated, not just castrated. He was also drugged. We didn't report that in the press."

She let out a howl. It was a terrible sound, like a wounded animal and she tried to loose her hand from his; he held it tight.

"Janet, for what it's worth, as an independent male, I believe your account of the rape," the solicitor's eyes widened. "Stevens had a record of abusing women, but was never ever convicted. He was a truly evil man. He preyed on women and I am sad to say that he exploited a female tendency to self-loath under stress. He was by all accounts masterful at it. We know that from several accounts from other girls we interviewed – all like you Janet. Did you hear that? All like you Janet? But none were as brave as you were. I mean that. Brave and spirited. You are the best Janet. Without people like you we would be hard pressed to convict thugs and I am so sorry that in this situation the court case collapsed."

Janet took a handkerchief from the solicitor and dabbed it against her sodden eyes. After a long pause she spoke.

"But I wish I had killed him, I do so wish I had."

"Yes, I can imagine. You really want his death to be according to your hand so that you can release yourself from the pain of the rape. But that won't do it. You need expert counselling and some help, but please remember that you've been courageous already – give yourself some credit Janet."

"What now?" she said.

"We call a halt, that's what. We forget your assertion of guilt. We get you some quality counselling, some contact with Victim Support and other help. And you start to build your life all over again. You are an attractive, lovely girl Janet; very attractive indeed. And for what it's worth you do not have a saggy arse!"

Hannah and the solicitor blanched at his blatant lack of political correctness – was this really Ramsden talking? He continued.

"I have a lovely daughter too and if anything like this happened to her I would feel mad as hell. I would be just like you Janet. You're no exception. At the moment, my little girl is fighting for her life in intensive care because some stupid boy thought knives were big and stabbed her. When she gets better, and I hope to God she will, I'm gonna watch her every move and tell her how beautiful she is. I will listen to all her fears, especially about saggy arses, and will give her the confidence that a father ought to be providing. If she is half as beautiful as you Janet, I will be so proud."

Hannah actually felt a lump rising in her throat.

Janet felt the tears coming again but didn't cry. She moved her free hand over his and smiled weakly.

"She's a lucky daughter. Thank you. I don't feel so silly now. I am so sorry."

"It all ends here, yes?" he said.

"It all ends here, right," she replied.

Ramsden then turned to the lawyer and nodded. He didn't need to tell Hannah what to do. They had access to a list of competent counsellors. Hannah switched off the tape without the necessary formalities. She would of course destroy it. She stared at Ramsden in silent awe, not quite believing what she had seen. He had bonded, actually bonded, with a rape victim. He stood up and made for the door, but turned and addressed Janet.

"Detective Inspector Hannah Sinclair will give you details of counsellors, good counsellors. But then I bet, knowing you, you told them all to 'go to hell' already eh?"

Janet looked up at him and they both laughed as if there was no one else in the room.

It had been a long and tiring day and DC Joe Grogan sat back in his chair and stretched his youthful frame, sucking in as much oxygen as he could, before he breathed out heavily. He enjoyed research, looking for clues, analysis and so on, but it took its toll of his physical and mental framework. If he worked too long at the computer his eyesight took on double vision and after too long in his seat his backside felt like hot coal and his spine and top neck ached.

"What a state to get in, all this and only twenty six years of age!" He grinned and thought to himself.

But Joe knew how to take care of his mind and body; regular breaks and exercise and a healthy existence outside the CID kept his life – and his body – in a decent state of balance. And talking of balance, he recalled that he was on a hot date with a delicious young girl who was a probationer police constable in the Chelmsford station. She was blonde, bright and had a bubbly personality. Sadly she didn't have any ambition, but she was intelligent and funny. She also had a beautiful body that responded to his every touch. He was going to meet her at his favourite pub, The Odds, in Springfield Road.

Joe met her at a party and they were attracted to each other at first sight. His fingers tingled at the thought of her and his mind raced, as all young male minds do, beyond the job in hand to the sensuous pleasures that might await him – depending on how he played the game of course! He yawned to get more oxygen and stretched again. He knew that he had to concentrate or else all would be lost.

Joe held on to those thoughts, brought his mind back to the job in hand shuffled the pages that he downloaded on his personal computer from the Chelmsford "The Knowhere Guide" web site. It was an amazing pot pouri of comments from anyone who wished to post a comment on a wide range of subjects about Chelmsford. Much of it he already knew, especially the comments relating to under-age drinking, fighting and so on; that was part of the local police environmental 'picture' of the town.

What was so enlightening was the language and the thoughts of teenagers and adolescents in Chelmsford. If you wanted to know how they thought, what they liked and disliked, then "The Knowhere Guide" had it all. It was a different world where kids spoke a strange language, with strong codes and understandings that bound groups together – all human beings like being in their own communities, however they are defined. Groups create a sense of belonging, an identity and that feeling of never being alone. Their observations on the world around them were also illuminating.

Joe settled down and read the latest bulletins, his eyes skimming the entries, stopping occasionally to take in information, if only to laugh out loud at the outrageous things that were being posted on the site.

There were a lot of teeny comments, but some items called the local council to account for not taking the town seriously and poor planning – although most teens wanted more clubs and pubs! One item attacked the sale of council houses to a House Corporation and a whole world of campaigning had grown from that. Joe noted the web site: www.defendcouncilhousing.org.uk and decided to give it to his Dad who was one of the council house residents who objected to the scheme and might not know about the existence of the campaigners. At least he was getting something out of all this review work. He laughed at one of the few intelligently written pieces that criticised the local councillors and officers for their lack of ambition, planning and community spirit despite professing to work in the interest of Chelmsford. It then spoiled the illusion of local democracy and free expression by calling them, 'dried up tossers,' who feathered their own nests.

He agreed with the assessment of the local pubs and clubs; it was surprising to see that the YMCA came out as being immensely popular despite the fact that it didn't provide booze. But he knew that most of them smuggled in small bottles of spirit if they could afford it. Most of the serious teen drinking went on down at the skateboard area in Central Park. He grinned at the almost cryptographic language that described the best places in Chelmsford.

- Like the sex shop down Moulsham street – kool.
- THE Y. THE Y. THE Y. THE Y. THE Y, is full of greebos but they dance better than trendies. Then get booze and go central park to get pissed wiv out getin arrested.
- The train station but mind them greebos and goths.
- Him…he's kool and knows all.
- The bridge of the A12 cos u kan piss of it wen u kum out of MacyyD's.
- Chelmsford's vibrant West End.

- The bats on the other side of the park are gr8 soze the cannal. Most of us greebos go down 2 da ramps to get pissed and pull. Never c girls sk8tin though.
- Buskers, joe bundey and goth girl…gr8 muzik….gr8 laff. They R the KoOlest people, buy them a drink, they no every1 and were police go and grungers hang out

Joe scrolled around the site for about an hour. If you wanted to understand the youth of today then this was the place to start. The items on the worst elements of Chelmsford included: p**s stinking greebos beggin' at the station, tarty girls wiv heads up their arses, crime, boy racers and puffa jackets and the bus station.

He was almost finished when, ominously, newer comments proved mor worrying.

- Good job dat bruv got nutted. He wuz bad news…and f*****d my sister wivout her permission. He deserved wot e got.
- Ackroyd was a wanker klepto druggie and theef – gud ridance.
- The Avenger loves greebos, grungers and trendies…heez kool. If U done something bad then yr 4alt…..police R krap anyway.
- Toms gave my bruvver the skud – they R dirty bitches and deserve all they get.
- The Avenger iz kool. The police iz krap.

Items posted went on to lionise The Avenger and Joe had to pause for a minute to think about the consequences.

Just then Hannah Sinclair passed his desk.

"Hey, guv, look at this lot. It's stuff I downloaded from 'The Knowhere Guide' on Chelmsford. Pretty childish stuff really, lots of teen comments and the like, but it is a microcosm of life in that age group. There are one or two things I'd like to follow up, such as the street buskers, who inevitably see and hear everything that goes on in a town and perhaps I can talk to some of the kids that congregate in the parks, especially by the canal. But look at these recent comments."

He pointed at them on the screen and Hannah leaned forward, quite unaware of the effect that her Calvin Klein Eternity perfume would have on Joe.

"Joe this is worrying. If The Avenger gets a cult following, and there are signs already that this is happening, then crimes may soon be committed in his name." Hannah looked worried and then, scrolling down further, she leaned even closer to the monitor. "Wait a minute, look at this one?" she said abruptly.

She highlighted a comment that stood out from the others. It was posted in good English and lengthier than the others.

- Sometimes bad things need to be done to make us all safe. We need our weak, old and young to be kept safe. This is the job of the police and they are not doing it at all. They must work for everyone in the community. If they cannot work for us then we must make them.

Joe and Hannah looked at each other.

"It's The Avenger for sure, guv. It must be – 'community' is correctly spelt!"

Hannah playfully thumped his shoulder.

"Enough of that you educated snob. Joe, I want you to monitor all the pages on this site daily for new entries and contact the people who manage it to see if they can establish where the entry was posted. I think tracks will have been covered, but we can only try. Well done on all the other checks by the way, I agree with your assessment and you should follow your nose on this one."

Joe smiled and gave her a wave as she walked away. He liked her style. When she needed to be tough she was, without question as sharp as a knife, but she welded it with care; rarely was anyone taken apart without good reason. Hannah cleverly utilised mature and down-to-earth praise, unlike the silky honey-tinged, patronising language that some female senior officers used that made him want to puke. They local force agreed they were lucky to have her strength of character especially to counteract the dreaded Ramsden factor.

Joe leaned back in his chair and stretched again. He just wished she wouldn't wear such alluring perfume.

Chapter Sixteen

Watching Randle come and go to his flat in Malden was a tedious task, but the hooded figure sitting in a blue Ford Mondeo was determined to wait for the right moment. The comments made by Gary Randle the criminal profiler riled a lot. Sure it made good copy for the tabloids, but how audacious to think that the crimes could be solved by profiling a killer using mere abstract thought and a bit of guesswork? It was insulting that the murders, which were designed to rid the county of anti-social and murderous scum and pillory the hapless authorities, were attributed to some sick bastard who worshipped a sloppy parent or had a fixation from cheap horror DVDs. This was the kind of rubbish that criminal profilers proffered for cash. It wasn't real. This work – vengeance - was real and it would get results – it would.

Then the moment arrived. Gary Randle rushed out of his flat ran down the main stairs and flew out of the front door, obviously late for something or called urgently into the police station. The figure knew that people who were in a rush forgot things. Randle drove off at speed.

Once inside the main hallway to the small block of flats, courtesy of a set of skeleton keys, the figure crept upstairs then gained access to Randle's flat. It felt good to be inside. The smell of the place, someone else's place, was electrifying. It felt as though it was there to be violated, but perhaps not in the way that the drug dealer's house had been violated last night. That had been done to rid the country of the stench and vileness of drug dealing. No, this flat was there to be manipulated. Yes, even a flat could be manipulated. This was a different exercise altogether.

After moving around the walls of the flat, the door to the study was slowly opened revealing just the opportunity that was being sought. Above the writing desk, was a notice board on to which had been placed a large number of pictures, letters from The Avenger and newspaper articles. Copies of the letters received a gentle stroking from a gloved hand. The figure smiled and said quietly, "lovely,

lovely, letters, they'll do the trick, I just know it. It's just a matter of time."

Wasting no more time, a small drawer was opened and a roll of tough sticky binding tape, a small disposable cigarette lighter and an envelope with characters cut out of a number of newspapers was pushed firmly to the back.

As the figure stood back to check that no clues had been left, a glance at the map showed a single pin, placed just outside South Woodham Ferrers, not far from Malden. What a coincidence, right in the middle of an area renowned for frequent trouble with kids in their teens and other youths who generally behave like animals. It didn't seem to relate to any of the other circles that were self-evidently where murders had taken place and, it surmised, where victim crimes had taken place. It was an odd pin. "Well," thought the figure, "South Woodham Ferrers it is then, if you really insist, Professor Profiler."

A quick search of the bedroom uncovered a cuff link box and one was removed and held tightly in a gloved hand. Then it was time to leave.

Leaving the flat quietly was not a problem and the hooded figure gently clicked the door shut without a problem. But just then, the sound of the front door in the hall being opened caused the figure to freeze. It was Mrs Fryer the cleaner.

As she slowly made her way upstairs the figure darted up the next flight of stairs. Mrs Fryer reached the door and, resting against the frame, gathered her breath. This work was getting too much for her, bungalows yes, but stairs to second floor flats, no; it had to stop. But not today, there was work to do. She unlocked the door and went inside. It took only moments to get her coat off and get the vacuum cleaner out. She plugged it in and moved towards the middle of the lounge. Then she saw the study door slightly ajar. She froze. Was it just possible? Could he be in there again?

Suddenly a large smile came across her face and she licked her lips. She let go of the vacuum cleaner and stood looking at the door. She willed it to open and reveal the professor stark naked again. Her mind worked overtime and she kept reliving what she had seen a few days before. Goodness but he was a well built man for his age, if Mr

Fryer couldn't fill a thong then this feller could do so three times over. She instinctively placed her hands on her lower belly.

"Er, professor," she said, as her voice cracked slightly, "are you in the study, professor?"

There was silence. She stood there for a few minutes, praying that his naked body would bound out, apologising and ever so sorry to have embarrassed her – she would of course put her hands to her eyes, ever so slowly, but to her enormous disappointment, there was nothing. She would have to make do with the mental snapshots that she had put away in her mind for posterity.

Mrs Fryer moved the door open with her foot and huffed loudly. The study was empty and a little untidy, but only needed a surface clean. Then she saw the notice board. Silly man. He usually put the curtain down over the contents, which of course she lifted and regularly read all she could; why not, it was very interesting after all? She idly reached up and freed the curtain, letting it fall and cover the board. Yes, silly man, fancy thinking that the average cleaner wouldn't be inquisitive.

Mrs Fryer got on with the cleaning, humming as she did so and outside the flat a hooded figure moved slowly and quietly down the stairs, then out of the main door and into the street, idly throwing a cuff-link into the air and catching it several times.

Gary Randle arrived at the burned out semi-detached house in Malden at the same time as Hannah Sinclair. It was a smelly, charred and, after being drenched by the contents of several fire tenders, very damp looking shell.

Hannah sighed loudly and said, "Thanks for coming. We're here by the way, because this is where Tommy Watkins lives, or should I say lived. A body has been found and it's suspected that it's the man himself. Tommy is, or should I say 'was', a very successful drug dealer. We busted him several times, but he always got away with it. Clever lawyers and lots of alibis." She kicked some discarded wood aside as she made her way into the shell of the house.

"I'll stake my pension money on the fact that this is another Avenger show piece," she said.

"Ah, so we're all calling the killer The Avenger now are we?" Said Gary.

"Oh, please, no psychoanalysis today, or parsing language, we've got some pretty bad stuff to deal with. And maestro, the latest is that the Super's daughter Becky has been stabbed."

"You're kidding?"

"No, I am not kidding. It was outside her school. A boy has been apprehended and is in custody, but apparently Becky is in a bad way; fifty-fifty chance I understand."

"Jeez, that's a tough break," said Gary frowning with shock, "I've been working from home so I hadn't heard. He must be beside himself with worry?"

There was no more to be said. It was awful news.

They walked towards the shell of the building and spoke to the duty police crew who were doing their best to cordon off the area as a crime scene, much to the annoyance of the fire crew who had yet to finish the job.

It was chaos and so they both decided to leave and go back to the station. Hannah went to the coffee machine, as it strained to stay alive, continuously pumping its brown concentrated caffeine liquid into plastic cups to keep policemen and policewomen awake. She brought two strong coffees to the table in the main office where Gary was seated making notes.

"It was an early morning fire, just the right time to catch someone off guard. Not many people will mourn Tommy Watkins' passing," she said.

Just then the telephone rang.

"Hello, Hannah, this is, er, Andy Ramsden."

"Oh, Guv, listen we're all so sorry, how is Becky?"

"Not good. But we should know much more some time soon. Hannah, listen, I'm not going to be in until later. I heard there was a fire, at Tommy Watkins place?"

"Yeah, it looked as though he was incinerated with the real estate," she said wryly, "we very strongly suspect that it was murder."

There was a long pause and she knew that he hadn't been listening.

"Oh. As I said, I won't be in until …"

Hannah interjected without apology, but firmly.

"Until everything's okay with Becky, Guv, that's when. Jack Rollo's a good guy and is the senior man. He will keep everything going until you get back and I will give him all the support that I can. Go and take care of your wife and son. They need you now."

"Yes, thanks Hannah," Ramsden said, in a tired and uncharacteristically listless voice, "I'll be in touch."

Then the telephone went dead.

Throughout the rest of the day information kept coming in, in dribs and drabs. The body was identified as Tommy Watkins. There was no one else killed or injured. The fire had been started at the foot of the stairs where all the plastic that could be found in the house including televisions, video tapes, and so on were placed, so that the acrid poisonous fumes would move upwards and into the bedrooms. The smoke alarms had their batteries removed. The windows were all locked and the small keys usually left in by householders were removed. Someone had carefully prepared the house beforehand. There was evidence that Watkins had tried to open the bedroom widow once he had been aroused, but as he frantically tried to do so the fumes had got the better of him. In addition to all that the external doors had all been secured with strong sticky industrial tape.

None of the team had any illusions about who was responsible; nonetheless, the process of interviewing neighbours and other criminals associated with Watkins was being undertaken. The team would have to be enlarged to cope with the many new tasks that this new murder had generated. The task of filtering yet more information would be horrendous.

By mid-day Hannah and Jack Rollo had rolled out new tasks for the team, but both of them realised that it would be the same as all the other situations; little evidence and a lot of heat.

Chips Johnson sat at his laptop tapping out his latest diatribe against the local and national police force of Great Britain. His lawyer forbade him from saying anything about his interrogation by the police, because he wanted to see how things panned out. But Chips was angry, really angry. He knew that he was well respected by local people who understood his mission in life, to expose corruption and to help those who could not help themselves. He stopped typing and looked at the letter on the table next to his laptop and read it aloud.

"Dear Chips,
Words fail me. The people support me otherwise why would they copy my work, Portsmouth, Birkenhead – see for yourself? So why doesn't the government?
A dirty drug dealer dies – so bloody what?
I wrote to the Home Secretary, sorry, I always write to you, but he didn't reply and all I got was grief in some of the press.
I don't believe in politicians anyway – they won't do anything. So, more work for me then?"

He marvelled at its simplicity and wondered just how this next letter would go down in the media and police circles – badly, he hoped.

The bell at the main desk in the Chelmsford police station rang a dozen or more times, until the desk sergeant arrived. He was none too pleased having only just arrived back from the canteen with a hot pasty and a large mug of tea; he had hoped to get a quiet ten minutes to himself.

"Sergeant I demand to see Detective Inspector Hannah Sinclair," said the Reverend Alex Allan.

After taking his name the Sergeant called upstairs to the CID room and Hannah made her way quickly downstairs. After quietening the Reverend down she guided him, still smouldering, to a small discussion room.

"Reverend Allan, what is wrong?" she said.

"It's that man Chips Johnson. He's a bloody menace. He came to see me some time ago regarding the murder of the prostitute Kelly Golding. At first he was asking questions about how I stumbled across the body and so on. Then he started to ask whether or not she attended the church and did I think it was a satanic killing, or could it have been a choirboy and all sorts of rubbish. I told him we didn't have choirboys and to get out. He did go eventually, but not after a considerable struggle."

"What's your problem then?" said Hannah.

"My problem, as you so cutely put it, is that he said he was going to write a speculative article about the murders linking them to church activities. It's just because we're different Hannah. It's not fair and it's preposterous. You've got to stop him, you really have to."

He sat back in the cheap plastic chair and it creaked as he did so.

"Reverend Allan, between you and me, there's nothing I would like more than to clip his journalistic wings, but unless he has harassed you or done anything illegal there is very little I can do about it. We must wait and see what he writes. You never know, it might even be a complimentary piece?"

"So that's it then?" he said, agitation spreading across his face like thunder, "just another piece of soft action by a police authority then? Let people get away with insulting a churchman, let this man behave how he likes? Well, why not indeed, after all this is the UK, free speech and all that? He has his human rights of course? Don't answer that, please, I couldn't take it. Well let me tell you this. If that man writes anything in any way defamatory about me or the church I love, then I for one will not be responsible for my actions."

"Please Reverend don't say that, you know you cannot say that to me without me having to warn you." Hannah was upset with his behaviour and it disappointed her.

"Oh dear, a warning? I counsel young men quite regularly, my dear, and I can always adopt their attitude to warnings. I read the other day of a woman harassed by youngsters who were smashing up her garden ornaments, who ran outside her house and swore at them. She was of course arrested, kept for four hours and cautioned. Is this the same kind of stupid behaviour by the law?"

"Reverend, please, I cannot answer for that situation and yes I did read about it and it does get to me too, but this is entirely different. Why do you use such an example? You seem to be just winding yourself up. Calm down, please, sir."

He suddenly looked chastened, his attitude softened,

"Okay, look I'm sorry, I just hate the misuse of authority and being insulted. It's my Achilles Heel I suppose. Let's just wait and see what he writes, as you say. Pigs might fly, Inspector," he said, exasperated, "he may even write something incredibly beautiful and complimentary. It's just that I am responsible for counselling dozens of young people many of whom have criminal records already. We are, all of us, only to aware of the voracious appetite that the newspapers have for scuttlebutt, whether or not it's true. The very institution that should be the mouthpiece of democracy and freedom is used in these days of plenty as a source of entertainment. If the kids I have worked so hard on lose confidence in me, because of some stupid badly written article based on invention and lies, then this will put their lives back several years. They will then become your problem and not, as they are now, mine."

Hannah understood the logic of it all and sympathised. Then a much less excitable Reverend Allan left the station. She was confused though.

When would Chips Johnson ever stop fomenting aggravation necessary and why on earth did Reverend Allan get so upset?

Constable Ritchie Dawson stood to one side of the bed in the intensive care unit looking at the bruised and battled face of his comrade Colin Robbins. Robbins' wife Trisha was there with their two little girls. It had been serious enough for a priest to be called, but Colin was a fighter and his body fought back from the horrendous injuries. A brain scan showed considerable damage to his skull, but surprisingly, once a few blood clots had been removed and excess fluid drained away his brain seemed unaffected. That would become a joke when he returned to work, for sure.

Trisha and the two girls, much relieved, kissed Ritchie and left him alone with Colin. After about an hour he began to regain consciousness. Ritchie leaned forward.

"It's okay mate. You're in good hands, really good hands. The doctors are great and the nurses really pretty, I'll swap with you any day. Trisha and the girls send their love. I don't know if you know but they have been here for ages and have only just left. You are in good company Col'. Superintendent Ramsden's daughter was stabbed and she's in the next side ward; he and his wife are there too. Not a good time for the force buddy. But we'll all get through like we always do."

Colin Robbins tried to raise a head but Ritchie stopped him. He was about to call a nurse when he got the feeling that his buddy was trying to say something to him. He bent closer.

177

Muffled words came out of Colin's bloated and blue mouth.

"Haphee Bushop. Haphee Bushop," he mumbled.

"Haffy Bushop?" said Ritchie,

Colin became agitated, "mo, mo. Affy Bushop."

Ritchie thought aloud. "Affy Bushop. Bushop or Bishop, or, Christ, that little bastard Alfie Bishop. Was it him Col' was it him?"

Colin laid his head back down on the pillow and breathed a sigh of relief. "Ess, Affy Bushop." Then he fell back into unconsciousness.

The nurse confirmed that his body was functioning well and that he was in a deep sleep as it went through the necessary healing process of which deep sleep is an integral part. Assured that all was okay he passed a message to Trisha that Colin had woken up and the gist of what the nurse had said.

On his way back to the car Ritchie knew what he wanted to do and how he was going to achieve it. He opened up his mobile telephone and called up a name he had frequently leaked information to.

He called Chips Johnson then some mates in the rugby club.

Chapter Seventeen

Jacque Peters' path to paedophilia had been a slow transition from one random sexual act, to a position of control over an Internet paedophile ring. He was aware of the misery he caused, but he had long since lost interest in the rest of the world, having created an exciting one that he occupied most of his waking time.

Peters grew up in a female dominated family and from the outset was mercilessly teased about being the male child by his older sisters. He joined the Scouts and this ordinary event was to trigger his already emerging sexual awareness along eccentric lines because of a series of unfortunate events. The Scouts were infamous for their 'initiation' ceremonies, almost all of which involved the new boys being stripped naked. If Peters had had peers to turn to for advice, they would've told him to grin and bear it then move on. It was no big deal. But he had no one to turn to; he was very much a loner. The resulting humiliation, which greatly upset him, set off a sexual trigger. He did get over it, but relived the experience over and over again, with all its humiliation and, oddly excitement, as his body went through youthful puberty. Then he fantasised about putting other weaker boys through even more bizarre rituals.

Then he became a senior scout. Part of his unofficial duty was to set up younger boys for initiation ceremonies. Had the adult scout leaders known they would've been horrified. It all started when Peters was left to tend to a boy who had been tied to a tree. He teased him and then, for reasons that he could not explain, even today, he touched the boy.

After that, he imagined the resulting feeling he got from this event, and it flowed through his body like an electric current. Thereafter, he would ensure that he became the virtual master of ceremonies for initiations. Incidents that took place would vary from stripping and throwing the initiate into a pond and pelting them with cow dung, to tying them to trees. Then he would send the younger junior scouts back to their tents and stay to tend to the initiate, ostensibly to ensure that the boy was re-clothed and released.

Once on his own, he would sexually abuse the boy in question. The usual threats to tell fellow scouts and schoolmates secured complete silence and meant that his secrets remained just that – secret. From that moment on he established a network of victims, some who would be quiescent only to ensure that their secret remained just that and others whom he skilfully 'turned' and who became fellow members of his paedophile ring.

The Internet was a successful way to plan conquests. It was technically interesting stuff that challenged the intellect in terms of learning Internet and computer skills. It also raised the enjoyment level as the worldwide web provided a sea of possible initiates that needed careful fishing. Peters was good at this.

Today, he was overjoyed. He searched the web and found an eleven-year old boy who had set up a personal chat room and was looking for friends. He apparently had no web camera, but had posted his photograph on his web page. Fair haired and wearing only the briefest of swimming trunks of the flimsiest of material – he looked a truly juicy morsel and he lived locally.

Jacque Peters contacted the boy often. He appeared to have problems with his parents and was not at all interested in girls. He seemed a sensitive soul and in need of a friend. During the previous weeks Peters masterfully built up a friendship where secrets were exchanged and promises to support each other were given.

Then the finale: he set a date to meet. It had to be late at night, the boy had said, because his parents were going out to a party and he was allowed the freedom of the house. He was to sneak out and meet Peters in the local park. Peters gave him a false description and the boy would be expecting another twelve-year old.

Peters could hardly contain his anticipation and when he switched off the computer his body was tingling.

Ralph Hardacre the Home Secretary felt truly beleaguered and sat alone in his office with his head in his hands. The Prime Minister's performances in the House of Commons in answer to questions from Moira Harold and the opposition parties about the chaos that was emerging nation-wide following a sequence of murders in the county of Essex had rebounded back on his desk. In addition, there had been a series of riots in Birkenhead and Birmingham, when gangs of youths taunted police and decided to act in a lawless manner, robbing stores and members of the public. The riots had been effectively dealt with, but it had severely stretched manpower.

There was considerable concern that it might lead to the kind of riots that swept through France not so long ago. He had given up telephoning the HMI, who himself had privately expressed concern that this problem was of the government's own making. Too much attention paid to the high profile stuff and little done to make the lives of ordinary people feel safer. Sooner or later those people who are criminally disposed take advantage of weak systems, as was happening now, or, the ordinary man cracks and takes the law into his own hands, as happened in Portsmouth and various other towns.

A demented killer had caused all this chaos – it beggared belief. For the moment there was no answer to it all.

What could possibly happen next?

Constable Ritchie Dawson considered the situation carefully. His best mate Colin Robbins lay in hospital, badly broken and it could have been much worse. Police work was becoming more and more difficult, and it seemed that the odds were tipping in favour of the criminals all the time. He laughed when he considered the popular view of law and order, what with the ASBOs and those criminals who were given derisory prison terms, or sometimes no sentence at all. What the general public did not know was that this was the tip of the iceberg. On many occasions, he and his fellow constables would deliberately avoid areas such as travellers' camps. Those who got up to no good in society had all the time in the world to prepare and rehearse their script – a police constable often has no more than a minute or so to make a decision. If it is the wrong one then the ramifications spread far and wide.

Ritchie knew that he had made the right decision. It didn't sit easily with him at all, but he knew that he would have to live with it. He had had enough and the beating of his buddy by travellers was absolutely the last straw. It was bad enough taking down evidence from people who had been robbed or molested and feeling impotent and unable to help in any way whatsoever. The time had come for the community to strike back – and to strike hard, so hard the lesson would be driven home and never forgotten.

Joshua and Naomi sat contemplating their situation. They had chosen the travelling life because he had lost his job as a welder and their lives had been one long chaotic ride in an increasingly surreal world of benefits, debt and increasing violence on their estate. Their choice was to do it alone and for two years it had been relatively easy. Their four-year old son Thomas loved the fresh air and was responding well to being taught at home rather than in school. Naomi was enjoying the time that she was spending with her young son. It made up for the sheer torture of saying goodbye to him when she was forced to put him into child-care from babyhood, paying out almost all she earned only to get someone else to tend to him.

But then, on their way through Essex en route to the south of England, their car had broken down. Money was hard to find. Joshua tried to do some casual work to cover the costs, but half way to reaching the cost of the car repair, some local people complained about their caravan and car parked in a lay-by just off the A12. A group of local lads were about to scatter the washing from a temporary washing line when travellers Dermot and Ardal Doyle turned up. The exchange had been short and some punches were thrown, but they easily saw the troublemakers off. Without asking for payment the travellers helped them hitch up their caravan and car and towed them to their main site where about twenty caravans had made a semi-permanent home.

Their help enabled them to survive the attention of the local thugs and later Joshua was able to make inroads into repairing the family car. They were helped with money and anything else they needed, to be repaid when they could and were well on the way to repaying that debt. Joshua was aware that his new friends were up to all sorts of mischief, much of it illegal. He tackled them about it once or twice, in a friendly way, but they just laughed at him.

"And what good did being a fine upstanding citizen do you then Joshua?" said Dermot. "A lot of debts, a bad landlord and redundancy from a company that cared little about you or your family is all you had before you hit the road. Now you've repaired your car you'll hit the road like the rest of us and you'll be as free as a bird, won't you?"

No matter which way Joshua came at the subject they had all the answers. Society was well insured so anything they stole was replaceable after a few tears. They made a virtue out of every scam they could, avoiding car tax and insurance, as well as all the other taxes on income and gains. Molly Tanner was the group expert on all these matters and offered her services to guide them through the maze of benefits available to travellers as well as a few that didn't exist at all – there was absolutely nothing she did not know about benefits. It was difficult to criticise their lifestyle; but he did have issues with some of the rougher younger lads who were not very well educated and had little to do around the site. Uncontrolled and arrogant they were the ones who did things that brought them into daily conflict with local people.

He knew that the travellers had helped him and Naomi a great deal and that they had made life so easy for them to could get back on their feet. The temptation to stay and increase the size of the group was great. Naomi was teaching the younger children to prepare them for school; she was an ex-Primary schoolteacher and knew only too well the parlous state of education amongst travellers. Strangely, although she was the most sensitive partner, she had settled better than Joshua, taking people as she found them, and he knew that if he suggested staying on the site she would readily agree. It was as though she blotted out all the things that she knew the travellers got up to.

"It's their culture," she would say. "They're no worse than people I dealt with from a sink estate in Birkenhead, in fact they're better."

Joshua and Naomi were locked into a kind of 'tribal bubble', a different and yet undemanding world where much was done on the basis of favours and understandings. They exploited the foibles of what they considered 'the outside world,' that was, in their view, full of dull people, living dull lives, content to pay through the nose for everything and get ripped off by the government as well as retailers. It was just a question of picking sides and making sure that they did the ripping rather than it being the other way around.

But now the car was repaired and Joshua and Naomi decided that they would go out for the evening to a local pub to celebrate. They would also consider their future in more depth. They had made many friends and were so very settled. Leaving the group would be such a wrench.

What to do?

Chips Johnson hastily packed up a small bag of notebooks as well as his elderly, but expensive Nikon digital camera. The events unfolding were a sure-fire hot story. He had already made contact with a couple of the 'red top' nationals and they awaited his 'copy' complete with digital photographs by midnight. Chips world was getting better and better. He basked in the respect paid to him by many professional editors as well as local people who saw him as a kind of saviour in the community.

He was still an outsider in many respects. He didn't have a partner and his life was all work; not having someone to share his life with made him self-centred and sometimes a little paranoid about criticism. There was no one to stop him from taking action that might at times be considered a little incautious.

That might have been different had the one woman in his life not been so angry with him after the police arrested him. She remonstrated with him about his methods, much of which might have never reached her attention had it not been for the heavy-handed police investigation. She simply didn't understand that sometimes you have to do wrong, to do good, especially when the person you are trying to nail in an investigative article is so well protected by lawyers. They had rowed and then, inevitably, slowly drifted apart. He pretended not to care at the time, but the wound was deep; as he got older it was with him almost every day and it made him more resentful. He found that he was frequently angry.

Tonight was one of those nights. Travellers were vermin. They dirtied the place, robbed at will and were a blot on society. The beating of his rugby club friend Constable Colin Robbins was the last straw. He and a few friends had whipped up the hatred amongst a larger group of men who all held similar views of travellers as he did. Perhaps what they were about to do would have far reaching ramifications; perhaps it would spur the government and local authorities to take proper action to curb their activities and regulate them; perhaps they would catch the bastards who beat young Robbins?

Whichever way the evening went, tonight would be a gift to a journalist.

Detective Inspector Hannah Sinclair discarded her clothes in a nonchalant, but tidy manner, onto a wicker chair in her bedroom. It had been yet another busy and confusing day and she was tired and ready for a quiet drink and some relaxing music. She didn't always stay over with Gary Randle in his flat in Malden. It was a mutual arrangement and gave both of them time to do the things they didn't share and to help to focus on their respective careers. Too many good relationships failed, because a decision to cohabit was made too early; they both wanted to ensure that their bond was a solid one and based on trust and mutual independence.

She ran the shower and after an invigorating salt scrub, dried herself and put on a fluffy dressing gown. Before she put the dressing gown on she caught her reflection in a mirror. Without thinking she covered up and disregarded the other person in the mirror. For a second she contemplated how silly this was. Hannah had a good body, but like most women she didn't spend too much time looking at it. She was happy to be saucy with a partner in a variety of ways, but on her own she was more reserved. How silly was this?

Hannah's best friend had given her one of those battery driven 'buzzy' things and they had giggled their way through an evening fuelled by Chardonnay, but once her friend had gone it ended up in the drawer and remained unused. True, several times she had got out of bed on a hot sleepless night and on her way to get a drink she paused by the sideboard with her hand on the drawer in question. But she never opened it and chose her own ways to get to sleep. Hannah remained conservative with a small 'c', something that had caused her a small problem during her school years and with earlier relationships with men.

She curled up on the couch, opened a book that she had been trying to get into for weeks and to the strain of Rimsky Korsakov's Scheherezade. Barely ten minutes later, and before she had time to even sip the brandy she poured herself, her telephone rang.

It was Jack Rollo. A contact of his with a national newspaper had called him to say that a fracas was planned at the nearby travellers' site.

It was a case of all available hands to the pump.

The operation had been planned down to the last detail. A dozen men dressed in track suits, wearing woollen masks, protective arm and leg pads, carrying a variety of iron bars and baseball bats had formed on the outside the travellers' site near Billericay. The brief had been clear, Alfie Bishop's caravan had been identified and the order of the day was to drag him out and beat him. To do this, those nominated with the task were to be protected on either side. A couple of shotguns were taken but were to be used in extreme circumstances only. All the men were intelligent and not the kind to cause trouble; but they were angry.

To add to the beating, they would damage as many vehicles as possible using a variety of hammers and petrol bombs. Then to everyone's delight, James Allington, a local farmer who had suffered badly at the hands of travellers over the years was to drive his muck-spreader, which had been filled with human sewage, into the site and was to spray all the caravans. This caused considerable mirth and the highlight of the 'rumble.'

All went well at first and Bishop's caravan was located and stormed. Alfie was then led out and stood alone in a circle of hooded men. His mother was frightened out of her wits and cried for help. Other caravan doors opened and men poured out in every direction. This caused chaos, as the locals did not expect the number of men on site. The fight that ensued ebbed and flowed between the two groups. Bishop was clubbed to the ground at the beginning and lost consciousness immediately,

Then the petrol bombs were thrown. There was a loud howl as expensive four by four vehicles were damaged and this incensed the travellers. Some of them rushed to a single caravan and when they emerged they were armed with shotguns. On seeing this, the locals loosed off several salvos and one of four travellers was wounded. Then it began to get out of hand and petrol bombs were thrown indiscriminately; despite the shouts of the leader of the locals several vans were torched. The muck spreader was duly deployed but in the chaos could only dump the sewage along five caravans in the middle of the site. The smell was disgusting. The fire and shouts of men on both sides was frightening.

Just as the locals were retreating Joshua and Naomi's car came over the rise and they raced to the entrance to the site. They got out of the car and ran up to the entrance; men pushed them aside as they made their way through the stink and burning vehicles and caravans. Joshua's heart beat faster as he shielded his eyes to look to his own caravan.

Then he heard Naomi scream, "oh God."

He followed her gaze and they walked slowly, as if in a trance, passing men fighting and other caravans hissing as water was poured over them. They were mesmerised as they came closer to their caravan. It was a ball of flame. Naomi sank to her knees and put her hands to her face. Through the already charred shell she could see several shapes on the floor of the caravan and their son's teddy bear half on the step and half in the van was a macabre sight. Tears flowed down their cheeks and their stomachs churned, as they had never done before.

Almost a minute later a blue flashing light caught their gaze. It came from a number of police cars. Then Joshua gripped Naomi's shoulders tightly. The blue light turned and turned, and in the light he saw Molly Tanner, transfixed, standing by a large tree, wearing a floppy dressing gown. She had not stayed with their son in the caravan as they had specifically told her to. Just as Joshua was about to launch himself at Molly, the anger in his throat preventing him from shouting at her, her dressing gown moved and a small head popped out. It was their son William.

Joshua and Naomi ran to Molly and without paying attention to her circumstances they tugged open her dressing gown and pulled out their son. Naomi held him tightly to her, she was crying and he was quiet - quiet with fear.

Nearby, Chips Johnson was busy, taking photographs.

Hannah couldn't get the smell out of her nose. The custody sergeant in the charge room was busy sorting out those who had been arrested and was none to pleased either.

"Right then, I don't care what anyone says, you can all get your boots off and they will be taken outside the station. I am not doin' my job with the smell of shit pervading the air."

Three probationers were detailed to collect all the boots and the smell was so obnoxious that no one complained; except the probationers.

One of those arrested was Chips Johnson. He was furious. He ranted about calling his solicitor and vowed to get even at the earliest opportunity. Detective Superintendent Ramsden arrived and was amused at Chips antics. He suggested to the duty staff that interviews be arranged and should take place with generous breaks in between and with Mr Johnson the journalist left to well after midnight.

Hannah quizzed Ramsden, "why's that guv?"

"Jack Rollo told me on the phone that his contact in a red top newspaper had heard that Chips had tipped them off. Quite apart from withholding information that could have prevented the violence, our Chips will be oh so upset to miss the midnight deadline for copy and photographs. That'll cost him a pretty penny in missed royalties."

Hannah laughed, "Ah, I see. So, there we go then. It's off for a coffee I suppose?"

As they turned to leave the custody area Chips caught sight of them and screamed abuse – but no one was listening.

The next day the Chelmsford Police Station was a hive of activity. Ramsden had been called twice by Her Majesty's Inspector of Police and the Chief Constable, who had both in turn been called by the Home Secretary. The previous evening's violence at the Billericay travellers' site had missed the morning papers, but would make the evening editions, local television and radio broadcasts. Ramsden sympathised, told them he was doing all he could with limited resources and refuted any connection between Chelmsford and Baghdad. He handled them well, partly because he was good at it and partly because he empathised with the pressure that they must be under due to the escalation of violence in the county. Several other incidents around the country had also been reported and the harsh fact of life was that if they didn't stop The Avenger soon, all kinds of normally reasonable people would be taking the law into their own hands. That of course was quite separate to the sporadic violence in inner city areas where respect for the law was quickly receding.

Ramsden, Hannah and Jack Rollo were locked in discussion about the charges being brought against those responsible for the attack on the travellers, in particular was the vexing problem of what to do with one of their own constables who was found with the group. To everyone's amusement, Chips Johnson was eventually brought forward to be interviewed. He shuffled, half-asleep and half-angry, and unwashed despite having the facilities to do so, to Interview Room One. He was upset that this had been arranged once everyone else had been dealt with. His anger and accusations of police brutality and wrongful arrest rang around the station. The more he shouted the more everyone enjoyed it; he had made few friends in the Police Force over the last five years or so; you reap what you sow.

Detective Inspector Jack Rollo remembered Jenny Ellis' account of her treatment at the hands of the smelly reporter and he was going to enjoy this. Chips solicitor was already waiting in the interview room. A young Detective Constable was assigned to accompany Jack and he started the tape. Jack went through the process of time, date and describing who was present, then began the interview.

"So how is it Chips that we find you at the scene of a particularly awful attack on a travellers' site?"

Chips bristled. "A tip off," he sneered. "Isn't that the way you boys work, tip-offs, snitches, informers? Aren't we in the same business inspector?"

"I think not, Chips, I think not," said Jack, "but I remain concerned that you were at a site where a crime was taking place and you failed to notify the police. In fact you were there with your notebook and camera all ready to go. What if someone had been seriously hurt, does a story mean more to you than that?"

Chips grimaced at Jack. "You are a 'holier than thou' shit, inspector."

Jack leaned forward equally menacingly, "I advise you to watch your tongue, sir," he emphasised the word 'sir', "it can be construed as threatening language?"

189

"Well go on then, do your worst why don't you," Chips brushed off his solicitor's light touch on his arm with a swipe. He didn't need anybody's help, he never did and he spat back, "if you think that's bad what about your boys then, eh? What about the police boy who was there too, the one who tipped me and the Rugby Club off that it was Alfie Bishop's mob who did over that young constable some time back. Pretty nasty so I heard? What about the times I turn up at a celebrity's house because he's been charged with downloading porn or eating whisky flavoured crisps? How do you think we reporters know about that sort of thing – because for a few quid you bloody tell us, Mr Plod, you bloody tell us!"

At the end he was shouting and wild in the face.

Jack was taken aback. This wasn't going to be easy and Chips was now making accusations that would need verifying. What to do now? He lamely re-entered the interview.

"Listen Chips we can't go on believing cock and bull stories to get you out of trouble …"

Chips broke in, "Yes you can and you know it. I know you want to charge me with withholding information to a crime that was eventually committed, I'm not stupid. Well I will tell you once and once only, you speak to someone who can arrange a deal for me, and I will tell you all the snitches you have in this rotten hole. If you fail to do that then I will simply tell the whole world, your choice big boy, your choice. Now I wanna go for a cup of tea and a piss. You brought me here so you're gonna have to put up with me for a little longer."

With that he, uninvited, pressed the stop button on the tape recorder and stood up. His lawyer did so too and as he left the room with the young Detective Constable, Jack was left to see to the tapes.

What on earth was he going to do now?

Upstairs in the MCIT room, Detective Superintendent Ramsden and Hannah sat contemplating the chaos of the previous night. As they refilled their coffee cups with dark brown liquid a young policewoman brought Ramsden a piece of paper. He read it and looked up.

"Well we've got some good news. The knife that sliced up the rapist chappie, has been traced. It's apparently an Italian item and only sold in one shop in Chelmsford. The salesperson remembers several people purchasing such a knife. It says here that she was most concerned about a woman who bought one some weeks ago, that is just before the murder. Jack, your team is now trying to trace two men who purchased a similar blade. Well that's something, let's see where this leads us?"

Ramsden ran through the priorities for the rest of the week, but the attack on the travellers' site had severely dented confidence all round. Manpower was short enough without having to interview stupid people. Just as he finished, Jim Barrell came rushing up to him.

"Guv, it's the hospital, your daughter, get there quickly. I've got a car waiting engine running, boss," he said, almost waving Ramsden out of his chair.

Jason sat watching his sister as she lay in bed with tubes and monitors all around her. He wanted to kill Wayne Prentice, but didn't know how to. He knew it was wrong to feel this way, but it was his sister lying there with a wound in her side and a bandage on her head. He was acutely aware of his mum, sitting close by, crying ever so quietly in case Becky could hear her. It was just like his mum to think of someone else; he realised it now more than ever. He realised the part that he had to play as a son to a mother and father who had been in turmoil and brother to a sister who would need him to look after her. He clenched his fists. He knew he had to grow up fast.

Sue Ramsden stood up and dabbing her eyes carefully, went over to Jason.

"I'm just off to get a coffee, Jason, do you want anything?"

"No Mum, you go. I'm okay," he said and gave her hand a squeeze.

After she left he reached for his CD player. He brought in a small loudspeaker to plug into the unit. This would allow him to play a CD so that it could be heard in the room. His Mum welcomed the injection of music, even if it tended to be Jason's weird stuff. Today, he cursed softly. He had grabbed a handful of CDs and one of them was Becky's. It felt like a heinous crime using one of her CDs when she was in this state. Nevertheless, he looked at the cover and the blonde artist, Cascada; she looked so attractive he thought he would listen to her. The album was called 'Every Time We Kiss'. He put it on, with the volume quite high and sat back, closing his eyes. The soft lyrics wafted around the room and caressed his mind, removing him from the smell of the hospital ward and taking him on a sensual journey; this was some chick.

All of a sudden he became aware of movement on Becky's bed and thought at first his Mum had returned. He opened his eyes and his jaw dropped.

Becky was moving her legs and staring at him through half open eyes. Just as he sat up Sue Ramsden came into the ward. She dropped her coffee and let out a short choked yell.

Ramsden got out of the car and raced past the hospital reception desk to the intensive care ward. He took the steps two at a time hardly tiring as he rose to the first floor. As he reached the ward he noticed some commotion near Becky's room. When he got there, his heart leapt with joy. He saw Becky, by now the breathing tube had been removed, being hugged by Jason and Sue. Tears welled in his eyes.

Becky looked past them towards Ramsden and said wearily, "so who said Jason could listen to my CDs?"

Chapter Eighteen

The whole of the Chelmsford Police Station turned out to welcome Ramsden back to work the day after the good news about his daughter's recovery. Every corridor he walked down, every desk he passed, someone would shout good wishes to him and his family. He had never felt such humility or such emotion. It was like being reborn. Jenny Ellis, so long the butt of his ire, gave him a card and flowers for his wife Sue. He felt enormous guilt and looked at her, and she at him; her eyes said, "it's okay, that's life, I can take it!" It was all he could do to nod his appreciation.

He and Sue talked long into the night and he surprised her. He had seen a job as a security consultant with a major retail outlet. The money was good and he was in the zone for voluntary retirement if he wished to take it. Ramsden held her to him and said he was going to apply for retirement and apply for the job he had seen. If he didn't get that he would get something else. A lot of things had come to him as being more important than the direction he had been heading in. She cried buckets and to his enormous surprise so did he.

The result was that today he was empty of stress and emotion and able to take in so much more. Of most importance was the fact that he had such a great bunch of people around him. He frowned at the thought that he might have to change his style, but corrected himself; it was not just the style, it was everything. He knew he could still be touch and yet retain that human element that turned a good manager into a leader. This would be an easier task in a completely new environment.

He approached his three Inspectors, Jim Barrell, Jack Rollo and Hannah and they greeted him warmly. Hannah kissed his cheek and he blanched slightly.

"That's for Sue, not you guv!" she said.

"Well, these are for you guys. Thanks for everything. Get stuck in," he said, and with a single movement swung a paper bag onto the table. It was full of jam doughnuts.

Jack smiled, "I'd better get the coffee and we'll resume our briefing in half an hour then?"

Ramsden sat down and pretended to busy himself with some papers. It felt strange to be popular and at first it didn't sit easily. He knew he mustn't allow it to dull his edge – but for now, it actually felt good.

Jacque Peters showered and dressed in a blue denim shirt and jeans and wore an expensive pair of sneakers. He carried a small pair of binoculars, mobile telephone and his wallet with enough cash to treat his new initiate; he would need treating because he would be expecting another twelve year old boy. No matter, he had worked through this obstacle many times before. Persuasion at first, then presents, then alcohol and perhaps soft drugs. Video film of the seduction never failed to bond the apprentice to his master, and then he was bonded for a long time to come. Too guilty and ashamed to tell anyone, too frightened to say no in case of blackmail.

Before he left he sent an email to some of his contacts, boasting of a potential good night out, supper and sport. Then he closed down his computer, locked his front door and left the block of flats on the south side of Chelmsford.

It was getting dark for the time of year because of heavy rain clouds, so he went back inside and collected a large golf umbrella. It was approaching nine o'clock. He made his way to the park and waited some distance from the bandstand. After about twenty minutes he looked at his watch and cursed; the little bastard had probably changed his mind. So far he had only seen two or three couples go by, one old lady and her dog and a jogger in dark tracksuit bottoms and hooded top. He was relatively well covered by the bushes and trees around him and wasn't therefore too unhappy to feel the rain suddenly patter all around him. This was probably why the boy hadn't showed up. The rain got heavier all of a sudden and he quickly reached for his umbrella.

As he struggled with the catch on the umbrella he saw through rain soaked spectacles a dark shadow bearing down on him. He turned to ask what was going on and received a blow to the centre of his face that snapped his spectacles and broke his nose. The pain was awful, his vision was full of bright lights and he could hardly breath because of the shock of the attack.

He lay in the wet mud and as he turned onto his knees the figure brought down an iron bar heavily onto his head. Luckily he slipped as he was trying to get up and the blow glanced off his head as he moved in the opposite direction. But it still hurt and he yelped not just with pain, but with fear. He received several more blows to the ribs and stomach.

"Stop it, stop it," he yelled, "why me, go away. Here's my wallet, look it's got money in it but don't hit me ag…" his pleas were cut short as another blow strategically hit his right arm breaking it above the elbow, then another hit his left elbow causing indescribable pain.

The shadowy figure watched as he writhed on the ground and seemed content to do so for a moment. Then the bar was prodded several times into Peters' face and body. He whimpered for mercy but there was none given.

As if waiting for the right moment to deliver the coup de grace the figure took a step backwards and raised the bar again, but just as it did so, several shouts stopped the blow from falling. A group of young men had been jogging in the rain and larking around as it drenched them. They hadn't retired to cover as many other people had and carried on around the bandstand. Peters' pathetic screams alerted them and they raced to the scene of the attack. They were about one hundred and fifty metres away and the figure realised that retreat had to be hasty; the approaching men looked fit and fast.

The iron bar fell to the ground and as it did so the figure dropped a silver cuff link alongside it.

Superintendent Andy Ramsden stood next to Hannah Sinclair and they both watched the bruised and battered body of Jacque Peters. The contents of his pocket had been emptied and the emails between him and a young boy were enough to indicate that he had been beaten by someone who had inveigled him into a meeting, or that he had been discovered in some sort of compromising position with a minor. They concluded that he had been set up; whether it was for retribution or sport they did not know.

"Hmmm, a 'rum do' no less," said Ramsden, "I'm torn between pity and nonchalance. I know that will shock you, but we are in private and I think we are getting to know each other a little more."

"Yes, I know what you mean. I don't share your views though. No one should be beaten like that, whatever their predilections. If they are caught, punished properly and then receive psychological counselling and treatment, their lives might change. We just catch them, that is what we are here for," replied Hannah.

"Yes, of course you are correct. Although, I am minded to remind you that it was you who couldn't stand the pace in the paedophile unit."

Hannah blanched.

"But let me say, that's what makes you a good copper Hannah, a bloody good copper. Don't quote me of course, I'll only deny I said it."

He turned and uncharacteristically smiled at her as he left. Hannah went to the policeman charged with guarding the suspect and spoke to him.

"Hi, PC Hall, do you want some tea?"

"No ma'am, I'm fine. My job is to stop The Avenger swooping down and finishing the job, leastways that's who we all think who did it?" He turned and nodded towards Peters' who was a mass of bandages and tubes. "Besides, he's not going to be going anywhere quickly in that state."

Hannah agreed and wished him a quiet night.

After the ambulance crew had attended to Peters and taken him to hospital, the police went to his flat to get him a change of clothes and at the same time take a casual look for clues to the incident. Peters had been extremely clumsy in his haste to meet with his supposed young initiate. He hadn't tidied away several pictures of young boys provided by friends in his 'special club'. This had given the police constables the excuse they needed to telephone for a full search warrant, which was duly agreed, and then a full search was carried out. The computer was removed and the Essex police force paedophile unit was currently breaking down the hard drive. Several arrests were already being arranged through connections to Peters' email address.

It would take several days before Peters was fit enough to respond to questions, but early investigation on his home computer revealed a number of emails that indicated a meeting was planned for that evening in the park in Chelmsford. Hannah had no doubt that it had been a set up and the computer wizards were trying to trace the respondent who apparently contacted Peters via a hotmail address.

Hannah arrived back at the station to a hard-pressed team who were all depressed about yet another murder, when she reminded them that this victim was still alive and was, according to the medicos, not going to die. There was lots of black humour, all part of police life, and arrangements were made to investigate this new crime which was probably going to be part of The Avenger sequence. No one questioned the use of this name now.

A fingertip search of the area was almost complete, but by now it was past four in the morning and she needed some sleep.

Unlike Peters, she would at least be able to undo her own buttons before going to bed.

Chapter Nineteen

South Woodham Ferrers is by all accounts a pleasant place to live, but like any number of towns in the UK it has problems with gangs of youths with nothing to do. Usually, there is a local resolution and the problems go away. However, in inner cities and the sink estates of Manchester or Birkenhead the situation remains volatile. Unfortunately for South Woodham Ferrers, it joined that elite group by hoping that the situation would improve as time went on. But it didn't.

There had been several stabbings and a terrible beating of a householder who had been brave, and unwise, enough to confront a troublesome group of teenagers outside his house. Night-time in the north of the town brought out the worst groups; no adult with any sense ventured out alone.

The regularity of nightly forays by teenage gangs made it easy to plot their next move. Watching their favourite haunts and routes around the town showed where they were most likely to strike if given the opportunity. That opportunity would be a stolen Ford Escort placed directly outside a block of flats. The distributor cap would be removed so that it couldn't be driven away and the door would be left slightly open, to encourage the inquisitive. A large street lamp lit the scene. It was that easy.

After this was done, a figure dressed in black quietly took up position in a nearby group of trees, behind which was a path leading to a car park and a quick getaway. A small branch provided a suitable place on which to rest the twenty-two-millimetre target rifle, complete with sights. Would there be some 'game' tonight or not?

The plan nearly went awry. A large lady with a tall lanky husband was walking their dog along the path outside the block of flats. She noticed the slightly open door to the Ford and wanted to close it; her husband objected and said they should leave well enough alone. But there were some nervous moments as they argued, before finally leaving the area and the door still ajar. The lady could be heard berating her husband for some time as they disappeared around the corner. Then there was silence, except for the noise of cars passing nearby and sounds from some of the windows that were open in the block of flats.

Sure enough, the figure heard the sound of teenagers, firstly the odd sounds of voices yelling and laughing, then as they came together a louder sound. As expected, some passed the Ford, but a couple walked along the roadside of the car and noticed the passenger door ajar. They looked around and seeing that they were not observed they hopped inside. Others joined them; they were like jackals falling on a rotting cadaver. They searched the inside of the vehicle and found some half bottles of whisky that were duly opened and passed around.

The figure took out several bullets and carefully loaded the rifle. Then the sights were checked for accuracy – the street lamp provided perfect light, illuminating the young jackals.

Eventually, a spare set of keys left in the glove box was found and the sound of whirring was heard as they turned the ignition. More swigging from the bottles and then the inevitable frustration as the vehicle refused to start.

Two boys got out and kicked the side of the car calling it a disgusting name. Some people began to look out of the windows in the block of flats, a young woman yelled at them to move on and so did someone else. All they received for their pains was a barrage of filthy abuse and threats as to what would happen to them if they didn't 'wind their necks in'.

Then there was mayhem, the combination of alcohol in young bodies and anger that the motor would not turn, led to a frenzied attack on the fabric of the vehicle. They ripped at the insides and jumped on the roof of the car and then started to siphon fuel from the tank. When a window was smashed, this was too much for an elderly man in a ground floor flat. He marched fearlessly towards them and demanded to know what the hell they were doing.

The rifle levelled at a spot immediately in front of the old man.

At first the boys taunted him, then, two yobs moved towards him menacingly. The larger of the two raised his hand, with the index and little finger sticking out, and thrust it towards the old man, who was not going to back down. Words were exchanged and the smaller of the two looked shifty, moving his body left and right excitedly.

Then in a moment he drew a knife out of his pocket – the blade glistened in the light from the street lamp and was noticeable even from forty yards.

As the yob with the knife approached the elderly man a shot rang out. The sharp sound made them stop suddenly; then the boy fell to the ground with blood seeping from his forehead. The elderly man took a step backwards.

The lanky yob looked around and cursed. Then there was another sharp 'rap' and he fell to the ground clutching his throat. The gang scattered in all directions and as they did so two of them fell to two more shots. By the time the people who lived in the flats, who were being so badly abused earlier, came out and administered to the boys despite possible danger to themselves, a dark clad figure was running down a tree-lined path towards a parked car.

More cleansing work done – one more task to do.

Despite his personal family circumstances, Ramsden felt it necessary to come into the office after discussion with Detective Inspector Jack Rollo. The shooting of the teenagers in South Woodham Ferrers, two dead and two injured, the previous evening was serious enough, but the real reason for his personal attention was potentially even more serious.

Items found near the site of the Peters' beating in Central Park were on the table and one was placed to one side on a white board; it was a single cuff link.

Jack had explained to Ramsden that when Hannah saw the cuff link, she blurted out that it belonged to Gary Randle. Immediately afterwards, the full implications of what she had said came home to her and she was distressed. The three of them stood by the table and went through possible scenarios. Had Gary been a member of the investigation team? No. Had he visited the sight of the beating in the course of his duties? No.

It didn't look good.

Just as they reached the end of the line, Gary came into the team room, his usual happy self, greeting colleagues left and right; they were unaware of the situation, as he was.

He approached the officers and read the expressions on their faces.

"Hey, guys, what's up, you've all got faces like Easter Island statues? Is it the shootings last night?" he said.

Ramsden got off the mark and held up the cuff link. "Gary, have you see this before?"

"Jeez, yes, where did you get it? I was looking for it this morning."

The officers looked at each other and Gary felt a sense of unease, perhaps even menace.

Ramsden said, "Gary, this was found at the scene where Peters' was beaten, do you have any idea how it could have got there?"

"Oh. Why no, I don't. What are you saying?"

Jack quickly intervened, "we are saying nothing Gary, but there has been so little evidence available, even this mish-mash of items on the table is almost worthless. Except that we find we have a cuff link and we know who it belongs to. Give us a break mate."

Gary looked at Hannah who said nothing, strangely, he felt for her more than himself. He sensed the weight of the evidence in that small object.

"What next?" he said.

"Let's just go through the motions," said Jack. "We won't frighten the horses just yet, I think we should carry out a search of your flat Gary, sorry, but that's standard procedure. Then we take a statement. For the sake of the team I think we all agree to keep this low key. I am sure this can be explained, but we have to do what we have to do."

Inwardly Gary blanched, he remembered the house rules about taking evidence and papers home; he knew he was in for a reprimand on that score.

"Okay, guys, let's go. The sooner we get this over with the better."

They went to his flat in Malden in unmarked cars driven by police drivers, Gary and the three main players. As Gary unlocked the door he had a terrible feeling of foreboding, but shrugged and let the party in. Ramsden and Jack Rollo moved around the flat with ease and out of respect let Hannah stand to one side. They suspected anyway that she was familiar with every stick of furniture and it would've been odd asking her to search.

Ramsden came out of the study and looked at Gary.

"So what's this then, Gary?"

"Ah! I knew you'd ask. I, er, set up a detached operations room in my study. Look, Superintendent, it is so much easier for me to sit and consider the evidence in the privacy and quiet of my own home rather than to be at the station all that time that's all. It helps me think without the noise generated in the office at the station."

Ramsden frowned and went back inside without a word. Jack followed him and uncovered the notice board. Then he began to go through the drawers, carefully putting items on the desktop. Ramsden stared at the pins and circles on the map in front of him.

"And this Gary?" said Jack.

Slowly he looked up at Ramsden, and put a large reel of masking tape on the table, followed by a cigarette lighter and an envelope. When he gently tipped the envelope out on the desk, fifty or more letters cut from newspapers fell on to the table.

"I thought you didn't smoke Gary?" he said.

Gary was shocked. "I don't. That stuff is not mine, it's the first I've seen of it. What's going on?"

"That's what we're asking Gary," said Ramsden and he pointed to the notice-board, "and this pin here, in South Woodham Ferrers, why there?"

Gary's heart was beating fast and he blurted, "well, I dropped the pins and when I was left with one I absentmindedly stuck it into the map."

"And that's of course where last night's shootings occurred. Well, you don't need to remove it do you? You seem to have predicted the next crime scene?" said Ramsden.

"God, I know how this looks…" Gary gasped and didn't finish the sentence.

"So do we, Gary. I'm sorry, but we really do need to follow this up with some questions back at the station. I am sure you understand?"

Ramsden was gentle, but firm.

Gary looked plaintively at Hannah who didn't know what to say or do and raised his shoulders and hands in submission. He turned and they left the flat. As he walked down the path he realised how it must feel when the full weight of the law comes down on you and you don't know what to say to refute charges made against you. It must be even worse if you are inarticulate or uneducated. He could not explain the items found in his flat. How the hell did they get there? Was this a police stitch-up? Surely not? Could his flat have been entered – perhaps? But why, and how? There were questions running around inside his head and he couldn't control them. He felt truly helpless and at the mercy of others.

It was not a nice feeling at all.

Walking to the car Hannah noticed that the drivers were not there. As they reached the vehicles, the two uniformed constables came round from behind the flats. One of them had an object wrapped in a piece of sacking.

"Guv, you'll want to look at this," said the larger of the two constables.

Ramsden took the bundle and carefully unwrapped it, revealing a twenty-two-millimetre calibre target rifle and a plastic bag of bullets.

The constable straightened up, "we found it out the back, behind some black wheelie bins."

Jack looked at Gary who was by now in a very confused state.

"Have you seen this before Gary?"

"Jack, the hell I have. What is this? It's getting worse isn't it? I have no idea what is going on, I promise you. And for the record, in case you are thinking it – I am not The Avenger."

They drove back to the station in an awkward silence. This was a difficult situation. Neither Ramsden, Jack Rollo or Hannah exchanged glances; the air was electric.

When they arrived at Chelmsford Police Station Gary was relieved of his personal items and went with the officers straight to the interview rooms. As he was escorted away, Ramsden turned and addressed Gary.

"Look, Gary, we have to do this by the book. You understand that. We should get you a brief and then take a statement. You surrender your passport and we can take it from there. Do you understand?"

Gary was dizzy with stress and simply nodded. Then he was led away by Jack Rollo to Interview Room Two, close to the custody area and the cells. The police custody sergeant was busy with several young boys who were swearing and creating a fuss, so, against standing procedures and because it was Gary, they simply took his

203

passport, but not his belt or braces, nor his shoelaces. They would book him in later; now it was time for a cup of tea and to let things settle in. They all felt a bit numb.

When Gary had gone to the cells, Ramsden turned to Hannah.

"I really am not sure whether I should keep him in custody or not. If I do and this gets out, then there will be hell to pay. But if I don't bang up a key suspect, then I will be hung out to dry. As if I don't have enough to worry about in my life." He rubbed his hands through his hair.

Hannah touched his shoulder.

"Guv, I don't know what to think. I know that he couldn't ever have done those things. We need to sort out his movements over the various dates and that will establish whether or not there is a case to answer. Where that stuff came from and the cuff link, I just don't know. Give us time and I will sort it out."

"Yes, I know, I know. But it does look increasingly obvious that we are going to have to hold him, probably at our local prison, until we can establish the facts. Look, I've got to go now. For what it's worth you need to keep a back seat. You know Gary too well and anything you say will taint any chance he may have. So keep your distance Hannah, do you understand that?"

Hannah looked at her shoes and nodded in agreement. Ramsden went on.

"Jack will take care of most of the action. I am aware of your professionalism even though you and Gary are an item. Let's just see how this pans out shall we?"

Without waiting for an answer he turned slowly and left the Police Station. Hannah just stared after him. She appreciated his concern for his daughter, Becky, but that was her man in the Interview Room, facing the horrendous possibility that he may be arrested on suspicion of being a mass murderer.

She could not let him go to the local prison on remand. Once he was in the system there would be no way out unless new evidence or alibis was placed before a court. Hannah also feared the insatiable appetite of the Police system when investigations have been ongoing for a long time, let alone the public reaction; he was warm and had evidence against him – that would do.

Hannah considered the situation. The custody and cells, together with the Interview Room used for Gary, were at the centre of the station. Next, came an inner cordon of wire mesh with two doors. Then, once exited to an outer area cordoned again by wire mesh and another locked door. It was not looking good. She had to think fast.

Gary sat in the Interview Room with Jack. Jack was too embarrassed to talk, but kept annoyingly asking him if he was, "all right?" The room was beginning to become claustrophobic. The weight of evidence was heavy and Gary had seen enough interrogations to know how it felt to be under the spotlight. The grey room, the whirring of the tape machine, the questions, carefully crafted to seek guilt rather than innocence. Then the countervailing factors such as the general nervousness of anyone being questioned, with slightly incorrect or inaccurate answers being pounced on as deliberate lies or dissembling. The human memory fails at the best of times – under interrogation is can make a man forget his own name.

Gary knew he was innocent, but he felt like a guilty man. He felt alone and exposed. It was the most frightening feeling he had experienced in his whole life.

The door to Interview Room Two squeaked as it opened and she saw Gary and Jack Rollo sitting away from the table talking. They looked up.

"We're just chatting Hannah, nothing to worry about. I don't get to beat the soles of his feet until the brief arrives," said Jack, but he failed to get a laugh.

She blew Gary a kiss, turned and shut the door. Without hesitation she formed a plan and walked quickly down the corridor. The custody Sergeant was busy and he looked up.

"Hello, Inspector, and how are we today?"

"Oh, fine Geoff, just fine," she replied with a smile.

Her eyes ran across the board of car keys behind him and fell on those with a VW badge. Just then, there was a clatter from one of the cells.

"Little bastard, I'll give him what for, excuse me will you?"

The custodyj sergeant left he desk and walked down to the cells shouting the name of the young yob causing the commotion. Hannah

205

took her chance and went behind the desk, lifting the VW keys from the hook and putting them into her pocket.

Then she went to the kitchen. It was easy to locate several pieces of stale bread and she put them under the gas grill, then on top of the grill unit she put a cardboard box with a lot of loose paper in it. She then lit the grill. Bread toasts then burns, smokes, catches fire; she hoped that it would set fire to boxes, and so on. She prayed that the smoke detectors would work.

Before leaving the kitchen she put a wedge in the door to ensure that it stayed open, leaving easy egress for the smoke.

Slowly, she walked back down to Interview Room Two. Her heart was beating fast and she knew she had to keep cool. She fingered the keys in her pocket.

It seemed like an age, but eventually she smelled the scent of burning toast. There would be no concern because the officers made toast every day. She waited and waited. Then she saw the smoke crawling across the ceiling like a spider's web, indicating that her plan was working. At last the alarm sounded. It was loud and continuous. The station practised the drills regularly and everyone knew what to do. To her delight, she saw that the smoke had by now got quite thick.

She quickly opened the door to the interview room.

"Jack, sorry about this. Some stupid bastard must have dropped a fag in his waste bin, whatever, but there's a lot of smoke around and we ought to make tracks. You are the key man in the department so you do the necessary and I will take Gary here to the fire assembly point – no handcuffs necessary?"

Jack smiled, "I should think not indeed. Okay, let's get this crap out of the way."

When Jack was a few yards away, Hannah turned to Gary and looked urgently into his face. "You've got to run," she said. "If you get banged up, I have this awful feeling that it will be the more difficult to find evidence to support your innocence – and I know you are innocent."

Gary's mouth hung open. "Run? But that's an admission of guilt, I can't do that."

"And what if you don't and Ramsden decides that this is a golden opportunity to close the case, what then? He's under such pressure at home Gary, what with Becky and all. I'm not sure which way he will turn. I don't know how the cuff-link got where it got, or how the stuff got into your study, but it doesn't take a rocket scientist to see that you are being set up by someone."

She kissed him quickly and hard on the lips and placed the VW keys in his hands.

"Just keep checking VW cars outside until one responds to the electronic signal."

Gary hesitated for just a moment then kissed her and walked quickly to the first locked door used to enter the custody area. It was slightly ajar as the custody sergeant was leading a reluctant drunken yob to the assembly point.

"Here, let me hold the door sarge," said Gary. "Rather you than me."

The Sergeant nodded his grateful thanks and continued to manoeuvre the yob out to the assembly point. "Luckily, we only have this little sod to deal with today. Thank goodness," he said over his shoulder.

Gary followed him down the corridor to the next door. One of the CID boys was holding the door open. The Sergeant and yob went through and the officer then stepped forward putting up his hand.

"You're going nowhere Doctor Profiler," he said sternly, then with a laugh he added, "we need you to work out who set the alarm off, what state their mind was in when they did it and if they will offend again."

Gary gently pushed him in the chest. "You guys are just jealous. Hey, you want borrow my raincoat?"

The young CID officer laughed and waved him through.

Within minutes Gary was outside in the main car park behind the station. He noticed the gate was locked, but a policewoman he knew was standing close to it with a clipboard in her hand. Looking around he saw two VW cars about five yards apart. Walking casually to one of them he was relieved to find that it responded to a click of the ignition key in his hand. He got in and drove to the gate, leaning out of the window.

"Hello Hazel and how are you?"

"I'm cool Gary, but I'm not supposed to let anyone out of this gate just yet," she replied.

"Oh, damn, Hazel, I've just got to go now or I will be late for a meeting with the Chief Constable. He wants to hear about my investigations. Please, for me, release me, child?"

She laughed at him and opened the gate.

He drove through slowly, then once outside picked up speed and headed out of town. His mind raced. It would take them time to sort out what had happened, so he needed to drive for only a few minutes, dump the car then talk his way into renting a small flat in a seedy area nearby. With nothing to pawn, no cash, cheque cards or driving licence he was at the mercy of the authorities. But Hannah would help.

He began to think that making a run for it was not such a good idea after all.

Back at the station all hell broke loose. Everyone was blaming everyone else. Hannah apologised profusely and said that she had left Gary in Interview Room Two whilst she sorted out what to do. He slipped out when her back was turned. All the officers who let him through got angry because they had no idea he was in custody, which technically he wasn't, and they wanted to know why they had not been told. As for the burned items in the kitchen, the perpetrator was not found.

Ramsden was furious. He ordered an immediate search, but forbade Hannah from joining in. He took her to one side.

"Hannah, you know the score. If I find that you had anything and I mean anything, to do with Gary's release then I will throw the book at you. Do you understand me?"

Hannah stared at him. She knew the consequences and said, without committing herself. "Yes, Guv, I understand what you are saying well enough. I am sorry that it happened too you know."

After watching the action at Randle's block of flats a hooded driver in a nearby car switched on the ignition and drove off. What satisfaction that had been. A plan perfectly conceived and enacted; the result was just as predicted. It really was a joy when things went well.

Driving through the Essex countryside seemed the best thing to do after such a harrowing evening. There was no question of conscience for the death of the two boys. They were scum and good riddance. Every man jack in the flats on the troubled estate would have done the same if they thought they could get away with it. Moreover, had not a stabbing been prevented? That was of course the problem with people today. They all know what they should instinctively do to 'right wrongs' but instead left it to the law to sort out. And what good did that do? Precisely nothing, that's what.

Now some poor sap had been fingered for something he didn't do. He would soon be released when the killings started again, but it would be interesting to see where the politics went on this one.

Sometimes this work could be so entertaining as well as satisfying.

Unluckily for Gary, the VW had a tracking device. Even toe-rags in custody can buy up-to-date extras for their cars. Within minutes, Panda cars were on the road and alerted to where the car was being traced.

Gary drove slowly through the west side of Chelmsford and to his horror saw a Panda car coming in his direction. The constable passenger had his radio to his mouth and he knew that contact was being made to say that he had been found. He cursed. That must be the shortest escape in history.

He gunned the VW right at a junction and raced along a narrow road hoping his manoeuvre had not been noticed. As he did so he kept looking intently at the rear view mirror to see where the pursuing Panda car was. Each time he did so he had to correct the steering. But this meant that he failed to look at the road ahead and as he gained speed to about eighty miles per hour, he drew level with a large petrol tanker backing out from a garage without using a guide. By the time his eyes went back to the road in front it was too late. The VW hit the rear of the tanker at high speed and there was a mighty flash of flame and smoke.

He died instantly.

Hannah looked at the smoke rising somewhere in the West of Chelmsford. It would take them some time to put that conflagration out. Just like Gary, to never do anything in a small way. By now the tears were streaming down her face.

Ramsden and Jack Rollo came up behind her.

"Hannah, what's done is done. Go home now. Nobody wanted this. None of us even wanted to arrest him, but the weight of evidence was enormous. I wish he hadn't run for it. Go home. Rest. Now," said Ramsden.

Hannah turned and nodded. She knew it was unprofessional, but she would visit her doctor and get some sedatives, then pull herself together.

But she was sad – agonisingly sad. Every fibre in her body ached.

It didn't take long for Chips Johnson to find out what had happened and even before the station had made the statement that Gary Randle was being questioned, he produced articles in the local rags as usual extending the truth more than a little. He quickly inveigled Randle's cleaning lady into one article where she was happy to say that Randle was very secretive and a bit strange. He also had funny sexual habits and had exposed himself to her. All of a sudden, Gary Randle was in the frame as The Avenger.

Hannah read the articles and fumed. She cried and fumed. Then she just cried. After a day or so she went back to work, or what there was left of it.

As she expected, the case was being scaled down. The evidence against Gary had been so damning that the Chief Constable had weighed in heavily saying that his escape and running from arrest indicated that he was indeed the guilty party. The Essex Police Force received congratulations and there was talk of promotions and commendations. The case had found its fall guy. It was all over.

Ramsden met her and explained that he had assigned her to oversee the filing away of the records and evidence. He was in the process of preparing the final report to close the case.

Another Ramsden success story.

It was halfway through the Friday afternoon, when Hannah decided that to save her sanity and help her grieve, she needed to talk to the one person in the world who knew her best; her father.

She dialled his number and Petronella's rich, chocolate brown voice answered.

"This is the Sinclair House, how can I help you."

"It's me Hannah. That's cute Petronella. Real cute – you sound quite posh. Can I speak to dad?"

"Oh, child. Posh indeed. Me and your dad have been following the newspapers. It was your man wasn't it? I'm so sorry. Look, he's been expectin' your call. I'll get him now. God bless child, God bless."

"God bless Petronella," said Hannah and she waited for her dad.

"High sweet pickle," his voice was warm and loving, "before you say anything I am so very sorry darling."

Tears welled up in her eyes and she couldn't speak.

"Don't say anything because I know you are crying, but just listen. Have a cup of tea or something, pack your gear and get down here for some home comforts. I'd like that and I'm sure you would too. I will be expecting you tonight. Goodbye darling."

Her response was barely audible and she turned away lest anyone in the office should see her sobbing.

Hannah drove carefully up the A12, through Colchester, towards Ipswich listening to loud music in her car to take her mind off her unhappiness. The countryside was beautiful in the mid-morning with tidy fields and hedgerows and occasional clusters of trees. The only drawback was the thickening traffic as she navigated the busy A-road. It was a product of national affluence that people owned more than one car and spent the weekends rushing to garden centres and shopping outlets. She drove on eventually reaching her turnoff point through a small village called, Tattingstone, then picking her way through small roads in the direction of Chelmondiston, then the short distance to Pin Hill almost by the sea shore.

Some people find small roads a chore, but Hannah loved them. They always seem to produce something worth looking at, at every turn. They force you to drive slowly, thereby taking more in – there was a lot to be said for country living.

After parking her car on the gravel driveway she made her way down the path and under the wood arch that formed the porch to the cottage. The door opened as she approached and Petronella stood there, beaming from ear-to-ear, arms outstretched.

"Come on in, Hannah, good to see you," she said, hugging the life out of her.

They held each other and through this one movement, two bodies just holding each other tenderly, Hannah knew that all was not well with her Dad. She eventually moved a little away from Petronella and when she did so she looked into her eyes and this confirmed the fact. But, true to family tradition, she kept matters at arm's length.

She kissed Petronella and said, "Well, let's go and see the feller then shall we?"

Despite her father's pallid skin and tired look, he was a bright as a button and cheerful. He was genuinely pleased to see her and she knew that he was itching to give Hannah the kind of emotional support that she had given him after the death of her mother. Petronella made so many tasty dishes for lunch, such as home made bread, pickles, cold meats and pate. This was then followed later with scones and jam for late tea, and she thought she would burst. As ever, Petronella knew when to remove herself and do some chores, always turning down admonishments and offers for her to stay. Hannah needed some Daddy time.

"No, you two have a lot to talk about and I have work to do. I'll catch up with you later," she said, and disappeared into the kitchen.

Without words, Hannah did what she had always done when she needed emotional support. She curled up against her father, head in his chest, a cushion over her feet and just hugged him. Then she cried.

After a while, they talked of the man she had loved and now lost and he comforted her. Then, she told of her frustrations: her boss, the unreasonable and particularly vicious journalist, the lack of clues and the fact that her lover may end up implicated as The Avenger. She went on to say that she had made some big mistakes and wondered how she would get over them – wondered if she ever would?

Her father half smiled, hummed a little, and remembering their favourite poem from the Rhubaiyat of Omar Khayyam, looked her in the eyes and said slowly, "the moving finger writes; and, having writ…"

Hannah smiled and took the cue, "Moves on, nor all thy piety or wit…"

Her father tapped her on the head, "Well done, let's see, oh yes, 'shall lure it back to cancel half a line' …"

Hannah ended the poem saying, slowly and solemnly, "nor all thy tears wash out a word of it."

"Yes, Hannah, and how many times in your childhood did we have to use this poem to describe how, when we have made a muddle of things, we have to be brave and push on regardless? We're now a bit older I guess and we can both see the poem in a different light. What's done is done, sweet pickle, we cannot change that, so we have to move on. When Omar Khayyam wrote his famous Rhubaiyat, and this verse in particular, I am not sure whether he knew how wise and prolific the words were."

Hannah sat up. "I guess you're right Dad. It wasn't easy when my baby brother died either?"

"No, it wasn't and thankfully I had some Moslem friends who taught me to look at life another way, celebrating what we have had, what we have now and what we may have in the future; each in its place. But enough of that. I take it the case has now closed since the august, Ramsden, has come to the conclusion that Gary is the killer?"

"Yes. I am now the one to do the tidying up."

"Then you are in a unique position to put wrongs to right," he said.

"How so Pops?"

"Firstly, let me tell you a story that I am quite ashamed of, but time is short so here goes. When I was working with 'Lieutenant Colonel Mad Mitch' in Aden in the sixties and one of the infantrymen, Lance Corporal Cherryman as I recall, was found guilty by Military Court Martial of theft and rape. The evidence was overwhelming. We did our job to the book. The trouble is, as most squadies would say, the book is for use when brains run out. In this case it was true. We failed on many counts to investigate further than our noses. I was young and keen and as far as I was concerned the man was guilty. He was sentenced to eight years in a civil prison."

He stopped to cough for a few moments and Hannah patted his back. He spat into a paper cup at the side of the bed.

"Uugh, sorry about that. Anyway, I was put in charge of clearing up the paperwork and I methodically did as I was told. It was only as I was doing so, and, as you do when you file I came at it from a different direction. When I looked around me, I became suspicious of various pieces of evidence on file; it was all too obvious and clear-cut. To cut a long story short, the theft was straightforward, but the rape turned out to be something else. It transpired that the girl, an ex-pat working in a local bar in Steamer Point, was sweet on the accused, but also liked one of our own Military Policemen, a rather nasty and arrogant Corporal with a penchant for violence. I was suspicious and got one of our boys to take him out and get him plastered in a local bar. Then he was to ask him all sorts of questions based on the 'wiles of women', saying he had woman problems and so on. Right on cue and full of booze and arrogance the Corporal admitted to the rape saying she deserved it and it kept her in her place. He said he then threatened to beat her and have her deported if she didn't implicate the hapless infantryman. That was his recipe for a happy relationship! I had the man immediately taken into custody and to my eternal shame arranged for his mates to beat the living shit out of him. He was never able to walk straight again and subsequently he was medically discharged later. Then the woman was forced to retract her evidence and Cherryman's sentence was immediately reduced. She never implicated the Military Policeman so our unit's honour was intact and justice was done. But I wasn't proud of myself by any means and I never did anything like that again."

"So the show is never over then?" said Hannah.

"No darling, the show is never over. For that matter, the book is never perfect, it is our rule and guide, no more than that. No amount of political correctness or Human Rights rubbish will ever help us to deal with what is right and what is wrong."

Hannah hugged him and they talked lots more. She challenged his old-fashioned values and he her clinical police procedures. They talked long into the evening before and after dinner about events in her childhood and things that they had almost forgotten. Sometimes they cried, for Mum long gone and the baby brother lost before he had a chance to see life, then they laughed until the tears ran down their faces about this and that. Petronella sat back in a large soft armchair by the bed and watched the flow of words – happy to see them both absorbed in each other's company. The morning after was long and lazy. Breakfast, Sunday newspapers, lots of coffee and chat, roast lunch, then reluctantly back to work. Hannah kissed her Dad long and hard. He smiled at her and told her not to worry about him or anything, but to rearrange her life and move on.

Hannah waved goodbye to Petronella as she drove out of the driveway. She guessed that Dad was right, and for that matter so was good old Omar Khayyam!

As she reached Chelmsford, Hannah switched on the local radio. After some music and general local chatter, there was a news flash. It was a report on The Avenger. She listened in tears to Detective Superintendent Andy Ramsden being interviewed outside the police station.

"I just wanted to reassure the people of Essex that we believe that the so called Avenger, the man responsible for so many killings in the county, was apprehended this week. The evidence against the person in question was about to be researched when he escaped and sadly, crashed his car into a fuel tanker, and was instantly killed. Naturally, we have a lot more work to do, but the evidence is so strong that we feel we can confidently say that we have our man."

There was a sound of cheering and clapping in the background.

"In answer to your questions, we cannot confirm or deny that the man was someone who was working for the Police Force for the last few weeks. It would be quite wrong to release a name at this stage. The purpose of this announcement is to lessen the tension not only in Essex but also around the country where people have been taking the law into their own hands. Be assured that the Police Forces around the country are determined to stamp out violent crime wherever it may be. We caught this man through good policing. This is what happens at all levels and the general public should have no fear at all for their future safety."

The interview ended with a few pathetic planted questions and that was it. Gary was guilty as charged, or at least he would be after a suitable period of deliberation.

Hannah was under no misapprehensions. The 'old' Ramsden would normally have loved this announcement. But she believed that the 'new' Ramsden probably hated doing it. It would've been something to be done under political duress, to settle the nervous general public. Doubtless the Home Secretary and Prime Minister would get at least a few more nights' sleep.

Then her Dad's words came back to her. So, it's back to work to shuffle the cards then – but, how would they land?

Chapter Twenty

Ralph Hardacre, the Home Secretary, sat glumly watching the hasty press conference convened by the Chief Constable of the Essex Police Force in which Detective Superintendent Andy Ramsden made the announcement that they had 'got their man.' It was of course politically contrived and he hoped that this would take the heat out of the violence in the country, but also, that it would relieve the pressure on the Criminal Justice System. Up until the end of Ramsden's speech things had been just fine, but only that frail under-the-surface fine, nothing special.

Then his spirits sank as the television crew switched to an impromptu press conference in a nearby hotel. Standing in front of a large fireplace, with cut flowers in evidence to her left and a small table of photographs to her right, was Moira Harold MP. His hands went to his head, "Oh God!" he thought.

With a smirk on her face she began.

"I am Moira Harold, MP for East Chelmsford, and I want to applaud the work done by the Essex Police Force to catch a particularly nasty criminal. But it's not that which I wish to talk about now. For some time now, I have been very concerned for my constituents. In fact, not just them, but for everyone in this country who values the rule of law and is concerned about the level of violent crime on our streets. It's time we stopped making excuses about deprived youngsters. Most of those who commit crime these days have ready access to education, wear hundreds of pounds worth of designer clothes and carry a vast array of items such as IPods and mobile phones. The fact of the matter is that we have all failed. We failed in our education, not just the academics, but the sense of right and wrong, we failed in the way we have molly-coddled teenagers rather than properly punishing them, and we certainly failed when we all thought that twenty-four hour drinking was no big problem. That means we have produced a breed of young people that think they can get away with any crime because they know that it will take years of cautions, ASBOs and soft punishments before they are properly punished, if at all. Is it therefore any wonder that law abiding citizens feel aggrieved when they fall foul of laws that sometimes they do not even know about and incur financial penalty or a criminal record for something quite minor. For that reason that I feel morally bound to tell you that this murder case has also opened deep wounds in society. As vile as the murderer was, I feel I must speak out and say his allegations were right, so terribly right."

She breathed deeply and took a sip of water from a nearby glass and the Home Secretary stared open mouthed at the television and waited for the coup de grace; it came quickly.

"For that reason, I have resigned from my party and wish to announce that I am forthwith to be classified as an Independent Member of Parliament. I therefore have no whip and am my own person. I can represent all my loyal constituents unencumbered by political chains. I promise those who voted for me that my key aim will be to deal with the lawlessness that troubles us at every level in society. Thank you."

The mood in the team room that Monday morning was sombre - Gary's death affected everyone. No one understood or believed the evidence that showed he was The Avenger. It just didn't fit. But it was all over now. He was dead and there would be an autopsy and post mortem to sort out the car accident scenario and allow for a funeral. Then a coroner's inquest would be arranged; it would be necessary to adjourn it for a couple of months to sort out the evidence already in hand and take in the outcome of an investigation into the car crash and Gary Randle's demise.

The team had been scaled down to leave only a skeleton force to sort out the paperwork and deal with any late evidence. This was expected to last about four weeks.

Hannah did her best to keep herself together. Her Dad's forthright but gentle advice helped a lot, but still her heart ached. She was not too proud to visit her doctor who prescribed a course of sedatives for a short period.

But it was still hard.

She put her papers in order and sorted various piles of reports, but had no real enthusiasm for the task. In the corner of the office, Detective Constable Mark Grainger flicked through copies of the letters sent to Chips Johnson. He was an intelligent young man and his English literature degree enabled his peers to give him the nickname 'the professor'. The bonus to Hannah was that his written reports were pure joy to read. He flicked through the papers, stopped at one, then absentmindedly read out loud.

" 'The cries of little children,' ho hum, a favourite of mine. It's likely to be by the poet Elizabeth Browning, an amazing lady, you know she…"

Hannah stood up quickly and stopped him mid sentence.

"Elizabeth Browning? Where have I heard that before? Where the hell have I heard that before?" she said.

Her mind was in turmoil because Grainger's off the cuff remark had connected with something in her memory.

"Mark, I need a black coffee can you get me one, I need to think really clearly and I am not at my best today."

Mark readily agreed and was glad to be of some use. Then she sat down and put her head in her hands. She slowly trawled through all the conversations that she had had with witnesses. Then as she sat back and relaxed a bit, the face of the Reverend Alex Allan came to mind. Yes, it had been the picture on the wall of his office at his People's Church in Chelmsford. The picture on the wall had been of a lady with a dusky complexion. She wore her dark hair long and had kind of white crocheted hat and a heavy black dress. She looked slightly sad in the picture and that was why Hannah remembered it.

Mark returned with the coffee.

"Well now, you look as though you don't need the coffee now?"

"Mark, I need you to carry out a full trace on the Reverend Alex Allan. I want to know everything, and I mean everything. This may be a wild goose chase, but your chance literary remark may have sparked something. I can't be sure," she pinched the top joint of her nose and blinked a few times, her body rising to the chance of new evidence, but at the same time, tired, so very tired, "I can't be sure but bells are ringing Mark."

Mark's eyes glinted and he set off without questioning any further. Hannah sat and made notes, carefully adding as many clues and links as possible. Just then Ramsden came into the office.

"Er, Hannah. How are you?" he said.

She looked up at him.

"Okay, I suppose, under the circumstances."

"Well, it's all over now. We can all move on. Why don't you hand over the administration clear up role to Jim Barell?"

For a brief moment Hannah considered telling him about her slim new lead. But that would be pointless. He would simply stop her from proceeding. It wasn't in his interest to follow new leads. There was a prime suspect, now conveniently deceased; Gary Randle. It fitted his immediate need. Until the next murder that is.

"No, that's good of you guv, but I just want to keep busy. Besides, it's all straightforward tidying up, not much brainwork really."

Uncharacteristically, he smiled and said, "okay, well done, I would've expected nothing less. I'll leave you alone. Let me know if there is anything you need."

He left without another word.

Detective Constable Joe Grogan sat in the Kings Arms pub in Chelmsford High Street where many of his police colleagues went to chill out after a busy day. He was on his third beer when he caught the eye of a bright-eyed young probationer policewoman. She smiled readily at him. Well who wouldn't? He was a good looking young man and well known to the girls in the station; owning a red Lotus Elan sports car, courtesy of his rich father, helped his image.

"Hi," she said, as she approached the table, "you look really fed up."

"Yeah, I am. There was a bad accident. We lost a lovely man, our criminal profiler. He died in an accident. I feel a bit miserable."

Then, ever alert to the prospects of a score, he added plaintively: "I need the warmth and comfort of a woman and some tender loving care for a while."

The girl smiled and was not at all taken in, but was quite impressed by his humour and charm. The evening continued with a tit for tat exchange of glances, drinks, jokes and the occasional touch of hands. He learned that her name was Jackie Weston and she had been in the police force for less than six months. His invitation to her for coffee and some tender care was accepted and she giggled with glee to have scored such a good looking date and they made their way by foot to her flat not far away.

Her flat was tidy and modern, if a little chintzy in places. She poured two drinks and they kissed.

"You know something," she said, as she stroked his chest, "you're quite a guy. I'm happy to administer some tender loving care to help your day improve. We have a half an hour before midnight and I am sure I can bring it to a satisfactory end."

Joe smiled broadly. Some days the Gods are with you and some days they are not; well, tonight they were all on his side. They kissed and slowly removed their clothes. Jackie's thong got caught in her heels and they both convulsed with laughter as it tangled and they wrestled to free it.

They lay together on the couch stroking each other. Joe nuzzled her neck.

"I am such a lucky guy, Jackie you are great. Just what I need right now. I've been studying files about murder and dead bodies for too long and I think I'm getting morbid."

"Yeah, I know what you mean. I don't know that I can continue in this job," she arched her body at his touch, "oh, boy, just there, ooooh, lovely boy."

She kissed his forehead and he followed her directions.

"The nearest I got to seeing a dead body was that lady that got killed by the thug Ackroyd. She died right in front of me, in intensive care at the hospital, poor old dear. Good job her daughter was an ex-CID from Herts Police otherwise I would've had to have stayed and identified the body. Oh, Joe, don't stop?"

Joe sat up and Jackie stared at him.

"What on earth is wrong?"

"Jackie, her daughter Angie McPherson, and you say that she is an ex-CID copper. Are you sure?"

"Yes, course I'm sure. She gave me her police number too, I remember, it was 521. She knew I was a probationer and let me go home."

As she was speaking she noticed that Joe was dressing.

"Jackie, I really am sorry, this is now urgent police stuff. It's not you I promise and by golly I will make it up to you, I promise sincerely I do, but for now I've just got to run."

He hopped out of the flat door without a backward glance carrying one shoe and tucking his shirt in as he went. The door slammed shut.

Jackie curled her body up, pulled the sofa blanket over herself and cursed her luck. But the couch felt warm and she could smell the remnants of his after shave and remember the sight of his young naked body.

There was nothing for it it; she settled down to finish the job in hand.

After continuing with her tidying of the administration, filing evidence in a seeming endless stack of boxes, and helping the administrators to catalogue the stuff Hannah went home, showered and had a light supper. Then, taking advantage of the quietness of the office she returned to the station and sat up late into the night, leafing through papers and scribbling on her notepad. She wanted to work hard, so that when she went home to the flat her mind would be so tired she would go to straight sleep; this hadn't been very easy of late. Besides, it was easy to just sit and drink black coffee and fiddle with the clues. Ironically, now the pressure was off and the blame had been placed squarely onto Gary Randle, the picture seemed a little clearer.

As she poured another cup of treacly thick black coffee, Joe Grogan burst into the office with a crash.

"Guv, guess what? The Angie McPherson we interviewed, daughter of the late Mrs McNulty killed by Ackroyd, was not the real daughter. Or if she was she was faking it."

Hannah gasped. "Joe what do you mean?"

"Guv, the real McPherson was an ex CID sergeant in the Hertfordshire Police Force. I went to see the Herts' boys today and they confirmed that she was indeed a CID Sergeant, very popular and a skilled one at that, and get this, only recently retired. Here's a photograph," he pushed a grainy black and white photograph onto the table in front of her. It showed a happy smiling young woman, slim and attractive, laughing with other police men and women at a social occasion.

"The trouble with our Angie McPherson was that she resigned from the force in high dudgeon after blasting the county Chief

Constable out of the water because of the, wait for it, failure of the criminal justice system, to support either the community or the police on the ground. This was a few weeks before her mother was murdered. I think we need to be asking why she would want to hide her identity Guv, what do you think?"

Hannah breathed deeply, trying to rid herself of her general malaise and to rise to the excitement of new evidence.

"Joe, this is doing my head in. Let me think about what you have discovered. But well done, how did you find this out?"

Joe winced and told her all that Jackie had said to him and how he had left her embrace in a hurry to get back to the station.

"Well young detective constable, that really is beyond the call of duty! Let's just say you need to pay this Jackie a return visit and reward her for information received," said Hannah with a raised eyebrow and a smile.

They agreed to meet again at noon the following day, but to say nothing to anyone else. Joe's information needed further corroboration, they would need to visit the McPherson house again and talk to her, this time in much more detail. But Hannah still had a funny feeling about the Reverend Alex Allan and awaited results from Mark Grainger's investigations. Funny old thing, you have a veritable drought of information and clues, then one suspect is identified and gets killed, the case almost closes and then others enter into the frame; it was three in all including the neurotic Chips Johnson

Was there a connection between all these suspects? She knew in her heart that despite the overwhelming evidence that Gary was innocent. But who was guilty? What did all this new information indicate? What would her Gary have done to sort all this out?

Oh how she missed him already.

Mark sat in the shadows of small shrubs across the main road in front of the People's Church. The air was slightly damp and the temperature mild, but his excitement hadn't been dampened. This was not quite what his guvnor had wanted, but he had seen first hand how laborious all the investigations were, how much time it all took. If he could find a magic clue then perhaps this would be just what they wanted to prove that Gary Randle was innocent. He liked Gary a lot, as he did Hannah. If he could do anything at all to help her he would.

After a long wait, Mark watched a group of people leave the church, it was late and they looked exhausted – probably some meeting on the meaning of life? They shook hands, hugged and kissed and loudly proclaimed that the meeting had been very useful and full of interesting 'issues'. Reverend Allan stood framed in the doorway with his hands on his hips an orange light behind him making his shape seem like a Chinese silhouette. Then, he watched them all drive away, before turning and closing the door behind him.

Mark watched the lights go out in the church one by one. After twenty minutes he made his way around to the Lead Lane alleyway and put his ear to the door at the rear of the church. There were no sounds whatsoever.

He reached into his pocket and took out a metal lock-pick. Mark worked his magic on the lock and it opened easily, which was more than could be said for the door, which scraped lightly against the concrete step, as it opened. He winced as he tried to open the door noiselessly. A smile crossed his face as he thought to himself, "Not all boy scouts were angels!"

After standing still for about four minutes, he was content that he had not attracted any attention and looked around him for a suitable entry point into the church. He spotted it easily; one of the downstairs windows was slightly ajar. It took only seconds for him to reach in and free the window from its latch – then it was open and he was crawling over the sill and into a room full of bric-a-brac and junk. The door was not one that had a lock and he quickly made his way into the corridor. It was so dark that he had to use his pencil torch that luckily had a low strength bulb that barely lit the way rather than giving off a sharp light. After dozen or so steps he reached a door and pushed it open. The scene took his breath away.

The inside of the church was lit by moonlight, shards of light piercing the interior of the church, illuminating the large photographs that hung from the ceilings and walls. At the same time, it made the shadows appear darker and more sinister. But it was a beautiful sight, this strange hall, full of large pictures, chairs in irregular groupings and a lectern at the centre. Then as the moon became shrouded for a moment in clouds, the light dimmed and the room darkened.

Mark spotted what looked like an office door at the far end of the hall and made for it. He bumped into a chair and the scraping noise of chair against floor filled the room – it sounded like an off-key trumpet blast. He stood stock still for a few seconds; no sound came and he continued across the room, this time feeling gingerly with his hands in front of him like a blind or partially sighted person in a new environment. He reached the door without further noise and pushed it gently; it opened easily. It felt strange walking into the warm dark interior. The air seemed fuggy from the warmth of human bodies, sweat and breathing.

The surroundings began to form in his view as his eyes got used to illumination from what must be a computer standby light in the left corner of the room. It was amazing how in a perfectly dark and windowless room, such a small light source could be so powerful. He was beginning to make out cupboards, a table, wall shelves on the left of the room and he turned slowly to take in the remainder. As he did so something caught his eye.

Too late he saw a figure bearing down on him. Despite raising his hand to protect himself he was struck on the side of the head by a very heavy object. He crumpled to the floor as though he was a blow up doll that had been punctured.

Reverend Alex Allan stood over Mark's body. After about a minute he reached into Mark's back pocket and pulled out his wallet. He walked to his writing desk, put on the small halogen desk lamp and switched it on. The wallet contained credit cards, some money and Mark's police identification card. He threw it on to the desk and sat back in his chair.

Alex Allan knew that at some time the police would begin to take a closer interest in him, but he did not believe that this young man was working to police instructions; they simply didn't work like that. This had to be an act of individuality or bravado. Well, whatever it was, he would deal with him. It was unfortunate but that was the way it was. He took a deep breath, picked up the wallet, got up and went to Mark's prostrate body. Bending down he opened the boy's jacket and put the wallet into the inside pocket.

It took barely twenty minutes to wrap Mark's body in the rug that he had fallen on, securely fastened with tape and then dragged into the courtyard to Alex's car. Getting the body over the boot lip and into the car was a little more difficult, but it was soon done. Alex thought for a moment, then got in the car and drove around the corner of the church and out of the courtyard into the Chelmsford High Street.

It was a patchy, sometimes moonlit and sometimes dark night and Alex drove carefully towards Chelmsford Central Park. There were few people around, those that were, were couples far too interested in each other to even know what direction they were walking. He stopped the car by the edge of the park, which he knew well from his frequent meetings with groups of teenagers, near a gap in the trees. Alex switched off the engine, pressed the button on the dashboard to release the boot lid then sat back and waited for the moon to be obscured by approaching clouds. As soon as this happened, and ensuring no one else was around, he quickly got out of the car and moved to the open boot lid. He quickly opened it and hauled out Mark's unconscious body. Without delay he first closed the boot lid then went to the body wrapped in the carpet and dragged it through the gap in the trees and into a small tunnel-like area of shrubs.

Alex was exhausted. Mark was not a big lad, but his almost lifeless body was awkward and heavy to deal with. After a short rest and again making sure no one was approaching, he bent down, removed the body from the carpet and gathered up the tape that he used to temporarily bind it. He took the carpet and tape back to the car and placed it into the boot, then returned to Mark's body.

As he opened a large clasped hunting knife, a present from a friendly African church member many years ago, he began to pray for Mark's soul. For a while he stood still, repeating prayers and words that he knew would speed his soul to heaven. Then he was jerked out of his meditation as he heard the sound of youthful voices.

"Stuff the greebo bastards, let's do 'em?" said one, in a slightly alcoholic slur.

Others readily agreed and the conversation turned to intentions of violence and mayhem. Alex stood stock still as they passed by, hoping that they wouldn't notice his unlocked Ford. He had to be quick. They might remember the vehicle or see him leave. He knelt down in front of Mark's body.

"I'm truly sorry young man, but God's work has to be done, we have to make changes, he will receive you in good grace..." but before he could finish, the sounds of running teenagers could be heard and he looked up, startled and cursed. He drew back his right hand to his rear and plunged it into the middle of Mark's chest in one action. Without waiting further he made his way back to his car, got in and drove away without lights, very slowly at first then, then after putting about a quarter of mile between him and the park, he put his lights on and drove quickly back to the church.

He felt no conscience. He knew what was right.

Angie stood straight with her hand clasped in front of her looking out of a large window and onto immaculately laid out gardens. She could see figures dressed in black and white walking in the distance. Her head was clear and her mind felt quite empty. She didn't have a headache and it felt wonderful. It was wonderful to breathe deeply without dizzy spells; they had all gone now.

It was time to take stock of things. What on earth had happened to her? What kind of despicable person had she turned into? A shard of fear pierced her as she confronted what she had done. What next?

Now she was dying. Fair punishment she supposed. Perhaps it was punishment for not showing mercy on those who knew no better and trying to play Solomon. Her beloved mother believed retribution was dealt out in heaven and not on earth. If this were so then perhaps this would release Angie's tortured earth-bound soul.

The pain below her navel was intermittent and when it hit her it was excruciating; it was like a hundred period pains all at once. She winced as it returned and put her hands on her lower stomach. This was punishment enough, she thought. It was punishment on a female, from a male God. She reached for a packet of pills and a glass of water and quickly swallowed two morphine-based Tremadol tablets. The relief would not be quick because they took a while to take effect, but knowing that it would eventually come and release her from pain was enough, although she wished there was something stronger she could take. Surgery was promised at the private hospital to which she had been admitted for a week or so from the Sacred

Heart Sanctuary. The consultant advised her that she would need an operation, but that this would only provide temporary respite of about four months or so; they were now treating the symptoms – prevention was impossible.

The consultant had been very kind. He had been gentle with the news and she appreciated his honesty. Then he left her with a young registrar who made a good start explaining the treatment, but within ten minutes burst into tears. Angie then had to comfort the doctor – strangely this had a beneficial effect on her, except that she wondered whether the young registrar would have pitied her so much if she had known her crimes and the pain she had caused to others?

At least Angie was at peace with herself now. The nuns had helped her enormously. So had He. She read a lot about mental breakdown and realised, not because she was trying to excuse her actions, that she had suffered a violent mental psychosis. Coupled with too much alcohol, the agonising misery of her mother's death in such awful circumstances and guilt had it had all led to a complete breakdown. The symptoms included hallucinations, irrational fear and the voice and vision of her mother telling her to do things, in schizophrenic episodes. It was this that had made her act the way she did. It was hypnotic and led to her living in a surreal fantasy world with no means of escape.

Angie didn't like the situation any better now that she could rationalise it; she would simply never excuse herself, ever, from the evil things that she had done. It was something that she could hardly bear to think about and left her empty and full of guilt.

She slowly packed her bag, it was not such a chore because she had not brought much to the sanctuary and would need even less at the hospital. The consultant had been quite insistent that despite the prognosis she should have the operation. She would do as she was told. Looking around the sparsely furnished room with its cream coloured walls and crucifix hanging directly above the bed that she had occupied for weeks and weeks, she felt enormous gratitude for the unquestioning and impartial help she received. The Mother Superior had known her mother Alice. She knew all Angie's pain and left it to her to find her salvation.

That was what Angie planned to do. To tell all and clear her conscience – it was like preparing to be reborn. Preparing her for her death. What a strange thought that was.

Her only disappointment was that she had not been able to talk to Him. For some reason there had been no contact. Although he was not a Catholic He was readily admitted by the sisters to help counsel those who needed counselling in the sanctuary. Angie had benefited greatly from His help. She looked upon him as her saviour and over time, shared her every thought with Him; she adored Him. He listened to her and never judged her actions. He really understood the injustice of her mother's murder and the suffering of others in the community; unprotected, preyed upon and abused. Most important of all He had wanted to know more about her relationship with her mother who had been a pillar of the community and a strong Christian? Interestingly, He had become fascinated in Angie and her mother's interest in the Celtic Priory, Peter-on-the-Wall, its history and the broader history of the Celtic religion in the region. At times he seemed quite in thrall of her views.

She was impressed by his worldliness and work in other areas of the world, such as Africa. He had such a strong sense of right and wrong, and explained that he had seen this strength in many tribal cultures in the world. He understood her suffering and the way the psychosis had released an almost primeval urge in her to seek vengeance. He had understood and not judged her. That's what had saved her sanity.

It hadn't been right just leaving a message, but there was nothing else she could do. She had made her mind up to go and had little time left.

Angie zipped up her Gucci holdall and left the room without a backward glance.

Reverend Alex Allan slept deeply after returning from Central Park. He had cleaned up and worked his way back from the open back door to the courtyard, the window in the store room and through to his study. He disposed of the carpet, which was not blood stained, but was nevertheless evidence, and buried the knife. He was sure that the young detective constable had told no one of his nocturnal adventure; he would have to wait and see.

He lay half-asleep throughout the night, thinking about the way he had managed to change life for many people in Chelmsford and the wider area. They had been grateful to him for the way he had revolutionised their lives and brought them back to religion, mostly Christian, but so very regional and English. He hated killing and was surprised at his total lack of conscience; he knew that was wrong, and yet, he excused it. After all, he had seen real violence in Africa, frightening violence in a continent where life was cheap. Many good people died, or had to die, just like that young policeman. If you gave in to violence you became a victim, and if you were a victim you were as good as dead. Tribal elders, witch doctors and latter-day religious leaders all controlled their tribe or flock, so as to provide them with sufficient protection from outside forces. When push came to shove, tribal bloodlines were thicker than God's influence.

The so-called better-educated western agencies were little better. Outwardly they posed as saviours and missionaries, but for many it was a scam to cream off value for themselves or for political gain. Aids had ravished countries, as casual sex and sexual crime abounded, paedophilia went unchallenged and drugs were often sold openly. And all the local authorities could do was to shrug their shoulders and accept their share of the 'dash' or, corruption money. To minister in Africa meant becoming part of all that, and that was something he was not prepared to do.

Alex believed in his heart that justice was spiritual and that we were all judged on high, by the successes we made, even if there had to be some balancing of the books along the way. He was ready to be judged. He could argue his case in any temporal court.

The enormously successful People's Church in Chelmsford would be his epitaph. Soon he would see people gain that sense of right and wrong that was needed in society as they were shaken out of their slothful skins. The Celts were right, the Devil must not be let in; and society had let him in, the doors were wide open. The trouble was that prison doors were also open and criminals came and went as they pleased. Elizabeth Barrett Browning had awakened consciences with her wonderful poems and writing – she mobilised consciences through her poetry and campaigning; but he would do it differently.

He stretched and looked forward to the coming day; each day brought him closer to achieving a more just society.

The alarm clock buzzed, almost too quietly, but it was enough to see him up, washed dressed and ready for another day. As he poured a cup of coffee from a Cafetiere his attention was caught by the red light blinking on his answer-phone. He went over to it, for some reason full of foreboding. People rarely left messages and he knew that he had been too busy with meetings to take any notice of it yesterday. He pressed the playback button and listened; it was from Angie McPherson.

The message finished. For a moment he stood motionless staring out of the window. Then, slowly, he began to go red in the face, his mood darkened and he clenched his fists and put them to his forehead. With volcanic fury his right arm swept the answer-phone and several picture frames and ornaments from the sideboard on which they stood, off the surface and against the opposite wall.

He shouted, "damned fool, no Angie, you will spoil everything, damn, damn, damn!"

She had to be stopped and quickly.

The next day Hannah rose with some difficulty. It had been a long and exhausting day before, during which she had consumed far too much black coffee. Caffeine stays in the blood for some time and she hardly slept a wink. She cursed her lack of discipline. She needed a good breakfast, which she took late in a nearby café then she walked briskly back to the office to get the endorphins moving around her body. She felt as though she had a hangover.

She sat down wearily at her desk and as she did so she noticed a brown file marked, 'Reverend Alex Allan' in her tray. She opened the file and began reading the content of a double space brief; it was from detective constable Mark Grainger.

Mark had done a thorough job during the previous day. He researched enough to corroborate Reverend Allan's background, his Scottish Isle of Stronsey upbringing with its high church influence, his strong mother figure and their home move to Glasgow. Mark had even obtained some school reports on Allan. Shy, introspective, intellectual, but hard to get to know, they said. He obtained a second class degree from Edinburgh University, but little was known of this almost reclusive young man.

Hannah's attention was instantly aroused when she read the last two pages of the briefing note. During his last year of university, Alex Allan's mother had been killed by a hit and run driver, who later turned out to have been loaded with alcohol and drugs. The punishment related to the driving offence only and he was given a risible sentence for driving without due care and attention. Allan had a nervous breakdown that year, but recovered and finished his degree. He was later accepted into the church, but preferred to work overseas and was out of the country for nine years.

Reverend Alex Allan's new People's Church was very popular and had a large and growing congregation, made up mainly of people who were fed up with mainstream worship, or those who had been waiting for 'something different' and yet 'the same'. There was a list of extramural activities gained from simply surfing the Internet and speaking to local church people; it wasn't long.

Hannah's eyes floated up and down the short list, past items such as lay adviser to the Anglican Church in Burundi, sometime writer in the Isle of Stronsey Quarterly Religious Journal and so on, then her eyes were held by one description: counsellor – Sacred Heart Sanctuary Convent near Malden, Essex. She remembered the receipt that she had seen on his desk along with the milk bill and other items. When Mark returned they would both visit the Sanctuary to find out more about the man and his work there.

Just then Detective Sergeant Jim Barrel came in, ashen looking.

"Jim, what's up?" she said.

Jim Barrel was a kindly, fatherly man who loved all the young constables as if they were his own children. His eyes were glazed and he said through a thick throat.

"It's Mark. They found his body in Central Park. He has been taken to intensive care at the general hospital; he's been stabbed."

Chapter Twenty One

The last twenty-four hours had been chaotic. There was a hunt for Mark's attacker, but with little evidence this was little more than going through the motions. But at least there was good news. Mark had been stabbed in the chest, but to his great fortune, his wallet had deflected the heavy blow from a large bladed knife to the centre of his chest away to the right, under the lower rib cage and out through the back. The blow avoided all his major organs, but nevertheless caused a very serious wound. It was the head-wound that worried doctors more and medical opinion was that this had occurred some time before the knife wound – it was so bad they said he wouldn't have felt the knife wound at all.

Hannah's blood boiled. They found Mark's car in Chelmsford High Street; two hundred yards from the church. Surely not? Not the Reverend?

Most of the officers were tied up with the inquiry, but after several sweeps of the station she caught up with Detective Constable Joe Grogan. Joe was the only police officer at a loose end and he readily agreed to join her. First of all they drove to Angie McPherson's house in the village of Steeple. It took only a few moments to gain entry, the back door had a standard Yale lock and it was quite insecure. The rooms were tidy, but had a damp smell about them; no one had lived here for some weeks.

Hannah explained to Joe that they should have a warrant, but that she would take full responsibility for their actions; after all they came expecting to find Angie McPherson and found a broken door instead.

Joe started to carefully search the lounge and Hannah started with the bedroom. There was abundant evidence of disguise. In one wardrobe Hannah found shabby clothes and various other items like a rather dowdy wig and theatrical face make-up. A large piece of quilted padding hung on a metal coat hanger. In the second wardrobe they found more elegant and stylish clothing. After searching the chest of drawers, Hannah concluded that Angie had left for a while. There was hardly any underwear left behind and no sign of any overnight bags. More telling, was the absence of a toothbrush in the bathroom.

Joe shouted, "hey Guv' look at this."

Hannah went into the lounge.

Joe looked up to greet her, like an expectant puppy ready to please, and said, "there's very little to link her with any life other than this godforsaken place. But, these crumpled papers that had fallen behind her waste bin show that she has been under the care and observation of cancer specialists, in Colchester Hospital Cancer Unit. She might be in hospital at the moment? Also, she has been in contact with the Sacred Heart Sanctuary, a Catholic Convent just outside Malden. There's a receipt for four thousand pounds; a lot of money for a donation?"

"Good work Joe and in the bedroom there is enough evidence to show that our Angie was competent with disguises. But the question has to be why?"

Joe couldn't answer that one.

"Okay, then, let's just review a few clues to get the facts straight. We were so convinced that Chips Johnson was up to no good. Then Gary Randle was implicated, arrested and," her voice choked a little. "Well, you know the rest. But Chips has always been there, like a toothache you cannot get rid of; a dull ache in the background. Then young Mark follows up on the vicar. Nothing too special there, except a vague reference in one of the Avenger's letters to words used by poet Elizabeth Browning, the vicar's pin-up girl. Then Mark gets himself nearly killed one night in Central Park, but his motor is parked close to the People's Church. And now we find that Angie McPherson has been disguising herself to hide the fact that she is ex-CID – why would she do that?"

Hannah stood up and walked to the window. "And you, Sherlock bloody Holmes, have found a link between Angie and the vicar. She has given a donation to, and he is a counsellor at, the Sacred Heart Sanctuary. Typical, weeks and weeks of no clues and a complete draught in terms of information, then suddenly the case is all over and it starts falling from the sky."

There was a moment of silence then Joe Grogan rattled his car keys.

"It's off to the Sacred Heart Sanctuary then Guv?" he said.

Hannah smiled. "Yeah, but remember, this case has been closed and we are acting outside our authority. If anything happens that is a tad unsavoury, I ordered you to help out, okay?"

Joe smiled broadly, stood to attention and said, "Achtung, Mein Fuehrer, I only obey zee orders!"

Hannah thumped him in the arm, "Go on yer big tart, get moving," she said, "and drive carefully it's getting late and misty and you have had a couple of late nights."

"Yeah, so I have, and I remember 'em well!" Joe said, as he closed and let the Yale lock click into place none-the-worse for their forced entry.

As he got into the car he added, "It's such a chore when a witness's memory needs encouragement, but frankly, it's all in the line of duty, Guv."

Alex Allan's mind was whirling. He must not let his plans slip out of his hands. The case had been closed courtesy of his masterstroke against the academic upstart who thought he could get the better of him. He really hadn't meant the Randle chap to die, only to be pilloried for a long period, perhaps put in Jail for a while. Then, just when the authorities thought it was all over and the politicos started to spout forth on the good work of the police forces and how lucky the people of the UK were to have such a dedicated and smart government and police force, he would begin again; this time with even more fury.

He would do this until they took him seriously.

But Angie was going to spoil it. She had been his catalyst. Alex had led a life selfless duty to others, but from the time of his mother's death at the hands of a careless drunk driver to the present, he had observed more than his fair share of institutional stupidity and political lying, at home and abroad. At least in Africa they had the excuse that they were tribal and that it would take generations to breed out the tendency to want to protect your own and kill or hurt all others. There was no excuse in the UK. That was what angered him most of all.

He called his contacts in the Sanctuary and they told him that she had left.

He knew where she would go.

Joe Grogan stopped the unmarked police car outside the Sacred Heart Sanctuary and took out the ignition keys.

"Don't suppose I need to lock it here, Guv?"

"Okay, wise guy, please no jokes here. We are not on a case and if we end up upsetting the Nuns I'm likely to be in more trouble. So, zip it please."

Hannah got out of the car and walked into what looked like a reception office. A young nun in her full habit greeted them. She smiled so sweetly it was like a ray of sunshine. Joe was speechless.

"Hello sister, I am Detective Inspector Hannah Sinclair and this is Detective Constable Joe Grogan, could we have a chat with someone who may be here today called Angie McPherson? It's just routine, we need her help to clear something up that's all."

The young sister thought for a moment the said in a beautifully soft lilting Irish accent, "Why you're the second person to want to track her down today, the other is Reverend Alex Allan. We know him well here."

Hannah stiffened.

The young sister continued, "but I told him what I told you, you are a day late. I must say that it is so good to see Angie leaving the Sanctuary in such high spirits, especially considering the state she was in when she came here. But then Inspector, it is our job here to allow people the space and time to find themselves and come to terms with their lives. When she left, she said it was for good, and that she was going to spend some time with her mother. That's what I told the Reverend and that's all I can tell you. Except to add for your benefit, because the Reverend knows already, that her mother is dead and is buried at a place called Bradwell-on-Sea about ten miles away. My guess is that she will be spending some time in reflection at a place that she and her mother loved. The priory of St Peter on the Wall. It's of early celtic origin, you know."

She was about to add that reflections were a necessary part of one's life, when the two police agents thanked her quickly and left the office quickly; such manners, or lack of more likely.

Joe Grogan gunned the car down the Essex lanes. It was hard work, because the light was fading badly and it was getting mistier. The aftermath of the now all too typical June downpours that seem to deliberately aim at events like Wimbledon or a much-planned local fetes or concerts, now seemed aimed at him. He cursed, as a large lorry pulled out in front of him on the crooked road back through to Steeple, luckily it had a delivery to make at the Star public house and this enabled them to pass.

It was early evening when they arrived at Bradwell-on-Sea and they made straight for the St Thomas's church. As they got there they saw a man locking the large front doors. Hannah got out of the car quickly and ran under the large lych-gate towards him.

"Vicar, hello, vicar, I'm so sorry can you help please?" she cried.

"No my dear, not vicar, but just a mere verger. Now what can I do for you?" He said patiently.

"Oh, dear, I am sorry," she said and went on to introduce herself.

"I'm looking for someone called Angie McPherson. Her mother is buried in the churchyard. Would you know of her?"

"Why yes, her mother was Alice McNulty. She was well loved and so very much missed. Well, Angie has been here for a day and a bit I think. She has been spending lots of time by the graveside. She doesn't look well you know. Do you know her?"

"No sir, but we do need to talk to her urgently, very urgently. Do you know where she is staying at the moment?"

Hannah crossed her fingers behind her back and hoped that Joe Grogan wouldn't see; it must have worked.

"As it happens, I do," said the verger, "Angie is staying at the Kings Head public house. They do rooms there, quite cheap I understand."

He had hardly finished when Hannah thanked him and ran back to the car.

"Kings Head public house, go, go, it's back down the road we came in on, we passed it. Quickly now," she said, and Joe obliged with a handbrake turn and burning rubber.

Outside the public house, Hannah turned to Joe.

"Joe, I am going to speak to Angie alone," she said. Joe intervened. "But, Guv, that's out of order she might be …"

"What, tooled up, machine gun in hand? No Joe, call it a woman's instinct. I don't think she was at the Sanctuary for nothing. Leave it to me. Just be there when I need you. For safety's sake, give me forty minutes."

Joe was irritated and grunted, "Thirty, at the outside – Guv!"

Hannah smiled and appreciated his loyalty. She got out of the car slowly and went inside. The publican, a great round man with a ruddy complexion, told her Angie was in room five at the top of the stairs. She went up the stairs and along the threadbare carpet to room five and when she got there she knocked on the door.

It opened and there stood Angie McPherson. As attractive as the picture of her had indicated, but a little hollow and dark eyed. She spoke first.

"I'm glad you caught me. I didn't know how to give myself up, isn't that funny? I'm also glad you are a woman. I couldn't bear some young arse of a DI all nerves and platitudes. You don't look like that at all. Come on in." She stepped back and beckoned Hannah inside.

"What took you so long?" she said. "I was beginning to lose faith in the Force."

She proffered a limp hand and Angie took it – her hand lacked strength and conviction; it felt tired and lifeless.

"Hello Angie, I'm Hannah Sinclair. Well, we had a few confusing moments I suppose, but it's all sorted out now. We came here from the Sacred Heart Sanctuary can you tell us why were you there?"

They both sat on either end of a large double bed.

"Where else would you go Hannah after killing three people in a brutal manner and with your mind shot to pieces so you cannot even stand up straight? They were wonderful. They asked no questions and I told them no lies. That's why I was there."

Hannah's mind was working at full speed. Three murders?

"How long have you been staying at the Sanctuary Angie?" she said, not anticipating the answer she got.

"Oh, I went there in early June, yes that's it, early June. I got bedrest, comforting prayer – and don't knock it, it really works you know – some sleeping tablets, then lots of counselling and advice. I'll always be grateful to them."

"Angie, tell me, I guess it all started when that thug Ackroyd killed your mum? But why all the others?"

Angie sucked air into her lungs. Even the mention of the little bastard's name made her feel stressed.

"Ackroyd, yes, little bastard he was too. I was confused about that for some time, you know? I was so angry, so violent and even thought that I was losing my mind. My whole body was in pain, real deep pain. I blamed the alcohol, but then talked to a coroner friend of mine up North – I pretended I was on the case - well they're all doctors aren't they? Anyway, he put me right. He said that the murderer was in a seriously bad way, mentally that is. That really frightened me. After the two other murders I really did feel that I was going mad, really mad – you have no idea. I actually saw my mother, who spoke to me, I felt her presence and heard her voice."

Angie gripped her hands together until the knuckles went white.

"Oh God, it was awful. I hated everyone, but particularly anyone who had ever done anything horrible. There is a plentiful supply of information in the press to get angry about, no difficulty in finding a suitable victim. If the truth be known Hannah, there are a hundred and one people in the pub' on a Friday night that would do what I did without the mental condition."

Hannah kept quiet and let Angie continue. Angie held her hands in front of her and looked down at her feet.

"I hope you don't hate me like I hated them? Anyway, my dear old coroner buddy up North, without knowing all the details of course, diagnosed, er, what did he call it? Oh yes, a brief chronic reactive psychosis due to the severe trauma, which of course in my case was my mum's terrible death. He said the symptoms of which disappear after about thirty days, after which the murderer was unlikely to kill again. Trouble is Hannah, it was only partly right. My little psychosis was organic; I was growing a rather nasty tumour. More reading on my part has revealed that this can sometimes have an effect on the mind. Then I got cancer of the womb. So I had a double whammy. You live and learn eh? It's terminal by the way, a few months to go, that's all. So if you arrest me, I'm not going to last long on prison food."

Hannah stared at Angie and ignoring her gallows humour said, "look, I'm so sorry I really am, but can you repeat something. You said the two others, well in the third one there was two victims, but there were six murder occasions in all. Can you tell me how that is? And the way you taunted the police and the Home Office, you became a nation's hero, 'The Avenger,' what about that?"

Angie looked perplexed.

"What are you talking about? I stopped after three murders, booked myself into the Sanctuary and it was there that they diagnosed that something was wrong and I attended the cancer unit in Colchester to find that I had a malignant tumour. I've not been out of the Sanctuary until I left yesterday morning. No newspapers, no radio, nothing. It was peaceful. Since then I've been with mum, talking to her. The Avenger you say?" She laughed out loud, a kind of comical laugh. "How stupid is that?"

Hannah frowned. "You said you got counselling, was this from Reverend Alex Allan?"

"Oh, yes. I told him all. He was superb with me, so gentle and so understanding. He's had a hard life too you know?"

"Yes, I do know Angie, his mother was killed by someone stupid too," she replied.

Angie went on to explain how she had told him about her mother and her love of the church and especially the strong celtic traditions of the area. It was all becoming a little clearer to Hannah and her head spun as she absorbed the information and tried to make sense of it against that which she already knew.

Hannah stopped Angie talking and asked for a glass of water, she excused herself and left the room and from the corridor dialled a number on her mobile phone.

"Joe, it's me. Everything is all right, I promise. Yes, please don't worry. Now listen, I know it's late, but get back to the Chelmsford nick and call DI Jack Rollo, tell him that I have a key suspect in the first three Essex murders. Tell him too that I have very strong suspicions that the Reverend Alex Allan is implicated, perhaps guilty of the rest and we should bring him in for questioning - quickly."

Joe didn't need telling twice. He sped off to Chelmsford to explain all to DI Jack Rollo. This was getting exciting and he wanted to be in on a key arrest.

Four miles away, the Reverend Alex Allan drove a stolen Honda sport car at speed through the Essex countryside. He knew where he was going, and although he did not know what he would do, he knew the outcome that was needed.

Hannah went back into the room and accepted a glass of water from Angie.

"Hannah, I know that you just made a call and that very soon I will be swept away by fleets of Panda cars. I was going out to my Mum's favourite place tonight, the celtic priory, St Peter on the Wall. It's not far from here. Can we just go there and watch the sea, perhaps catch the sound of a bird or two? Let me breathe the fresh air and try and remember how it used to be with me and mum?"

Hannah hesitated and Angie added, "sorry, this cancer means that I can't move quickly let alone run. If I did abscond I wouldn't get far without my painkillers."

That was enough for Hannah and she readily agreed. They locked the bedroom door and made their way down the stairs and out of the public house. It was gloomy and misty, but occasionally the moon would peak through the grey patches and light the way. They walked slowly along the road towards the priory, passing the mobile homes and St Cedd's Café, which Angie claimed served the best cream teas in the area. As they walked farther on, Angie was surprised. Someone had hired the field to the right and there were funfair roundabouts, a disco' and a barbecue in progress. Doubtless they had hoped in vain for a sunny June evening. The noise was deafening and everyone was determined to have fun despite the weather.

They passed the party and walked down the road that turned into a hard path then on to the priory. When they reached it, Hannah felt as though she was looking at something particularly holy; she could make out a simple oblong structure with a gabled roof. Despite its simplicity it had tremendous presence. Once inside, she let out a little gasp. Someone had lit some candles and it gave the whole place a beautiful smell and glow. The rough stone walls were evidence of its great age and the high wooden ceiling seemed to make it bigger inside than it seemed from the outside. The floor was made up of black stone slabs and apart from some small wooden benches; there was only a simple stone altar at the front and centre of the priory. But above it, right in the middle of the far wall, was a beautiful crucifix about four feet long and three feet wide in a Celtic design with the cross painted red. Christ's image was simple, not agonising and uncomplicated and on each side stood a person, angels perhaps, in a red and a blue cloak respectively.

Hannah looked around her.

"No wonder your mum loved this place," she said, "it's got a beauty and peace all of its own."

Angie held her tummy slightly and winced. After a minute she spoke.

"Yes, we talked and talked as all families do. And we used to go outside and imagine what it looked like hundred of years ago. Come with me."

Hannah followed her outside and around the priory to the opposite end. When they got there she noticed a semi-circle of stones.

"This is where the nave used to be. There were two small wings, like a cross, either side too. Guess what? The place was used as a hay barn before a local trust was formed and it was brought back into use as a religious building. Services are held here quite often now."

Hannah felt good about herself. She could've simply cautioned Angie, held her at the public house, then gone home leaving it to others to sort out. Giving her this little bit of time to herself seemed fair and reasonable, despite what she had done. She would leave others to sit in judgement on that decision.

Angie took Hannah by the arm and they walked towards the sea shore and she could see the crests of the waves as they tumbled onto the long beach. The grassed area dropped down towards a fence and a ditch so they stopped and stood close together, collars up against the breeze, looking at the mist. Angie put her head on Hannah's shoulder and began to sob.

Alex Allan drove the Honda sports car up the badly made-up road towards the priory and cursed the people enjoying themselves at the funfair party nearby. Some cars were leaving and they pressed their horns to ensure he got out of their way.

Unperturbed by their antics he drove on and at length he reached a large metal gate. But he knew the area well and also what he had to do. Without a second thought he got out of the car, lifting a set of bolt-croppers from behind the driver's seat. He went to the gate and snipped through the padlock as though it were made of plasticine. Then he opened it.

He drove very slowly along the path, past the wide-open spaces full of wavy merongrass on the right and the hedgerow on the left. Ahead of him, he saw through the gloom, for the first time, a branchless tree covered in ivy, its body thinner towards the top. It looked almost like a dark finger pointing to the heavens. Then his gaze fixed on two figures ahead of him. He was sure it was Hannah and Angie. He gripped the wheel tightly. The noise of the fairground behind him was deafening. Then he smiled. If he found it difficult to hear anything so would they. He put out the car lights and gently revved the two-litre engine and after a short prayer for both women, he slowly let the clutch out. The sports car launched itself forward at high speed, gathering even more speed as it sped down the flat track towards the two women. Hannah and Angie heard nothing but the din of the fairground and did not even turn around.

Faster and faster it went until it was almost on them. Just then Angie turned to walk back and saw what was happening. She held Hannah tightly. Both women were transfixed.

The car raced towards them. But as it reached the edge of the priory, it suddenly hit a large rock which knocked the left-hand wheel off its suspension. The force was so great that the left-hand side of the car was flipped up into the air and when the left rear wheel hit the stone too, the whole vehicle rolled over onto its right side, bouncing twice, flattening the windscreen and roof against the body of the car. Fuel leaked quickly and sparks from the battery ignited it into ball of flame.

Hannah and Angie held their hands up against the flames, and walked towards the burning wreck. There were shouts from the fairground party and people were running towards them. They peered into the bright wreckage, but saw no one.

Then, just as they assumed that the driver must have perished, they saw a crumpled heap moving some yards off; the driver must have been thrown clear. Hannah immediately reached for her mobile telephone and she dialled spoke to the emergency services. Then she called Joe Grogan, explained the situation and told him to get to the priory quickly. After she finished her calls, she looked up and saw Angie leaning over the driver. She seemed to be comforting the person, but then, to Hannah's horror Angie stood up, then reached down and grabbed what looked like a large rock in her hand. She raised it above her head. Hannah screamed, but to no avail. Angie brought the rock down on the person's head with two hard strokes. Hannah ran over the rough ground and when she reached Angie, roughly pulled her to one side.

"My God. What the hell did you do that for?" she said.

Angie looked at her. "It's Reverend Alex Allan. He tried to kill us." She let out a little laugh, "pity he didn't come here as often as me. He would've known about that large stone set in the ground on the right of the priory. We used to sit on it when we were kids."

She wiped her brow with her sleeve and looked at the lifeless corpse.

"I reached down to him and he looked near to death. He looked up at me, said he was sorry and asked me to forgive him because he had done the other murders. He didn't want to be pilloried. You know what? He said that my stories of mum inspired him. I couldn't have her memory besmirched like that Hannah. I just couldn't. I let her down once and I couldn't do it again. He had to go."

Hannah put her hand on Angie's shoulder.

Angie dabbed her eyes and went on, "I think I knew what had gone on when you were talking to me in the pub. It was kind of dawning on me that the counselling sessions were cathartic for him too, but as you talked I was denying it. I should've been smarter all along. Perhaps I would have been if I'd been living in the real world. Anyway, Hannah, he didn't want the People's Church to perish. He begged me to confess to all the murders, which I hereby do, of my own free will, and of course I will deny everything else I have said to you."

In the misty grey of the night, with flashing blue lights coming towards them, Hannah could see in Angie's face that this was her salvation.

How the hell was she going to untangle this?

In a dark bunker, one of the many that were constructed around the coast of Britain in 1940 to provide for machine gun nests to defend against attacking Nazi forces, three men sat chained to the damp wall. There was little light and it was cold and damp. Their food had long since run out and they were in an emaciated state.

On the walls, although they couldn't see them, were newspaper cuttings of paedophile crimes against children in the area. Several of them reported angrily that paedophile criminals had been let out of prison early following successful rehabilitation. Others warned parents to keep children under close watch at all times.

"D'you think he's gonna come back soon, I'm so thirsty?" said the oldest of the three men.

The youngest man lay in a coma. The other survivor said, "yeah, he's a man of the cloth, he'll be back, you wait and see. Back to give us bread and water and lots of forgiveness. You see if it ain't true."

He let out a hacking cough that rattled his lungs.

Suddenly, a gust of strong wind forced its way in through the narrow gap in the metal cover over the mouth of the concrete bunker. As it did so, it rustled a piece of paper taped to the wall that read:

Do you hear the children weeping, O my brothers,
Ere the sorrow comes with years?
They are leaning their young heads against their mothers,
And that cannot stop their tears.

Elizabeth Barrett Browning 1841

The End